THE MAGICIAN

DETECTIVE

AND OTHER WEIRD MYSTERIES

By Charles Fulton Oursler

Off-Trail Publications
Elkhorn, California

*With thanks to Adventure House, Monte Herridge,
and Bill Vande Water.*

OFF-TRAIL PUBLICATIONS
Elkhorn, California
offtrail@redshift.com

Printed in the United States of America
First printing: April 2010

CONTENTS

FULTON OURSLER
Drawing by James Montgomery Flagg
Writers 1934 Year Book & Market Guide

Fulton Oursler
The Magician Editor
By John Locke

CHARLES FULTON OURSLER (1893-1952) led a rich life in the world of letters, both as editor and writer. Much has been written about his life, including his autobiography, which he was working on when he died. Fulton Oursler, Jr. filled in as much as he could from his father's notebooks, eventually publishing the book in 1964 as *Behold This Dreamer!*, taking the title from FO's first novel. FO had completed his memoirs up to 1925, and this section of the narrative provides a detailed description of his career. The post-1925 narrative is understandably spotty and leaves many interesting questions unanswered.

Fulton Oursler spent two decades (1921-41) as Supervising Editor for Bernarr Macfadden's publishing company. Macfadden was the famed physical fitness advocate who originated the magazine *Physical Culture*. When he introduced *True Story* in 1919, a publishing empire was born; FO eventually became his right-hand man. An important perspective on the Macfadden-Oursler partnership comes from *Dumbbells and Carrot Strips: The Story of Bernarr Macfadden* (1953), coauthored by Mary Macfadden, Bernarr Macfadden's third wife (of four), and Emile Gauvreau, former editor of the newspaper BM started in 1924, the notorious New York *Evening Graphic*. Additionally, *Family Story* (1963), by FO's eldest son Will Oursler, describes in rich detail many aspects of family history unavailable elsewhere.

One becomes aware, in examining these sources, of the competing agendas at play. For instance, Mary Macfadden married BM in 1913; they were permanently separated in 1932. She blames the entrance of FO into BM's life as the beginning of the end of her marriage, for the two men quickly developed a rapport that made BM closer to FO than he was to his wife. *Dumbbells* portrays the union of the pair in dark psychological shades:

> All I know is that I didn't feel I was rotating helplessly in the magnetic vortex of Bernarr's ambitions until Oursler came on the scene. He had a way of increasing the momentum which could always be created from the central spark my husband was ready to furnish. With his five-hundred-thousand-candle-power imagination, maybe Fulton couldn't tell, finally, whether he was dealing with reality or chimeras when the Father of Physical Culture turned on his own brain power. I have often wondered whether our Richelieu felt he was compelled to say yes in order to hold his job. That might have been the main reason for many things that were to happen when our stream of gold was tapped.

Mary and Bernarr Macfadden disagreed over which of them had the idea for *True Story* in 1919, the first confessional magazine—a significant point since the windfall profits from this wildly successful magazine financed the rise of the Macfadden magazines and newspapers in the '20s. Mary bolstered her argument by giving FO as much credit as possible for the good ideas that occurred during his reign as Supervising Editor, and by denying that credit to BM. FO, on the other hand, published a biography of BM in 1929 that gave BM credit for all the major decisions. But that book's agenda was to advance BM's standing as a national figure, and is in fact contradicted by points made in *Behold This Dreamer!* So what we end up with is disagreements over key events in the history of Macfadden Publications among the only people who knew the answers.

Gauvreau, for his part, left the *Graphic* after five years, then turned his experiences into a virtual side-business. He published a 1931 novel, *Hot News*, an exposé of the tabloids that was admittedly autobiographical. Universal turned it into *Scandal for Sale*, a 1932 feature film. Gauvreau followed up *Hot News* with a similar 1932 novel, *The Scandal-Monger*. He published his autobiography in 1941 as *My Last Million Readers*, in which the sordid details of tabloid editing were no longer veiled in fictional form. In short, Gauvreau made the ideal coauthor for a "now it can be told" book that would properly situate BM within the "Era of Wonderful Nonsense."

Other agendas emerge from FO's fractured family life. He had two children from his first marriage, Helen and Will; and two more with his second wife Grace Perkins, April and FO, Jr. After FO died, Grace wrote the two oldest children out of her will. Thus, Grace's death in 1955 revealed that FO's considerable estate, two-thirds of which he had intended to split evenly among the four children, would only go to the two youngest who claimed Grace as their mother. The outcome was a costly legal battle that ended with the two pairs of siblings alienated. Thus, the section of *Behold This Dreamer!* completed by FO, Jr. eliminates important portions of FO's life that involve his first two children; they are barely mentioned. Will Oursler's *Family Story* fills in the point of view of the disinherited, the grim details of the estate battle and the family frictions that led up to it, namely Grace's resentment of any reminders of FO's first marriage, including, sadly, the two older children.

Further complicating matters, *Behold This Dreamer!*, *Dumbbells* and *Family Story* are all occasionally inaccurate on dates, magazine titles, and other specifics which makes pinning down the history of the Macfadden magazines problematic. Even FO's portion of *Behold This Dreamer!* contains errors, suggesting that his notes were inaccurate, or that he had deferred fact-checking the manuscript. In either case, FO, Jr. didn't correct the record. As a result, all three books are filled with faulty decades-old memories, in addition to the selective memories of their competing agendas.

Much of this gets ahead of the story of FO, but does serve to illustrate the difficulties in getting to the heart of matters relevant to his career. But on to the story. . . .

Fulton Oursler was born in Baltimore to a poor family, January 22, 1893. A sister, May, died of scarlet fever two years before he was born; a younger sister, Florence, died after a year. Consequently FO grew up lonely. His family was Baptist, and fervently religious, but FO turned agnostic. His real passion was reading. His father worked for the city transit system and brought home all manner of unclaimed books from the streetcar lost-and-found office. FO devoured everything, from literature to dime novels. His favorite authors were Oliver Optic, Horatio Alger, and G.A. Henty; his favorite book, the collected poems of fellow Baltimorean, Edgar Allan Poe. Another passion was answering ads in the back of magazines.

One of the big events in FO's young life occurred when he was ten. The family received proceeds from a lawsuit against the city. With his share, FO purchased a bookshelf for $3 to house his growing collection. That Christmas, he received a desk. He figured, with the bookshelf and the desk, he had all the equipment he needed for life. At that early age, he began to write short stories and novels.

Another passion was the theater. He performed would-be plays in his backyard, most of which climaxed with Buffalo Bill saving the day. At age six, he was mesmerized by a magic act performed at Sunday school. It began a lifelong interest in magic and the desire to be a magician. "Even as a child," wrote Will Oursler, "there were forces drawing him toward . . . the darker corridors of mysticism, magic, hypnotism, spiritualism, crime, and mystery." FO occasionally performed his magic act at amateur events.

At 14, he discovered a book, *The Stolen Story*, which introduced him to the newspaper business. His many dreams boiled down to two: magic and writing.

The family remained poor, though, and Fulton dropped out of school to work as an errand boy and clerk in a law office. One of the key benefits was access to a typewriter. He spent much of his earnings at a Keith's vaudeville house in Baltimore. He saw acts like Will Rogers, the Marx Brothers, and Houdini, and other notable performers, many of whom he would meet later in life.

After two years with the law office, Fulton set his sights on a newspaper job. A year of persistence landed him a position, at age 17, as a reporter for the *Baltimore American*. A couple of years into this job, the paper's elderly music critic took ill. The managing editor, eager to confirm a pet theory that criticism required no qualifications, determined that FO had no musical background, and sent him to the symphony. FO rose to the challenge and for 1912-18, wrote music and drama criticism.

In 1911, against his parents' better judgment, he married Rose Killen Karger, whom he had been dating for two years. With the added expenses of marriage, he supplemented his income by obtaining a correspondent's job with *Farm Implement Age*, published in Springfield, Ohio. Their daughter Helen was born in 1912, followed by Will in 1913. With his expenses rising accordingly, Fulton continued to look for outside income. He sold his first attempt at a short story to *The Black Cat* ("Before the 'Amen,' " May 1913), which gave him a false impression as to the ease of writing fiction. "I wasted a great deal of time writing unsalable short stories." The 900-worder has the requisite punch for a short-short. It also shows a sensitivity to poverty, befitting his upbringing, combined with a touch of black humor, befitting a future writer of mysteries. He had much better success selling articles to religious magazines like *Adult Bible Class Monthly* and the *Baptist Pastor*. He wrote a regular feature for *Boys'World*, describing himself as "vocational counselor for half a million trusting boys." All the known early work was bylined under his full name, Charles Fulton Oursler.

Oursler nurtured his interest in magic. He was a founding member of a local organization of magicians, the Demons Club of Baltimore. His first known published work—outside the newspaper—was a column about the club's activities for the December 1912 issue of *The Sphinx*, a journal of magic (1902-53). The column appeared intermittently into 1915. He flirted with the idea of becoming a magician, but the established magician Howard Thurston, for whom FO worked for a time, talked him out of it, calling him a "born amateur" in the field. Thurston did convince him of the necessity of moving to New York.

For Christmas 1914, he received as a gift Carolyn Wells' *The Technique of the Mystery Story*.

> Under the spur of her exciting coaching, I could hardly wait to get to the typewriter. The first piece I mailed out was called "The Thousand-Dollar Thumb," and four days later I had a letter from Frank R. Blackwell, editor of the first detective story magazine, enclosing a Street and Smith check for my yarn.

It was, of course, *Detective Story Magazine*. But this passage is a good example of the confusing detail to be found in *Behold This Dreamer!* Trivially, he gets the name of Frank *E*. Blackwell wrong; he also misspelled Wells' name as Caroline. More significant, "The Thousand-Dollar Thumb" was actually his second appearance in the magazine, appearing in the February 5, 1917 issue. His story, "Chief Bob Carter, Foe of Gamblers," appeared in the issue of September 20, 1916. It's possible that Blackwell held onto "The Thousand-Dollar Thumb" for many months before running it, but not as likely as FO misremembering the chronology. There is also a space of over a year-and-a-half between when he received the Wells book and appeared in *Detective Story*, which doesn't match the abbreviated period FO implies in his anecdote.

FO added: "From then on, with many misses, I was able to write detective stories for cheap pulp magazines at Grub Street prices, but nevertheless with the feeling that I was on my way." He described an incident from 1917:

> . . . one day a short story was returned to me from *Mystery Magazine*, a sad little pulp, with a letter signed by a name that will always sound magical to me: Lu Senareus.

It's another unmagical recollection, which FO makes repeatedly; the spelling is Senarens. Senarens, best remembered for writing the Jules Verne-inspired Frank Reade, Jr. dime novels under the pseudonym of "Noname," had sent back FO's submission because he was overstocked with shorts. He asked whether FO could supply a 30,000-word novelette within a week. Not having any unsold manuscripts, FO banged out 10,000 words a day for three days. It was his first sale of a long story. "The Sign of the Seven Sharks" appeared in the May 1, 1918 issue. The thin, saddle-stitched *Mystery Magazine* became FO's best market, for number of sales, if not word-rate. He made almost two-dozen appearances through 1924, and was often the sole name featured on the cover. He became friends with Senarens. FO describes taking him to the Ziegfeld Follies and introducing him to showgirls backstage.

"The Magician Detective" is another long one, 31,000 words. It's padded with excessive reiteration and we can probably blame Senarens' requirements for that; Oursler's shorter works demonstrate his understanding of concision. The idea of a magician moonlighting as a detective would have been tasty wish-fulfillment for Oursler, allowing him to explore the life of a stage magician while elevating him to heroic status; showing that he isn't just a performer, but that his skills have practical application. We can't say with authority that Oursler's hero is the first bona fide magician-detective, but we couldn't identify an earlier one. A possible inspiration was Harry Houdini's entry into film acting, in the serial *The Master Mystery*, coauthored by the top detective-story writer of the day, Arthur B. Reeve. The serial hadn't been released when "The Magician Detective" was published, but its production had been discussed in the press. Houdini doesn't play a magician-detective in the story but that possibility might have been assumed by Oursler, who, as a well-connected amateur magician, an acquaintance of Houdini, and an arts journalist, was likely to have known of the project. The magician-detective concept would be infrequently revived in the pulps by other authors, and later in comic books.

"The Magician Detective" pays subtle tribute to people FO admired; the name of the heroine, Rose Kellar, is drawn from his wife and a famous magician of the time, Harry Kellar (1849-1922); the mysterious villain, Raven, is clearly a nod to Poe.

Oursler continued to supply material to *Mystery Magazine*, although the length of the stories gradually decreased. The plot-heavy "The Mystery of the Seven Shadows" measures under 27,000 words and reads as less wordy than "The Magician Detective." "Seven Shadows" features a scientific detective—the province of Reeve's Craig Kennedy—but Oursler's Gordon Keene, paradoxically, prefers intuition to deductive reasoning:

> Keene was not a logician. He was a scientist with imagination, who, once he knew what course to pursue, could bring surprising results forth by using unsuspected secrets of his laboratory. But he arrived at that proper course more by inspiration from his mental pictures than by theorems, hypotheses and logical thinking.

All of FO's early stories collected here feature magic in one form or another. The strengths of the *Mystery Magazine* pieces are strange characters and situations; thrills, often in the form of cliffhanging chapter endings; vivid, occasionally lurid prose; and generally weird atmospherics. These strengths more than compensate, as a piece of pulp fiction, for bits of shaky logic when the mystery is unraveled. An example of the latter is "The Hand in the Dark." Much action, we discover, has taken place under the noses of the baffled protagonists, yet no sounds were heard. It's as if Oursler had been writing for a silent-film audience trained to imagine an echoless world—short of the effects that could be mimicked by the house organist.

Soon after the first sale to *Mystery Magazine*, FO was hired as a reporter by *Music Trades*, a New York City trade paper with a weekly circulation of 3,000. He'd finally gotten out of Baltimore. Within FO's first three days with *Music Trades*, the managing editor was called away for duty in the World War, and FO was hastily promoted to take his place. He held the position for four years. Broadway became his indulgence, which put his salary under stress:

> To pay for the tickets I had to earn more money, because my salary at *Music Trades* was only enough to keep me comfortably as yet and no luxurious extras. So I redoubled my efforts on outside activities—writing at night in order to go to the shows at night, plus a little saving. This brought me to the office of Frank Blackwell in the old Street and Smith Building, now abandoned, on lower

Seventh Avenue. It was more like a warehouse than a publishing headquarters; the walls shivered with the grind of presses; the air smelled of ink and oils and the corridors were formed by gigantic spools of gray-white pulp paper waiting their turn to be changed and processed into *Popular*, *Ainslee's*, *Detective Story*, *Western Story*, and other unintellectual monthly storybooks. The fortune this firm was making was still a secret—income tax returns were not yet being published—and so this venerable firm had only a few competitors on the newsstands. But when their profit and loss statements became public property, the scramble to publish pulp magazines was like a new rush to Klondike.

Blackwell introduced him to Harold Hersey who was to edit "a new type of story magazine, the name of which must remain a secret." Hersey described FO as "a slender, energetic fellow who made an immediate appeal to my heart." The two became friends. Hersey's magazine became Street & Smith's *The Thrill Book*, which lasted a brief sixteen issues in 1919 but left a legend. Oursler had a short-short in the April 15 issue, which he had no doubt forgotten by the time he wrote *Behold This Dreamer!*, since it goes unmentioned.

After his initial sale to *The Black Cat*, Oursler continued to submit stories but was met with nothing but rejection, until he finally gave up on them. But in Spring of 1917, he wrote a Christmas story with no detective tie-in. He tried *The Black Cat* again, "with high hopes." Weeks passed with no response. In July, he happened to be in Boston on a family vacation and since *The Black Cat* was published in Salem, Massachusetts, he phoned the editor, Harold E. Bessom. Bessom invited him to visit the office, where he informed FO that although he didn't like the story, he'd been outvoted by the publisher and the two manuscript readers, and would thus buy it. This led to an unlikely friendship between the two. The story, "The Golden Adventure," appeared in the December 1917 issue to wide reader acclaim. Like "Before the 'Amen,' " it features a lonely man who finds a touch of salvation in a sleight of hand trick.

Two years later, *The Black Cat* had been sold and moved to New York, and FO had relocated there from Baltimore. *TBC* had been reduced to a one-man office, so FO helped Bessom plow through the hundreds of manuscripts. The friendship blossomed. But after about a year in New York, *TBC* went under. This would have been in 1921. Unemployed, Bessom answered an ad in the Sunday *Times* seeking an editor for a new magazine. The publisher was Bernarr Macfadden, and the new magazine was to be *Brain Power* (quickly renamed *National Brain Power*), intended as the above-the-neck companion to Macfadden's flagship, *Physical Culture*, and an addition to Macfadden's fast-growing chain. Macfadden made Bessom's hiring contingent on receiving, in short order, an acceptable outline for *Brain Power's* content. FO and Bessom stayed up half the night hashing out a proposal. Bessom was hired. He asked FO to supply two articles for the first issue. He appointed him dramatic editor to write a monthly review column. Macfadden wanted to start with a serial, so Bessom recruited FO for that as well. Macfadden had a paranoia about his editors, fearing they would hire their friends to fill the magazines (which explains the editing-by-committee approach that prevailed within the Macfadden offices); thus when Macfadden saw four checks going to one name, he called in Bessom and asked whether FO was his brother-in-law. This led to FO coming into the offices to meet Macfadden. FO described the scene:

> I found [Macfadden] in a pitifully small office barely large enough for a desk and two chairs. His business occupied one whole floor of an extensive building, but prosperity was coming so swiftly that the space was not nearly enough. Many of the offices that had once been eleven feet high were now only five and a half feet high, with a ladder running up the side into an upper compartment where some editorial clerk labored in a cramped position all day long.
>
> Men and women were rushing about in a frenzy of production, waving proofs, layout sheets, toting paintings and drawings, and all shouting as if by sheer vocal power they would get copy to the printer.
>
> In the midst of this bedlam Macfadden sat in a dimmish light, each wiry hair of his mane standing erect. He looked at me with a serious and inquiring air. "I like to know the men I am doing business with," he began. "Tell me about yourself."

By Christmas of '21, Macfadden offered FO a job with the organization. FO refused, preferring his *Music Trades* salary and outside writing income. Macfadden's fallback was to offer FO an irresistible $100 a week to spend an hour every lunchtime talking about manuscripts Macfadden was dissatisfied with. There wasn't enough time to actually read the manuscripts, so FO ended up taking them home to peruse in the evenings. In June 1922, FO finally joined Macfadden for fulltime employment, responsibilities unspecified. Two weeks later, Macfadden appointed him Supervising Editor of Macfadden Publications, a job he was to hold near-continuously for twenty-one years.

(Three other accounts of FO's hiring are less detailed, and less convincing. 1) In Will Oursler's account, FO had been selling articles to Macfadden's *Physical Culture*. BM saw four checks going out to one individual and asked his chief editor, John R. Coryell, about it. Coryell talked up FO's talents, and

December 1923   Cover artist *unknown*

The Oursler influence is evident in this crystal-gazing cover. The magazine's failure was attributed to reader embarrassment at being seen with a magazine named Brain Power; *they feared it would brand them a moron. Adding* National *to the title didn't save it.*

FO was brought in for a meeting, at which FO came up with the idea for *Brain Power*. This led to the paid lunch meetings. 2) In a profile of FO in the inaugural issue of *Writers' Journal*, March 1940, FO had been supplying material to *Physical Culture*. BM called him in and offered a regular job supplying more material. After three weeks of writing articles and stories, BM appointed him Supervising Editor. 3) In Mary Macfadden's account, it was FO that answered the Sunday *Times* ad, with a lengthy and persuasive written reply, and was brought in for an interview. He hit it off with BM, conceived of *Brain Power*, and was hired as chief editor the same afternoon. Bessom is absent from all three accounts.)

Macfadden and Oursler made a genuine odd couple. To BM, the human body was everything. He viewed the world through the prism of health, fitness, and diet. Jesus was the original physical culturist; Mussolini was the fittest leader in Europe; all problems were amenable to physical culture solutions; etc, etc. FO, on the other hand, was a flamboyant writer, a would-be artist, who smoked, drank, spurned health food, and didn't exercise. He was famous in the Macfadden offices for striking matches on the "no smoking" signs. On the surface, the two men couldn't have been more different. But FO was about the only blatantly unhealthful person that BM tolerated. He told Mary early on: "The best thing I ever did was to hire Fulton."

What the two men shared was ambition, energy and a desire to produce publications. And behind it all was a deeper purpose, which is explained in great depth in *Dumbbells*. It's a purpose so audacious in scope one is apt, from the perspective of history, to dismiss it as farcical, except that it explains so much of what was to happen with BM, FO, and the company. As Mary Macfadden writes:

> I knew in 1922 that [FO] felt that the Father of Physical Culture was a man of destiny. . . . It was soon to become apparent that both agreed destiny could be nudged a bit in order to bring about the desired result, which, in this case, was no less an ambition than to make my husband the first dumbbell-swinging President of the United States. . . . Bernarr felt that with Oursler's help and guidance almost anything could be accomplished for him, editorially and politically. But political power was to be the goal of it all. Publications were to be merely puppets. . . . Anyhow, here was the blueprint:
>
> First the country had to be made conscious of the fact that it was sick, and that, in Bernarr Macfadden, it had a national leader who could restore it to health. His power, in this respect, had to be worked up by degrees, from the bottom; obviously not from the top. As Fulton said, the people were not ready for it. The post of Health Commissioner of New York City was one possibility at the beginning. That, with proper manipulation, might lead to the creation of a new position in

the cabinet—National Secretary of Health. Secondly, a step-by-step process of international promotion was necessary in order to build up Bernarr into a politically significant figure worthy of vast public confidence.

What made this dream seem possible was the huge income from *True Story*, which allowed magazines to be launched and killed on a whim. In FO's words, BM "was addicted to giving birth to new magazines and then strangling them within a few months if they did not show a quick and lively sale on the newsstands." *Physical Culture* had given BM a platform to editorialize and present his health-minded evangelism; the creation of new magazines widened the platform. Macfadden magazines generally had BM-bylined editorials leading off the issue. New titles would open new audiences to his views. Of course, the gambler's approach produced successes and failures. In addition to *Physical Culture* and *True Story*, the successes include *True Detective Mysteries* (1924), a variation of *True Story* proposed by FO, the first true-crime magazine; and the love-confessionals *Dream World* (1924) and *True Romances* (1925). Among the failures were the aforementioned *Brain Power* (1921), *Fighting Romances from the West and East* (1925), *Red Blooded Stories* (1928), *Flying Romances* (1929) (BM was a private pilot and aviation enthusiast), *Tales of Danger and Daring* (1929), and *True Strange Stories* (1929). FO's stamp was on every Macfadden issue published under his authority. His energy was infectious, or, as Mary Macfadden put it: "With Oursler as top dog the Macfadden fiction foundry was to become known to the hard-driven hacks under him as the 'magician's sweatbox.' "

A particularly interesting failure was *Midnight* (1922) (later *Midnight Mysteries*). In content, it was a sensationalistic mixture of fact and fiction; in frequency, it was published as a weekly; in both respects, it was a stepping-stone in Macfadden's ambition to start a daily tabloid. A daily would provide an editorial platform much larger that the one afforded by monthly magazines. According to Mary Macfadden, *Midnight* "introduced a technique which Fulton Oursler, as an editorial director, was to follow for years with Macfadden Publications. First, you denounced and deplored, in a blazing editorial, what you were going to print: then you went ahead and printed it with astounding illustrations." *Midnight* covers and many of the interior photographs, featuring near-nude women, were risqué for the times, though to body-worshipping BM, they were completely natural. As *Midnight* progressed, FO made the contents hotter and hotter, and saw the circulation rise accordingly, until one day John S. Sumner, morals czar of the New York Society for the Suppression of Vice, visited the office with a summons for everyone connected with the magazine. Rather than duke it out in court, *Midnight* was canceled. It was known thereafter in the Macfadden offices as "Fulton's Folly."

In January 1923, on FO's encouragement, Macfadden bought the higher-class *Metropolitan* magazine out of receivership. FO became the new editor. The Macfadden era, starting with the February-March issue, was launched with much fanfare. The issue opened with an abridged serialization of Theodore Dreiser's novel, *The Genius*, which had been pulled off the market eight years earlier under pressure from the very same Suppression Society. Reprinting it was, perhaps, in part, an act of defiance toward Sumner.

According to Mary Macfadden, FO's ulterior motive was to use *Metropolitan* to establish himself as a popular writer, something his many pulp mysteries had failed to do. The magazine was to be FO's platform. And, indeed, his short stories began appearing in the second Macfadden issue. (His byline in Macfadden publications was Fulton Oursler, though he continued to use his full name for the increasingly sporadic pulp appearances.) His first novel, *Behold This Dreamer!*, was serialized in *Metropolitan* in seven parts beginning with the October '23 issue. He was paid no extra for these contributions but, through the intercession of western author, Harry Sinclair Drago, the serial received book publication. FO: "That is how I became an author." The book was positively reviewed by Upton Sinclair in the *New Masses*, a Marxist publication; then denounced a week later—by the *New Masses*. With the October 1924 issue the *Metropolitan* changed title to *Macfadden Fiction-Lovers Magazine*. It launched with the first part of FO's second novel *Sandalwood*. Upon book publication, the *New York Times* called it an "impressive assay of contemporary manners and morals." Still, *Metropolitan/Fiction-Lovers* was to be another failure, ceasing publication with the March 1925 issue which contained the sixth and concluding part of *Sandalwood*. Surely, not a coincidence.

The *Midnight* affair had only whetted BM's appetite to enter the daily field, which he felt would be immune to intimidation, given the protections of the First Amendment. When the cash reserves generated by sales of *True Story* reached $3 million, he started the New York *Evening Graphic* (1924), a top-selling, money-losing paper which earned the nickname the *Pornographic* for its beyond-tasteless muckraking. Emile Gauvreau, editor of the *Hartford Courant* and contributor of effective pieces to *True Story*, was hired to edit the paper. FO hired Walter Winchell to write a daily column, his first, for the paper. Another staffer was Ed Sullivan, future variety show host. In time, attempting to rival William Randolph Hearst, Macfadden purchased a number of regional newspapers.

In July 1924, FO received a visit at the office from an actress and aspiring 24-year-old writer with the manuscript of a novel under her arm, Grace Perkins. (According to Will Oursler, they met at a party for literary folk.) It was love at first sight. FO confessed to Rose, and soon he had separated from her and the two children. Grace joined the staff of the *Graphic* and wrote a daily children's column for two years. FO wanted to marry Grace but Rose wouldn't consent to a divorce. In the summer of 1925, FO met the man who was to be his personal lawyer for the rest of his life, Arthur Garfield Hays. Hays, a civil libertarian and wealthy private attorney, became famous for his pro bono work on famous cases like the Scopes monkey trial (1925), the Sacco-Vanzetti murder trial (1927), and the Scottsboro Boys trial (1931). Hays advised FO to get the proverbial "Mexican divorce." With a leave of absence from Macfadden, in September 1925, the couple traveled to the Yucatán, got a quickie divorce and a quickie marriage. Neither the divorce nor the marriage was legal in the U.S.; the strategy was to pressure the reluctant spouse with a fait accompli. But until a legal U.S. divorce was completed, FO would have to stay out of the country or risk a bigamy charge. Rose held her ground and the newlyweds traveled to Europe to wait her out. FO worked on his third novel, *Stepchild of the Moon*. He and Grace churned out copious copy for Macfadden magazines, and the *Graphic*. Hays finally coaxed an agreement from Rose, though it cost FO a whopping $10,000 a year in alimony. The divorce was granted in 1926 and FO and Grace returned to New York. They had a daughter, April, born October 15, 1926, and a son, FO, Jr., born in 1932. In 1928, Helen and Will came to live with FO and his new family.

FO's interest in magic had never waned. In his early years with Macfadden, his "ghost-hunting days":

> I became very active in investigating the phenomena of spiritualism. My interest in this area had grown naturally from my hobby of magic. As an expert on legerdemain I could detect almost any mediumistic fraud. But I was a benevolent, not hostile, skeptic; I have seen phenomena I do not believe can be explained by methods known to performers. This is especially true of telepathy, clairvoyance, psychometry and other forms of seeing the past, present, or future. Thus I exposed false mediums and occasionally sent the more outrageous ones to jail.

He attended and held séances—over 500, he estimated. He became a friend of Sir Arthur Conan Doyle, and exposed fake mediums to Doyle during the latter's 1922 Carnegie Hall lectures on spiritualism. Another friend was Houdini, whom he'd known since the Baltimore vaudeville days, and with whom he worked many times to expose frauds. Houdini's views were more in tune to FO's "benevolent skepticism" than Doyle's True Belief:

> Houdini spent much of his time tracking down fraud. His tragedy was that he wanted to believe but his hard common sense would not

let him. So he pursued fakes like an angry demon because they could not give him what he wanted most. It is no secret that he entered into compacts with his friends—the one who died first was to try to communicate with the other.

Fulton Oursler, Jr., wrote of his father:

> Like Houdini, he kept an open mind on the subject of psychic phenomena; he believed in the possibility of spirits, but did everything in his power to expose any hoax he encountered. In 1912 he had served as chairman of a committee of magicians formed to investigate mediums. He also became a member of the American Society for Psychic Research.

This is the backdrop for a magazine that Macfadden introduced with the issue of July 1926, *Ghost Stories*. It was an ideal blend of FO's interest in the paranormal and the Macfadden confessional style. Officially, *Ghost Stories* contained a mixture of fact and fiction; realistically, it's all fiction told in the first-person. Many of the pieces were bylined in the "as told to" form, with the narrator being a fictional name and the writer being a professional, some of them Macfadden staffers, some of them freelancers. The subject matter ranged from true-blue ghost stories featuring actual ghosts to exposes of frauds selling the fascinations of the afterlife. A number of stories centered around fake mediums and other spirit-peddling con-artists. The confessional style was made-to-order for stories of the spirit world. The first-person approach removed the pretense of objectivity from the stories, placing them all in the "you, dear reader, decide" category; it's fiction for the skeptics, and fact for the believers. The magazine mirrored Oursler's open-mindedness.

The magazine is such an uncanny reflection of his personal predilections, we can assume FO was enthusiastic about bringing it to market and shaping its content. We do not, however, have his account of its creation. With his divorce from Rose and remarriage to Grace, the completed portion of FO's autobiography ends. When *Ghost Stories* is mentioned in the narrative, it's simply another title on the "crazy list" of Macfadden magazines. Will Oursler states outright that *Ghost Stories* was started on FO's suggestion, no doubt repeating what his father had told him.

Oursler supplied copy for many of the magazines under his authority, in varying quantities. An indication of his engagement with *Ghost Stories* is the amount of material that appears under his bylines. He used at least three names, including his own, and all three appear in the first issue (July 1926). Under his own name, he launched a six-part serial, "The Phantom of the Fifteenth Floor." Under his occasional pseudonym, Arnold Fountain,

October 1926   Cover artist *unknown*

A moderately successful Oursler creation, Ghost Stories *blended his interest in the outré with the first-person confessional style pioneered by Macfadden's wildly successful* True Story.

he supplied a short story, "He Fell In Love With a Ghost," a reprint from *Midnight*. And he supplied an article, "Superman or Clever Trickster— Which?" under a name he'd used before in *Midnight Mysteries*, Samri Frikell, which combined the names of two stage magicians, Samri Baldwin (1848-1924) and Wiljalba Frikell (1817-1903). The bulk of his contributions to *GS* appeared under the Frikell byline. They consist primarily of fourteen articles, some of which, with material from other sources, were collected in *Spirit Mediums Exposed* (1930), essentially a book in the form of a magazine published by Macfadden. It resembled an issue of *GS* in size, was printed on the same grade of pulp-paper, and had a painted cover by the *GS* regular of the time, Dalton Stevens.

That first issue of *GS* may even have contained a fourth piece by Oursler, the editorial published under the byline of George William Wilder. Editorials under the Wilder name appeared in the first fourteen issues of *GS*. FO submitted a letter of resignation to BM in March '27, and stayed on until he was replaced; the last Wilder editorial appeared in the August '27 *GS*, so would have been written very near the time of FO's actual departure. FO's job as Supervising Editor was conveniently filled by old friend Harold Hersey, on FO's recommendation.

In the context of the company's history, *GS* was of middling success, lasting almost four years (45 issues, July 1926 - March 1930, after which it was transferred to Hersey's Good Story Magazine Company where it ran an additional 19 issues). It probably turned a modest profit. It's reasonable to assume that BM wouldn't have let FO publish it at a loss for very long. BM lost millions on the *Graphic* before finally killing it in the early '30s, but it was the indulgence the other magazines were expected to subsidize.

Why did Oursler resign? He had always dreamed of being a successful freelance writer, and had met up with the ideal moment to make the break. He was working on his fourth novel and, most of all, had an unexpected triumph on the Broadway stage.

Like his interest in magic, FO's love for the theater had never gone away. His early novels all received theatrical adaptations. In 1924, during a lunch with Lowell Brentano, of the Brentano's, Inc. family publishing firm, the two cooked up an idea for a play. In 1925, Oursler began its development in earnest. Brentano and Oursler worked nights and weekends together in 1926. The play finally debuted on March 22, 1927 at Chanin's Forty-Sixth Street Theatre. Called *The Spider*, it was an immediate hit. The play is a tour de force of novelty, weirdness, gimmicks, and spooky music. Houdini helped with advice. *The Spider* centers around a vaudeville show featuring a mind-reading magician, Chatrand. Shortly into his act, the theater's house lights go out, a shot is heard in the audience and, when the lights come back on, an audience member—a plant—is discovered murdered. Sirens wail; police

1930   Cover art by Dalton Stevens

This one-shot magazine reprinted Oursler articles examining paranormal matters, mostly from Ghost Stories. *Samri Frikell was an Oursler penname combining the names of two prominent magicians, Samri Baldwin and Wiljalba Frikell.* Spirit Mediums Exposed *was the title of an 1879 book by Baldwin.*

swarm into the theater; ladies faint. Later, there's a séance. *The Spider* was a huge success, with audiences and critics alike praising its thrills and clever construction.

The Spider played Broadway for over a year. Touring companies took it around the U.S. It made a hit in Europe. Grace Oursler wrote the novelization which became *Ghost Stories'* longest serial, with eight parts (December '28 - July '29); the novelization was published as a book with scenes from the play. *The Spider* was twice turned into feature films, 1931 and '45.

But with success came strife. Within a year, Oursler sued Brentano over the profit split, and lost. Worse, the play was hit with a series of plagiarism suits, four in all. All plaintiffs charged that *The Spider* owed its origins to works copyrighted from 1922-26. The best-remembered plaintiff, today, would be Robert H. Rohde, a familiar name in *Short Stories* and other pulps. Rohde claimed that Chatrand resembled his character, The Great Macumber, who featured in a 1924 series in *The Popular Magazine*. Arthur Garfield Hays managed to roll all the suits into a single case, and dismiss them as one. Bothersome as these suits may have been at the time, without them the origins of *The Spider* may never have come to light. The germ of the play was "The Mystery of the London Music Hall," a Sherlock Holmes tale that Oursler had written in childhood. It featured a murder that interrupted the act of a vaudeville magician. When Harold E. Bessom had asked FO to supply a serial for the first issue of *Brain Power*, it was this very story that had been adapted, appearing in the magazine as *The Man With the Miracle Mind* (1921), and obviously predating all the works claiming inspiration for *The Spider*. However, the plagiarism suits weren't resolved until March 1930. In the meantime, FO's legal bills mounted, adding to the burdensome alimony he was paying Rose. So, after about eight months away, he returned to his old job at Macfadden. *Ghost Stories* survived his absence. Harold Hersey moved on to publish his own line of pulps.

Oursler continued to write on the side. The reviews turned sour for his third novel, *Stepchild of the Moon* (1926). The *New York Times*, for instance, called it "an exhibition of true talent gone astray," a bad book. The fourth novel, *Poor Little Fool* (1928), was barely reviewed at all. FO hired a literary coach to supply some objectivity. A 1929 novel, *The World's Delight*, and a 1930 effort, *The Great Jasper*, both received reasonable reviews. FO feared that some of his negative reviews stemmed from an article he wrote for *Theater* magazine excoriating critics. To test this—no doubt, paranoid—theory, he published a 1930 mystery under the penname Anthony Abbot, *About the Murder of Geraldine Foster*. The detective hero was Thatcher Colt, the police commissioner of New York City. The book was a bestseller, leading to a number of other Colt mysteries, several film adaptations, and a radio show (1936-38).

In 1928, BM tested the political waters by showing interest in running for Governor of New York. He didn't get very far. Thus, 1929 became the year of Bernarr Macfadden biographies, in an attempt to convince the American public that BM was a Great Man. Three books about BM were published and the keenly observant may have noticed that all three came from the same publisher, and that all three were written by members of BM's circle. FO's contribution was *The True Story of Bernarr Macfadden*, also serialized in *Physical Culture*. For the ladies, Grace Perkins produced *Chats with the Macfadden Family*. The third book, *Bernarr Macfadden: A Study in Success*, came from Clement Wood, an author as prolific as FO. Wood may have been drawn into the fold by Harold Hersey. Hersey had co-founded *The Quill*, a Greenwich Village literary journal, in 1917, before moving to Street & Smith; Wood had been one of his editors. H.L. Mencken, in *The American Mercury*, appeared to have the most fun in attacking the three works:

> The authors of these brochures . . . do not spare the goose-grease: poor Macfadden chokes and gurgles in it on every one of their eight hundred and twenty-five pages. I can recall no more passionate anointing of a living man, even in the literature of campaign biography. He appears as a hero without a wart, spiritual or temporal, sworn only to save us all from the Medical Trust and make us strong enough to lift a piano with our bare hands, with maybe a couple of gals and a bartender sitting on top of it.

The Stock Market Crash roiled the company, of course, but with BM's fortune at $30 million there was no real danger. Negotiations to sell the *Graphic* to Hearst (which predated the crash) fell through; it continued to hemorrhage the profits made from the magazines and was eventually shut down in July 1932. A second true-crime magazine, *The Master Detective*, was added to FO's responsibilities in early '30. His workload may have been lightened, however, when several magazines—*Ghost Stories*, *The Dance*, *Model Airplane News*—were transferred to Hersey's Macfadden-subsidized Good Story Magazine Company over the course of 1930.

The inaugural Hersey issue of *Ghost Stories* (April 1930) featured the first of four installments of *The House of Sinister Shadows*, an Oursler serial written under the Samri Frikell byline. In actuality, it was a significant rewrite of "The Mystery of the Seven Shadows" from *Mystery Magazine*. Note the similarity between the cover illustrations for the August 15, 1919 *Mystery Magazine* (p. 110) and the April 1930 *Ghost Stories* (p. 27). "Seven Shadows" lays out a series of weird events that ultimately have a rational explanation. *Sinister Shadows*, however, adds a supernatural element which is left as an open question: "There were things that Keene could not solve."

In "Seven Shadows," Professor Rust, who brings the case to Keene, was a scholar of the classics, as near as we can tell. In *Sinister Shadows*, they are old friends, in conflict across an ideological divide:

> Professor Rust was the principal research officer of the Eastern Society for Psychic Research. His life work was the investigation of spirit mediums, the pursuit of ghosts and reports of ghosts, a career made of the collection and collation of the evidence of things unseen—a long quest of phantasms, the unceasing hunt for proofs that man has a God, a soul and a hereafter.
>
> On the other hand, Gordon Keene was a rationalist of the first rank, a materialist who despised anything that could not stand the test of his reason; a skeptic who hated all fraud and whose sole religion was a desire for truth.

Sinister Shadows also solves a storytelling problem inherent in the original. In "Seven Shadows," the lovely damsel-in-distress has two suitors, both of whom are suspects. In the rewrite, she is unattached and, of course, available to Keene by the end of the tale. Oursler had learned to put his detective-hero at the center of the romance as well as the mystery to be solved.

The prominence of Oursler's serial in Hersey's first issue suggests two possibilities. Either that Oursler supplied the story to help start the Hersey era with a flourish; or that the story was part of the inventory Hersey inherited when the magazine was transferred from Macfadden. The fact that the Samri Frikell byline was used for a piece of fiction, when it had been formerly used in *Ghost Stories* strictly for articles, suggests the first explanation, as if this had been treated as a special occasion.

Macfadden shocked the publishing world in April 1931 by acquiring *Liberty*, one of the three leading national weeklies (*The Saturday Evening Post* and *Collier's* being the competition). FO was installed as editor and, indeed, his decade at *Liberty* did much to establish his reputation as a top editor. *Liberty* also provided a unified platform for the Macfadden brain-trust. BM had a new national megaphone to put his views before the public. FO and Grace had a new market for their fiction. *Liberty* serialized FO's Thatcher Colt mysteries; and Grace, who had established herself as an effective writer of women's serials in *Physical Culture*, came on board.

Oursler had been conducting his job as Supervising Editor from the Cape Cod home he named "Sandalwood." In July 1932, it was his turn to give BM a shock. He and Grace were moving to Hollywood to write screenplays. He would perform his job from an even more remote location. It wasn't completely out of the blue. FO had already had two novels turned into films; Grace had done even better with three. BM consented. In Hollywood, FO

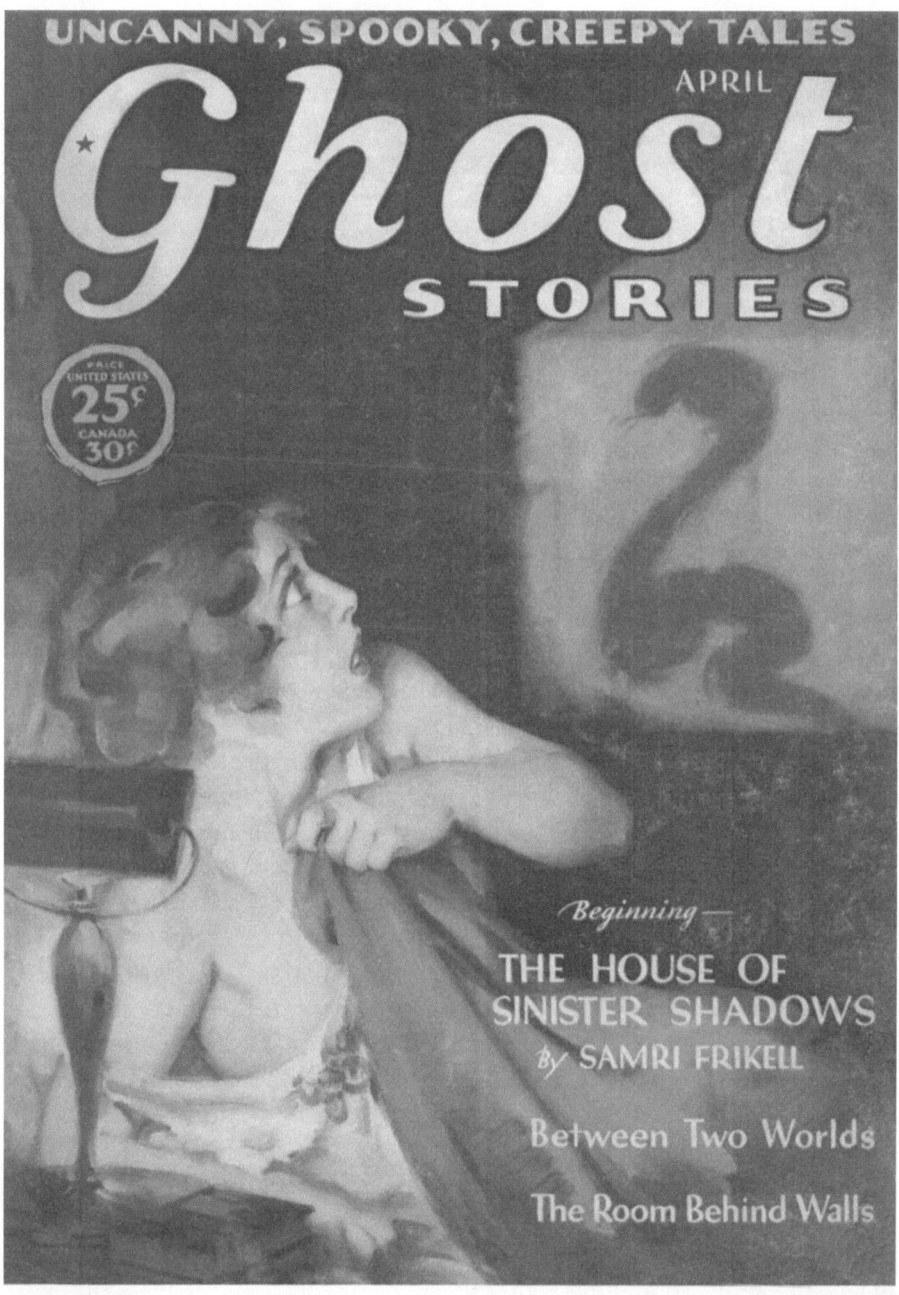

April 1930   Cover art by Dalton Stevens

The first Hersey issue of Ghost Stories *kicked off with a serial by Oursler writing as Samri Frikell.* The House of Sinister Shadows *was a significant rewrite of* The Mystery of the Seven Shadows *which added, among other things, a supernatural element.*

started by selling *The Great Jasper* to RKO. Then he sold a Thatcher Colt screenplay to Columbia, which led to him taking charge of Columbia's story department. Grace sold a novel to Paramount. At one point, five Oursler-family films were in different stages of production. It was a great time: red carpet treatment, fabulous parties, famous people wanting to meet *them*. The couple left an indelible mark. As a *Los Angeles Times* column noted later: "When Grace Perkins and . . . Fulton Oursler . . . were in Hollywood they amazed everyone by their capacity for work. Novels, scenarios and other literary efforts flowed from them as from inexhaustible fountains." Will Oursler described it realistically as "a horrendous work schedule." Things soon turned bad. Grace was hospitalized with phlebitis. MGM lured FO away from Columbia, but the assignments were a comedown. And just like that the Hollywood adventure ended. It was back to Sandalwood by March 1933 as Tinseltown success rained upon them. *The Great Jasper* came out the same month, followed by the Thatcher Colt film in April. Grace's play *Mike* reached the screen as *Torch Singer* in September, her last Hollywood hurrah.

Oursler's presence on the radio began in 1934 with a series of 15-minute shows called *Stories That Should Be Told*, during which he shared his favorite experiences and anecdotes. Later in the year, he moderated *Liberty's Forum of the Air*, a weekly discussion show. He would be heavily involved in broadcasting and radio-writing for the next ten years.

In January 1935, FO, with Grace and the two younger children, took a boat trip to Egypt and Palestine for three months. On the trip FO studied Egyptian magic; still agnostic, he began writing *A Skeptic in the Holy Land*, which would be published in 1936. Meanwhile, the April 1935 *Author & Journalist* listed this solicitation: "*Liberty* offers to buy 'Strange Stories,' involving true incidents that are stranger than fiction," harkening back to the eight-issue run of 1929's *True Strange Stories*. But in fact, the Middle Eastern trip had begun to undermine FO's interest in the outré. Christian faith began to seep into his thinking. In 1938, he and Grace made a second trip to the Holy Land, with his skepticism greatly diminished. He began contemplating a biography of Jesus.

Editing *Liberty*—"fifty-two nervous breakdowns a year"—continued to dominate his time, in addition to the other Macfadden magazines, whose numbers always seemed to increase. If asked how many magazines he edited, FO would reply something like, "when I left the office it was thirteen." *Liberty* had a constant need for timely reportage. It was aided in this by FDR, even before he became President, who chose it as a favorite to give interviews to. When BM turned against the New Deal and contemplated a run for the Presidency in 1936, his *Liberty* editorials attempted to lay the foundation. The Lindbergh baby kidnapping received heavy coverage, but led to a strange incident. Mary Macfadden, now separated from BM, accused FO in a letter to New Jersey authorities of being party to the kidnapping in order to generate *Liberty's* scoops. With BM's blessing, FO sued Mary, prompting Mary to denounce the letter as a forgery by a probable blackmailer. FO withdrew the suit.

As *Liberty's* editor, FO helped shaped public opinion during the Depression, toward FDR and the New Deal, the problem of crime and gangsterism, and the war threats brewing overseas

Much changed in FO's life in the '40s. In 1941, BM was forced out of the company for having used company funds to finance his political campaigns and other non-company activities. FO resigned soon thereafter. He had a radio show and wrote magazine articles. An experienced public speaker, he gave a series of lectures describing the propaganda techniques of Nazis and Communists. For three years, he helped the FBI root out the Nazi espionage network in Latin America by providing cover to US agents acting as reporters; the details are murky. He worked sporadically on his life of Christ.

Grace became a liability. Long a heavy drinker, by the end of the '30s she was an acute alcoholic, and her long-productive writing career was shot. She blamed her guilt at abandoning the Roman Catholic faith for her Protestant-agnostic husband. She urged FO to help save her soul. He began to receive instruction in Catholicism, and in 1943 joined the church. For her part, Grace cured herself with the help of Alcoholics Anonymous. She became editor of the religious magazine, *Guideposts*. In 1944, FO became editor of *Reader's Digest*, a job he held until his death. In January 1947, his plainspoken biography of Christ turned into a long-running radio show, *The Greatest Story Ever Told*. His book of the same name was a huge 1949 bestseller, and an epic 1965 film. Of his father's faith, Will Oursler wrote:

> Perhaps subconsciously even his love of magic had a part in his decision. There was in this interest no irreverence for things spiritual. Magic was to him a special world, a part of his personality, a private backroad through a rampageous life. . . . The mystical and the magical haunted him not because he held such things lightly, but because he always believed, I think, deeply and sincerely, in a magic of the universe. . . . To be sure, the magical was throughout his life a hobby only. But it was also a part of the trait that had led him to delve into the occult, into theosophy, into Oriental beliefs, into spiritualism, and mental telepathy. These had occupied his personal interest, but all of them, in truly spiritual force, had left him unconvinced. . . . The Christ story that he had followed in the Holy Land, the Christ story that grew under his own pen day by day, and the need he had to find an answer for himself, for Grace—here began his road, here began his way into the Church.

In all of this, one can draw a more or less direct line from FO's childhood fascination with magic tricks, to Houdini in vaudeville, to FO's involvement in stage magic and debunking, to the early stories collected herein, to *Ghost Stories*, to *The Spider*, to *The Greatest Story Ever Told*.

It's not much of an exaggeration to say that this brief biography only touches on the highlights of FO's career. He was extremely productive, and knew and collaborated with a great many well-known people. He wrote many books, including serious novels and mysteries. Most of his latter books were religious in nature. However, his dream of resigning from the ranks of the employed and living the life of a great novelist never came to pass.

His work continued to show up in films, but not spectacularly as a rule. A notable exception is the pioneering true-crime noir, *Boomerang!* (1947), based on one of his *Reader's Digest* pieces. He had a number of works produced for the stage, but his last play, *The Walking Gentleman*, written with Grace, opened in 1942 and closed after three performances.

Fulton Oursler died on May 24, 1952 at his New York apartment of a heart attack, age 59, survived by Grace and the four children. At his burial, the honorary pall-bearers included Bernarr Macfadden, Herbert Hoover, Thomas Dewey, Lowell Thomas, Dr. Norman Vincent Peale, and others.

Reading about FO's life leaves the impression that he passed through life like a tornado, leaving clouds of copy swirling in his wake. Most of it is inaccessible now, the newsprint, the magazines, the radio shows. His hardbound fiction has long been out of print; his nonfiction, too, though some of his religious books seem likely candidates for periodic revival. A succinct way of remembering him is through this improbable list of attributes with which Fulton Oursler, Jr. concludes his introduction to *Behold This Dreamer!*:

> Fulton was a man of seemingly inexhaustible talents and careers—a reporter, novelist, biographer, playwright, journalist and screenwriter; an editor, critic, radio scenarist and broadcaster; a magician, detective-story writer and columnist; a world-traveler, ventriloquist, and psychic investigator; a lecturer, criminologist and undercover agent for the F.B.I.

Before the "Amen"

It was not grief at the death of his wife that made old Gregory Mack pace restlessly through the three rooms he called his home, stopping every now and then to stare at the plain black coffin and the candles in the parlor. It was not grief that made him morose and mean and muttering; that made his soul peer out of his shriveled old body under bleared lids, and snarl and snap; that made him finger a rotten old pipe in his pocket and heave whispered curses. It was not grief.

All morning he had paced the floor; all morning he had been muttering; all morning he had fingered his pipe. Women moved silently back and forth in his little rooms, afraid of the old fellow and wondering what he was thinking about. At length he had the bed chamber all to himself, and stood staring abjectly at the squat wooden bed in the corner.

"Charity"—he snarled, as he kicked a pillow resentfully, "I call *that* charity—come and take the last cent a man's got to pay the expenses. Come with a smirk and a pityin' face and say, 'Poor man, oh dear, oh dear, and how much have you got, now? Well, then give it to us here, and we'll add enough to it to bury your woman.' Bats! Vultures! Death scorpions! Not leave a poor old man a penny for his pipe."

He shuffled to the door and peered down the steps. Perhaps—in the street, in the gutter, under an old box, he might— Enough! He hobbled down, pausing every moment or so to rest, but with his eyes ever on the oblong light at the bottom. The rattle and clattering and clanging of the street did not affright him. He moved slowly down the sidewalk, his gaze downward.

But the District Street Cleaning Commissioner of these late, these hard years, must have been in league with the charity workers. Clean, clean, everywhere; clean asphalt streets, clean brick pavements. The men in white had done their work well. Old Gregory Mack peered on behind posts, in corners, and under boxes, but to no avail.

As he crept on, the noise about him increased; the confusion grew greater, the crowds more pressing. Boys ran by him, pretty girls avoided him, young men jostled him, old men ignored him, as he trudged slowly forward, his eyes slanting downward to the curb. And still his long bony fingers crackled and twined lovingly, feverishly, around his pipe. And still he muttered.

It was after he had gone a great way, and his worn-out legs were trembling and tired, that he spied an empty box before a shop window. It was an oasis: a landing with a chair to boot, interrupting an interminable flight of stairs that led to nowhere. Old Gregory Mack stumbled his way through the crowd and sat down.

His battered black hat pulled over his eyes like a mask, he shrank from the gaze of the crowd and turned to examine the shop window. It was a jeweler's store—one who dealt in second-hand things, old coins and curios and such. A large sign was at the back of the window on which, printed in big black letters, Gregory read: "Highest Prices Paid for False Teeth."

Old Gregory Mack stroked his chin and stared; then straightened up and started on his way back. Yet the way was not weary, and the old man did not gaze downward, but limped on, his eyes burning bright enough to blaze a trail home.

At his door he saw a hearse and a mud-bespattered rickety coach. The first was for his wife, he knew; the second for himself, he supposed. He snarled inward oaths as he reflected that the "charity ones" were even then busying themselves in his affairs in his home up the steps. With no respectful quiet, then, did he climb the stairs. He planked his old feet heavily at every step.

There was a crowd in the parlor; something Old Gregory resented. Idlers, and street urchins, and dirty neighbor-women were glancing from the two prim settlement workers, sitting calmly near the coffin, to the dainty and demure clergyman who was saying something over his glasses.

Gregory poked his head in the door and grinned. This was the funeral, eh? The grin faded into a scowl, as he surveyed the "charity ones." And as the old man scowled, every head was bowed while the clergyman offered prayer.

The opportunity! As the saccharine tones of the preacher rose and fell in an abjuration he had composed at college, the old fellow tip-toed across the floor to the coffin. All eyes were closed, except those of a group of dirty children, too frightened to do anything but stare.

Old Gregory bent trembling over the death box, patting each cold bony cheek of the thing within. He bent far forward and placed his own face close down to it. One of the "charity ones" said afterward she remembered hearing a croaking, rattling sound, and a sob as if of joy.

As the sweet clergyman whispered "Amen," the door closed behind Gregory Mack, and he was gone.

The Golden Adventure

IN THE BLOOD OF THE BINNS FAMILY THERE WAS FIGHT—and failure. Airy Binns had fought all his life and lost. When a boy he fought against school ma'ams and lost an education. In manhood, he fought against work and lost decency. When he grew old, he fought against everything and everybody crossing his twisted pathway and lost again. Airy Binns was a fighter, but he was also a loser.

Bitterly enough he realized this, as he staggered down the edge of Albemarle Street, late one bleak afternoon, with the shrill tide of Misery Flats rising to his ears. He muttered about it as he felt his legs twitching; he choked on it as he pitched forward into the gutter.

But that was not the end of Airy Binns. Some of the squat children, who play queer, old-world games of hide and seek under the wheels of the carts that clatter through Misery Flats, found him. They pointed at him with derisive little fingers, laughed at him with their dirty little mouths, and stared at him with impudent eyes. They even fingered his preposterous clothes, and one of them took his hat, which had no crown, and fitted it over her tangled mop of gold. Another little one, prettiest among them all, then called the policeman who struts imposingly through the Flats.

Meanwhile Airy Binns was better off than he had ever been in his life. He was as unconscious of what was going on around him as the drunken tombstones in the ancient burial ground near where he had fallen.

It was a very long time before he knew he was still alive. His first sensation was of riding in a farm wagon over a rough road. Then he felt that someone was shaking the life out of him. In feeble protest, he opened his eyes and saw a horrid face.

A bearded man with long, gray locks tangled about his ears was bending over his bed and shaking him. He was clad only in a night shirt.

"Can ya hyere me, mate?" he whispered hoarsely.

Airy shook his bandaged head in weak assent. He felt quite peaceful—a new sensation for one who either felt the racing of rum in his head or the clutch of hunger in his stomach.

"Then listen quick," urged the bearded stranger, glancing down the long, low-lighted room, as if in terror. "Yer in a charity hospital. Ya get me? Ya fell down and busted yer top. Well, ya ain't gonna live—ya gonna die! I hyeard the doctors saying so."

Airy shifted uncomfortably. It was the first time he had looked upon death. And this was a bad time to begin.

The bearded man gave him no time to answer. He pointed far down the hall to the doorway. Airy's eyes followed the man's yellow, knotted finger and saw two crouched old men, nodding in slumber.

"Old Peter and Paul we calls 'em," whispered the bearded man. "They ain't got nothin' to do but wait for us to die. They expect ya to go off tonight. I hyeard 'em say so. I'm likely to go most any time—if I move around too much my heart'll stop goin'. But Peter and Paul ain't nothin' to us, hyere or hyereafter. What we gotta be thinkin' about is—*Gawd!*"

That name moved Airy strangely—the name his lips had so often defiled.

He cast an appealing glance at the man with the beard, standing there by his bed.

"And the preachers that come hyere ain't no good," the stranger went on sourly. "All mouth, full of bull. It's *works*, mate. And we ain't got 'em!"

He turned and stumbled over to his cot, close to Airy. From under his pillow, he brought forth a greasy bag, stuffed to the mouth and tied with a string twisted into amazing knots.

"I can't move much and live," he chattered on. "Ya've got a little more strength and a little less time. Only tonight, mate. If ya don't want hell-fire and the devil's pitchfork through yer rotten ribs, ya've got to get busy and so have I. Here's gold, mate. Get outen that bed; sneak out while old Peter and Paul are asleep. Git outen hyere and do some good with this money before the devil gits us both. Listen to me, fer Gawd's sake. I give ya this gold—that's *my* work. When He asks me up yonder what I ever did, besides steal yaller gals for the East Side when I was over the sea, I'll tell Him I give ya this money. That lets me out. Quick mate! Yer clothes are hyere. There's a windy; git outen that to the fire-ladder thing and run across the fields to town. Do something good with this gold tonight, or Gawd help us both!"

The bearded man had watched the changing eyes of Airy. He saw the frightened sick man try to raise himself on his elbows and fall groaning back again.

"Ya've *got* to do it," rasped the stranger desperately, as he pressed the bag of gold into Airy's hands. "Wait!"

With prodigious care he raised himself on his huge brown toes, and stole like a ghost in his nightgown, down the corridor, where the lowered gas flames, tortured by a breeze, threw his gaunt shadow into fearful shapes. He reached the side of the guardians of the door, fast in their dotard dreams. His blazing eyes studied their wrinkled faces and were satisfied. He slipped one great hand into a bulging pocket of Peter's coat and drew forth a bottle. With this held tightly, he scurried back to Airy's bed.

"Drink this!" he commanded, and poured half its contents down the parched throat of the man for whom death was ready but who was not ready for death. The stranger would have withdrawn the bottle, but with new vigor, Airy grabbed it and drained it to the last.

Presently, a shaking figure, gaunt and hideous, stood beneath the stars. Black and sullen, the landscape stretched away, far down to a group of twinkling town lights. To the ears of the fugitive came the sound of many bells, and once he saw a rocket.

The wind whipped new courage into him and the cold made him hasten. Unsteady of foot, but with high purpose for once in his heart, he floundered down the hillside and reached the road. The fighter was in his last battle, and only God knew what was waiting for him if he lost.

The distant clamor of the bells, the cold night air, impressed the pilgrim. As he staggered on, queer phantasms, old memories came to him. A star that seemed fixed over a ghostly spire brought a leer to his lips and a pain to his throat.

"There was three of 'em, wasn't they?" he ruminated. "Three wise guys from the East, bound for—some place!"

It is hard for men like Airy to understand much, if it is not just beneath their bloated noses. Airy didn't understand, but he felt, somehow, that the wise men from the East and he had something now in common.

This point in his vagrant thoughts found him tumbling up against a fence from sheer weakness. As he clung to the shaking rail, he saw a woman, wrapped round with a shawl, plodding on in the gloom. To the fence he clung and watched her, as she came on toward him.

Suddenly she darted to the other side of the road and quickened her steps—she had seen him. But Airy was a fighter. Now he was fighting his way against death to win one good action for his record, so he raised his voice and found he had power still to call.

"Come here, lady!" he croaked. "I got somethin' fer you."

He raised his bag of coins above his head and staggered after the woman. Her screams broke on the night silence as she saw him coming after her. But there was no one near by to hear, and the bells kept her cries from the town people.

She picked up a stone and hurled it at her pursuer. Her arm was strong and her aim was good—so sure that the stone hissed by Airy's head and tore his ear, and the blood came. Airy turned his face toward the town again, and another stone rattled at his heels.

At first he did not understand. He cursed the woman for a fool, and rubbed his ear. Then, feeling ill once more, he pulled himself together laboriously and trudged on.

"She could have had this money," he reflected, "and I bet she needed it—but damnation, *I* see! She was afraid of me!"

Suddenly Airy realized the truth. Barroom memories; memories of the fierce, menacing face that had frowned at him from the bar mirrors of Misery Flats. This was he; this was Airy Binns. Small wonder she had stoned him.

Above the spire, the star still glowed, just at the edge of the town. And the bells, too, were still tolling, as if the sextons in all the churches were gone mad, and were trying to out-do each other at the ropes. The star and the bells once more warmed the heart of the lonely man—they seemed beckoning, calling him from the road.

He trudged toward the edge of the town and into its streets, where the bells were clanging in deafening concert, and the people were going up and down gaily, as if it were some great occasion. In a few moments, Airy was a part of the throng; but all who passed him kept as far away as possible. Even the Salvation Army women drew back their tambourines and looked the other way when they saw him coming.

Forward, and then toward the gutter and back again they pushed him. He was in everybody's way. Without the will to resist, he let himself be caught in the current. It carried him in eddying whirls to many places and finally to a dark recess in a huge building off the seething thoroughfare.

"It must be Christmas!" muttered Airy.

Dully he let his gaze settle out on the pavement, but only for a moment. Something small and soft and cold had touched the palsied hand.

She was a little girl, not too well wrapped up. Her face was pale, but wistful and tender. Her childish stare went straight through his ragged shirt, straight to the tatters of his worn-out soul.

"Say! Ain't you supposed to be a dead one?" she ventured.

"No! No!" shuddered Airy. In terror at the thought, his shaking fingers closed around the little hand. "Don't I look alive?"

"Ye-ah!" she answered simply, "but I seen you when you *was* dead."

Airy's stare was uncomprehending.

"You fell down near our house in Mizry Flats," she explained. "Yes, you did, and I called the cop. Gee, you was a dead one then, all right. Maybe you're a ghost!"

In anguish, Airy held up his hand for her to stop.

"What do you want, anyhow?" he asked wearily.

"I want some poor guy," she answered briskly. "And you look the part. You see, it's this way. My maw and my daddy ain't got no coin, and course *I* know there ain't no Santy Claus. If there was, I wouldn't be here. But my six little brothers and sisters b'lieve there is, and it looks like they're gonna git a bum Christmas. But that ain't gonna faze me none—I got a hunch! Miss Lucy, up at the Sunday school where I goes, give me a hunch all right.

"Miss Lucy says if we give a whole lot away, we gits a whole lot more back. Gawd Jesus told her. And Gawd Jesus told her a little kid can do more'n the big ones. A lit-kid shall lead'm; he told her so. Are you listening to me, dead man?"

Airy signified his close attention.

"Well, I got ten cents, see? I found it on the stone steps of the Jew church on Fleet Street. I want to give that ten cents to somebody 'at needs it. Then I'll git a whole lot more back, maybe—if Gawd Jesus gits wise to what I done! Say, dead man, don't *you* need ten cents?"

But Airy couldn't answer. He couldn't open his tired old lips, they were quivering so. He could scarcely think—for ideas were flooding into his mind and their glory bewildered him.

"Wait a minute, kid," he begged huskily. "Wait a minute!"

His grip tightened on her little hand, and she squeezed back comfortingly.

"All right, dead man," she said. "You know, I like you."

He brightened immeasurably then. It all became so clear.

"Look here, kid!" he began with a feeble attempt at drollery. "Did you know I was a magician?"

"A magician?"

"Um. A real magician—a feller what can do tricks. Lemme see that dime."

She held up her other hand and the bit of silver gleamed like a baby star in her thin little fingers. He regarded it with his shaggy head to one side, quizzically.

"It's gotta be a good dime," he wheezed.

She held it nearer to him and he blinked.

"Bite it!" she defied.

Furtively he glanced down at her. She was regarding his face with a curious interest, in which there was mixed pity and infinite faith. She did not notice his other hand, with the bag of gold, as he slipped it behind him guiltily.

"I *gotta* bite it, I guess. It ain't that I misdoubt you," he apologized, "but little girls don't know about them things!"

He held out his hand and she placed the dime on his palm. He clutched both her hand and the coin, shut his eyes and bending low he kissed her baby fingers.

"Now," he commanded, in a singular treble, unlike the voice she had heard before. "Now for the trick, little kid. You know I ain't got nuthin' but these old rags and the dime you give me. Shut yer eyes and kneel down like yer Miss Lucy told you to. And kid—say a good word for me, will you."

She dropped down on her knees, but didn't let go of his hand. She shut her little eyes, laid her face against his hand, and whispered things he couldn't hear.

Stealthily he brought forth his bag of gold and held it over her head. He glowed with a warming peace, and there dropped away from him all bitterness.

"Look kid!" he sobbed. "Gawd Jesus heard you. Look!"

He pressed the clinking bag into her hands, as she opened wondering eyes. He tore the knots away and spread out the mouth of it so that the she could see the bright gold coins. He watched her delight and suddenly hugged her tighter as he heard her crow with glee.

Slowly he set her down upon her feet and stroked her hair.

"Go home, now, kid!" he cried. "Go home quick and show that to yer daddy and yer ma. And say," he choked, "don't forget yer dead man."

Impulsively, she reached up to his face and kissed him. Then she was off.

Up the street she raced until she was at the edge of the crowd. Then she turned and waved her hand, but there was no response. In the shadow behind was only a crumpled form, gripping a wonderful ten cent piece.

In his last fight, Airy had won.

MYSTERY MAGAZINE

VOL. 1. N° 20   SEPT. 1, 1918

PRICE TEN CENTS

FEATURE STORY

THE MAGICIAN DETECTIVE

BY

CHARLES FULTON OURSLER

The Magician Detective

CHAPTER ONE
THE MEDIUM'S THREAT

AT THE DOOR OF THE STAR DRESSING-ROOM, behind the scenes at the Globe Theater, a stage-hand knocked loudly.

"Come in!" a hearty voice called from within, and, as the stage-hand turned the knob and pushed back the door, he found Gordon LeMar, the celebrated conjurer and illusionist, just completing his make-up before the mirror. The magician gazed inquiringly at the reflection of the stage-hand in the glass.

"Mr. LeMar," faltered the man, "the princess lady—the blonde one in No. 10—asks you to come there right away."

The eyes of the magician were troubled for a moment, and he stared a little uncertainly at his uncouth visitor.

"You mean to say," responded LeMar slowly, as if he were repeating a most unusual thing, "that Miss Rose wants me to come to her dressing-room? Is there anything wrong?"

"I—I am afraid there is, sir."

LeMar was on his feet in an instant.

"What is it?" he demanded, and there was more than casual concern in his tone.

"I'm afraid the princess lady doesn't feel very well," answered the stage-hand diffidently.

Without replying, LeMar brushed past him and strode to the stage. Outside the curtain he could hear the musicians testing the strings of their instruments, and the excited buzz of a large and growing audience. With no ear, however, for these usual sounds, LeMar hurried across the stage, already completely set for the evening's first part, and arrived finally at the door of a dressing-room, on the panel of which the figure "10" was painted in black, bold characters. At this he rapped quietly.

Instantly the door opened, and the face of a beautiful girl gazed out at him. She was one of those rare blonde creatures, with blue eyes that seemed always dreaming and pouting, lips that seemed formed just for ardent kisses. But now her face was drawn and pale; in her eyes there was a strained, haunted look, like an animal that hopes to hide from its enemies, and beneath her long lashes there lurked the gleaming traces of her tears.

The sight of the girl's grief was evidently a great surprise to Gordon LeMar.

"Rose!" he cried. "What has caused this?"

Ignoring his question, the girl, clasping her hands together and holding them out to him in moving anguish, almost groaned the words:

"Do I have to go on to-night, Mr. LeMar?"

LeMar took her hands in his own. He was surprised to feel how cold her fingers were, and his heart was touched at the helpless way they closed about his own powerful hands.

"You mean you don't feel well enough for the performance?" he inquired gently.

She bowed her head.

"Just that!" she murmured.

"But, Rose!" he protested soberly. "Isn't this just a bit of stage fright? Isn't it your nerves, more than anything else? I realize, little girl, that this is your first night before a real audience. And I know what that means. I know how tired you must be, after all these rehearsals. Breaking in a new show is always a job, and when it's your first, I know how badly you must feel. But cheer up! Take a little ammonia to steady your nerves—the first plunge and it's all over. Just like a cold bath."

His tone had turned from gentle kindness to kindly bantering, and he was smiling at her hopefully. But she raised her head then, and he saw that his effort had failed. The look in her eyes, too, told him why. She was in mortal terror. She was trembling and her mouth was parted, her breath coming forth in quick, startled gasps. In dumb suffering she looked at him piteously.

"Rose!" he cried, alarmed. "I will get you a doctor!"

But with unexpected strength in the fingers which still were twined about his hands, she drew him back, and with a struggle conquered her emotion for the moment.

"It isn't that!" she protested. "I'm not afraid of them—out there! I can't tell you what I am afraid of, Mr. LeMar. I am just a foolish girl. I suppose you are right, after all. A girl's nerves! Aren't they foolish things to have? Hurry up, now, Mr. LeMar. They've made the last call; there goes the orchestra now!"

Even as she spoke there was a crash from the musicians' pit and, with a mighty blare of trumpets and blowing of brass, the lively overture, with which LeMar insisted his performance begin, was on in full swing.

The rush and gay swing of it seemed to enthuse the Princess Rose.

"Who could resist such magic music?" she said bravely, and her wan little smile went straight to the young sorcerer's heart. "Never mind, Mr. LeMar. I just felt ill for the moment. I am sorry I disturbed you. Finish putting those funny little touches on your eyebrows, and straighten your tie when you get it on. You know your tie always slips when you produce those bird cages from the shawl. I'll be there when the curtain goes up, and—"

She paused, and into her eyes the old frightened look came back again.

LeMar saw a strange pair of human beings approaching him. One was a white-bearded old man; the other was a yellowed old woman.

LeMar saw it and wondered. In his mind a hundred wild schemes had been whirling, by any one of which he sought to readjust his magical entertainment so that Princess Rose might not be needed. But he knew how useless such a thing was. Either she went on, or the performance would be a failure, because the principal illusions had been built around her. LeMar intended taking on an understudy, but had not done so. Now, as he watched her, his heart sank again; for her cheeks were actually blanching beneath her rouge, and her head was tilted to one side as if she heard something which filled her with dread.

LeMar listened, and he heard as well. It was a peculiar, wooden sound, that tapped imperiously above the waltzing strains of the orchestra; that rapped imperiously, as if it would not be denied; that came nearer and nearer to them as they harkened. It was right behind them, LeMar suddenly realized, and he turned quickly.

He saw a strange pair of human beings approaching him. By what means they had passed the tightly guarded stage-door he could not then surmise; for what purpose they had set out after him he could not guess, but the settled look of determination upon their wrinkled faces told him they were come to him on no trivial mission. One was an old man, white-bearded, whose tapping cane had first apprised them that visitors were at hand. The other was a yellowed old woman, whose face had lost all semblance of life, looking more like a crinkled old Chinese manuscript, except for her marvelous eyes. They were like two burning white coals, and from the moment LeMar turned to look, those penetrating, unfriendly eyes were turned full upon him in a weird sort of stare that disturbed him.

As if bidden by some influence outside himself, LeMar turned to see how these two affected the girl, in whose physical condition at that moment he was deeply interested. To his infinite relief he saw that her face was no longer frightened, and that she gazed with some tokens of curiosity, though with some apprehension, at this strange old couple.

Two feet away from the magician the withered old man and his decrepit companion halted. The old man raised his stick and pointed it at LeMar's knees.

"Are you LeMar?" the old man asked, in a harsh, snarling tone that proclaimed at once his errand was not for good.

"I am LeMar," replied the magician, with just a trace of asperity in his voice.

"Then I've come to talk business to you," the old man spat out viciously. "I'm here on important business with you, Mr. LeMar. You've got to talk business to me, and that's all. So—"

LeMar made a step forward and gazed sternly at the unpleasant old man.

"Whatever business you have with me, sir," he answered coldly, "will have to be at another time, and by appointment. That curtain will rise in about ten minutes, and I shall be quite busy for the next three hours. So I shall have to ask you to arrange to see me at another time."

The old man pounded his cane furiously on the floor and shook his head with dotard malice.

"That curtain don't go up until you settle with me," was his ultimatum, and he squared himself before the magician in spirited opposition. The old woman beside him let out a hectic little chuckle, glanced amusedly up at the flies, and relapsed into nonentity.

"My business don't take more than *five* minutes," the old man continued, "but them five minutes is important, and don't you forget it! Now, will you listen to me?"

LeMar was on the point of ordering the couple from the stage, but a second thought restrained him. After all, their mission might be a very simple one. Possibly they had some fancied claim on him and wanted passes to see the show. Possibly they were beggars. Like every other man or woman behind the footlights, LeMar was superstitious, especially about his opening nights. Here he was, opening an entirely new show in a large city, and he meant to take no chances with his luck. With a quick smile toward Rose Kellar, the girl behind him, he spoke again to the old man, this time in a more conciliatory tone.

"If you will state your business quickly, I will listen to you for three minutes," he said. "After that, you will have to leave the stage, as we have to make ready for the performance."

"Three minutes is long enough for me," the old man wheezed, lifting his stick again, as if he didn't know whether he should strike the magician or wait a while. "All you've got to do is answer my questions. Do you stand by all the show pictures you've pasted up around this town?"

"My playbills tell the truth, I hope," replied LeMar with a whimsical little smile. "I will confess, however, that all those pictures of little devils whispering in my ear and smoke arising from skulls is largely the imagination of the artist."

The old man blinked at him slowly before continuing.

"I'm not so Jerusalem sure of *that!*" he observed with a knowing shake of his head. "Not so *Jerusalem* sure, now. Well, how 'bout them notices that you're going to expose the mediums? How about them, hey? Do you still stand by them?"

"Most assuredly," answered LeMar with dawning wonder. "I have no quarrel with the psychologists who believe in spiritualism—such men as Professor Hyslop, Sir William Crookes, and the others—and I respect the faith of those who hold it as their religion. But I have a big quarrel, old man, with the crooks and the thieves who prey upon the most sacred emotions of the gullible who become their dupes; who prostitute the beautiful art of conjuring, and who pass off the feats of a magician as real phenomena and get money for it! They are the crooks! Those are the gentry I expose during my performance!"

"Who gave you the right to decide what's true and what's false?" demanded the old man.

"I haven't time to discuss that with you now," replied LeMar shortly. "I must beg you to excuse me."

"You leave the mediums alone!" the old man snarled, "and we'll leave you alone. But you trouble us, and see what happens. That's all. You better cut out that part of your show to-night, Mr. LeMar."

Again the old woman turned her burning eyes from LeMar's face and cast them in silent imprecation to the top of the theater. She grinned at LeMar with a feline malice which startled him.

"Good-evening," the magician said angrily. "Don't make it necessary for me to enforce that hint."

The old couple were turning slowly, when the old man suddenly paused and lifted his stick again. This time he pointed it at Rose Kellar, still in the doorway.

"Don't you be no party of it, gal!" he said, threatening. "Take a tip from a medium—and look out for the man with the scar on his left cheek!"

At this both, old and withered though they were, shook with croaking amusement. Then they slowly picked their way past wires and bolts in the floor, past towering scenery, to the shadows that lay before the door to the street. With a puzzled air LeMar turned to Princess Rose.

She was reeling. In her eyes the old horror had come back. But now their glance rested on the bent backs and feeble forms that were moving away from her, to the accompaniment of that inevitable tapping of the old man's cane. She clutched at the knob, as if to steady herself, and a convulsive shudder writhed her body. Then, with set teeth, she mastered herself.

She turned a wan face but a courageous smile to the magician.

"I'll be ready!" she whispered, and the door closed upon her. With a heart strangely weighted down with only half-understood forebodings, the magician hurried back to his dressing-room.

As he sat down to finish his toilet he heard the tapping of the old medium's cane on the flagstones outside.

CHAPTER TWO
AN UTTERLY IMPOSSIBLE THING

FIVE MINUTES AFTER THE BIG GRAY DOOR at the stage entrance of the Globe Theater had closed on the shriveled pair of ancients who had intruded themselves on Gordon LeMar, the curtain rose on the opening performance of the magician's new entertainment. It had been designed to create a sensation with the public, and it certainly made a profound impression on these "first nighters."

As the curtain soared groaning to the roof, the darkened stage was illuminated with quick, sharp flashes of lightning, while rumbling thunder and howling winds made the blackness fearsome. The intermittent gleams of light over the stage revealed a singular business. There was a huge caldron, suspended from a tripod, in the center of the stage. Beneath, a dull fire, and steam poured from it in great, ghost-like clouds. Around the caldron trooped three weird old women, while every second or so the audience caught glimpses of hideous faces in the vapor. All about were rushing storm clouds and the flying creatures of night and storm.

To the imaginative, it was truly a Black Art festival, such as one reads of in old story-books. But suddenly there came a change. There was a piercing scream as one of the old witches raised her broom. A blinding flash of light followed, and instantly caldron, fire, smoke, witches, evil faces and the darkness with them vanished into nothingness. There was the stage, brilliantly illuminated, laden with the glittering tables, the gorgeous draperies, and the beautiful apparatus of the necromancer. At even paces across the stage were the assistants, ready for the approach of the wizard. The purple hangings at the rear were seized by a lovely girl, whom many in the audience recognized from the playbills as the Princess Rose. Laughingly she drew back the curtains and Gordon LeMar stepped forward.

In his hand was the small black wand, carried as a conventional custom for a thousand years by magicians. He was in evening dress; his poise was perfect and his smile engaging as he stepped to the center of the stage and bowed.

"We will begin the evening's entertainment," he announced, "with the Silk Worm's Dream."

From the orchestra pit a low, mysterious melody stole out as LeMar began his work. He had that deftness, that grace and ease about his movements, the ready smile and the winning glance that made his art wholly distinctive from his weaker contemporaries and imitators. As the spectators watched they saw him produce great handfuls of radiantly tinted silk handkerchiefs. They seemed to grow beneath his fingers like magical bouquets, until the stage was covered with them. All the while that mysterious melody glided with him as he worked as if a phantom were dancing beside him. And as he passed on to the production of the flowers, and then the manipulation of playing-cards and the exhibition of the chosen cards that rose like butterflies from the decks and floated over the heads of the spectators, the audience was simply transported with delight. For LeMar had an elusive personal charm to which it is hard to give a name, but by which he managed to create a real Arabian Nights atmosphere over the house. It was to be a night of miracles and, with settled satisfaction, the audience sat back and watched.

At his gayest, LeMar worked on through his new and fascinating program. He produced pigeons from a net while standing in the audience; he cut off the heads of a duck and rooster, and in replacing them got the duck head on the rooster's body and the rooster's on the protesting, writhing neck of the duck, to the huge delight of the juvenile element in the audience. He caught fish at the end of a line he tossed over the heads of the bald-heads in the front row; he vanished a famous bronze lamp which was said to have come from a heathen temple in Benares, and finally, as a climax, he approached the *pièce de résistance* of the first part, and, in the opinion of veteran magicians, of all magical entertainments, the Levitation of Princess Rose.

With a rather serious look upon his face LeMar stepped somewhat closer to the footlights than was his wont and slightly held up his hand. A deep hush fell over the throng as the lights gradually were dimmed, and a mysterious crimson glow bathed the stage. There, in the silence and the strange twilight of the stage, LeMar began to explain to them how it was a favorite feat of the Hindus, especially the Yogis and the Mahatmas, to make bodies to remain suspended in the air without support, as a proof of their highly developed spiritual powers. In this connection he related some personal experiences he had encountered during three years he spent in India.

Then LeMar announced solemnly that he was prepared to duplicate the chief feat of the Hindu holy man. He promised to levitate the body of his assistant, until it would remain floating in the air, without visible means of support. He would pass an examined hoop around her body, and if a physician in the audience, or even two physicians, cared to come upon the stage and feel her pulse during the period of her suspension, they would be welcome. In conclusion, LeMar insisted that absolute quiet must prevail during the presentation of the illusion.

"I must ask you not to make a sound," he said, slowly but firmly. "Any sudden sound, any unexpected noise might result in serious consequences for the young lady."

Of course, LeMar was only acting; he was heightening and making realistic the scene, and he worked upon the fancy of the audience until many actually feared for the safety of the girl who was thus to be lifted up before their eyes. LeMar turned to the left wings.

From one of them now stepped a lovely vision. Attired in baggy Persian trousers of white satin, with flowing bodice of green, and wide, drooping sleeves, a girl stepped forward, her face turned toward the enchanter. But it was impossible to catch a glimpse of her face. It was covered, as is the fashion of Oriental damsels, and her lids drooped over her eyes. Her manner was timid, as if the very glance of the magician filled her with fear. This was all clever acting, over which LeMar and Rose Kellar had spent many hours in careful rehearsal.

He approached her now and took one of her hands in his. It was hot; so burning, indeed, that LeMar was startled. He wondered if she were suffering from a fever, and he inwardly determined to close the show after this evening until she was well enough to go on again, or until an understudy who could take her place could be secured. Meanwhile the illusion proceeded.

Passing his hand in fantastic circles over her face, LeMar pretended to be sending her into an hypnotic trance. She tottered and swayed backward. Frightened gasps came from nervous spectators, but before she had fallen to the floor an attendant rushed forward and caught her. This was all part of the *mise en scène*, intended to heighten the interest of the audience.

They placed her on a low couch, sat in front of an Oriental background, amid soft lights that added a touch of Eastern beauty to every new moment of surprise. Standing behind her, the magician renewed the passes and slowly a miracle came to pass.

With a slow, easy movement that seemed to be of another plane, of another sort of world, the body of the girl was lifted in a lying position. It rose higher and higher, perfectly rigid all the while. It moved neither to the right nor left; it did not shake, or bend or sway. As inevitable as fate itself it went up slowly through the air, until it was high over the conjurer's head. He stood regarding it with a fixed awe that already had communicated itself to those watching the scene.

With a grave air LeMar stepped again to the center of the stage.

"There," he said softly, "the young lady rests comfortably in the air. She might remain there for hours, for as far as she is concerned she is practically dead to the world. I shall now pass this hoop around her body, and then cause her to descend to the couch, after which I will restore her to consciousness."

While the orchestra breathed out fitfully the strange, sad music of the East, LeMar passed the solid hoop about the form of the sleeping girl; then he caused the body slowly to descend, until again it was resting easily on the divan. He clapped his hands vigorously, but it was only after considerable effort that the girl's form stirred, and she rose doubtfully.

It had been magnificently done. The girl had acted so cleverly that the people were genuinely glad to see her safe and normal again. They clapped and cheered, and the little princess bowed in repeated acknowledgment.

It was here that something utterly impossible occurred.

So insistent were the curtain calls, that LeMar, thinking it a gracious thing to do, lifted the Persian veil quickly from the face of his assistant. He did it so quickly she could not prevent him.

Then he stepped back with a hoarse gasp of astonishment.

The girl was not Rose Kellar at all. It was the face of a girl he had never seen before in his life.

CHAPTER THREE
A LADY OF SILENCE

FORTUNATELY, THE AUDIENCE DID NOT GUESS THE SITUATION.

All those in the front of the house saw before them was the finish of a perfect bit of artistic deception; the climax of a marvelous illusion. The wistful, uncertain air of the girl and the startled manner of LeMar all seemed to fit into the picture.

As the curtain dropped on the tableau, no one in the crowd had understood that they had witnessed a greater marvel than they had bargained for. Men climbed over their feminine neighbors in the seats and gathered in little knots in the lobby and smoking-rooms, there assuring each other that the effect had been produced by "wires" or "mirrors" or any other of the scores of methods which occur to the mind of the uninitiated. To not one did it occur as remarkable that the girl, as she was revealed when her veil was lifted, had not appeared previously during the entertainment. It is unlikely that any of them had noticed that she was not the same laughing Princess Rose who had given such a gay, buoyant touch to the earlier mystifications. This girl who had been caused to rise in the air was of the same size and build as the girl they had first seen, and such is the fallibility of human observation and the prevalence of human laziness that it is practically certain that not one knew the difference.

Therefore, they had no conception of the tense situation on which the curtain had really descended.

So soon as his body was hidden from the eyes of the audience, LeMar placed his hands on the shoulders of the strange woman and demanded:

"Who are you? And where is Miss Kellar?"

She looked very awe-stricken and frightened, but she said not a word. So wrought up was LeMar that he shook her, almost roughly, and his voice was angry as he repeated his question.

"Answer me!" he commanded. "Who are you? There is something radically wrong here! Who are you, I say?"

She put a finger to her lips and then to her ears, signifying by distressed little signals that she could neither speak nor hear. It was a dilemma. With a helpless little gasp LeMar glanced about him at the knot of wondering assistants who looked upon this newcomer with genuine amazement.

Just then another figure stepped into the picture. It was Jack Brown, the dapper, sporty young business manager of the show, and Gordon LeMar's best friend under the stars. Brown's face was dripping with perspiration, as if he had come on a mad run from the box-office to the stage.

"Great Jericho cats!" he exploded. "I saw it from the back of the house. What in hip-hip-hooray has happened, Gordon?"

LeMar turned a thoroughly puzzled face toward his excited chum.

"I don't know anything more than you do," he answered, "except that Rose—er, Miss Kellar—was taken ill just before the curtain rose. She at first wanted to stay out, and then decided to go on. All went well, until she—at least I thought it was she—came on in costume for the levitation. But when I lifted the veil it was this girl, and she has indicated to us that she's deaf and dumb!"

"Good-night in the morning!" Jack Brown exploded again. "Where in jumping Juniper did she come from? And how did she know what to do in the show?"

Gordon LeMar shook his head impatiently.

"The big question to me, first," he declared, "is where is Rose Kellar, and what has happened to her?"

Roy Carey, one of LeMar's most trusted assistants, stepped forward respectfully and touched his hat.

"I went to her door, Mr. LeMar," he said, "and knocked. And I didn't get no answer. So I tried the door and it was unlocked, and so then I looked in. Miss Rose ain't there!"

LeMar and Brown stared at each other, and then, as if by the same impulse, they turned to the girl who had impersonated the missing Princess Rose.

"She knows," said Brown, half under his breath. "She knows, all right. We've got to make her talk somehow."

LeMar had been pounding his right fist into the left palm in an absent-minded fashion, but now he suddenly straightened up as if he had come to a decision.

"Come here, all of you!" he said quietly, addressing his assistants. With a subdued air hovering over them, as if a tragedy had occurred, they gathered around him. His face was serious enough to impress even the lightest-minded among them.

"Miss Kellar has been missed," continued LeMar seriously. "We don't know where she is. She may have left the building. I want you to scatter and look in every room for her. And, Roy, send the doorman to me. I will be in my dressing-room. Come, Jack!"

The magician placed his hand on the arm of the strange girl in the gorgeous, barbaric Eastern attire. He indicated to her that he desired her to follow him. In her eyes, as she looked up at him, there was an appealing sort of childishness, a trusting confidence, that struck a responsive chord in the troubled enchanter's breast.

"Wherever this girl came from, Jack," he said, as they walked across the stage, "I believe she is an honest girl and a good girl!"

"Be careful!" warned the business manager, who suspected everybody, and who, it was hazarded by some, would not have believed implicitly in his own grandmother. "She may be just shamming, you know. She might have good ears, after all!"

If the girl, however, had overheard these words, she gave no token. As one who walks in a dream, she trod the thick, green velvet that overlaid the stage and stopped as if a little frightened at LeMar's dressing-room door. With a bow LeMar stepped aside to allow her to pass. At this evidence of courtesy she was plainly abashed and blushed furiously. They both saw the blood mantling beneath her artistically treated cheeks.

Inside the cramped little room—the Globe Theater was built a long time ago, and its dressing-rooms are the bane of all who play there—LeMar offered her a chair. Jack Brown climbed on top of a wardrobe trunk and lighted a cigarette. LeMar faced the girl, who had not spoken.

"If you are bluffing about your speech and hearing, you can't keep it up long," said LeMar sternly. "You know that. You're too sensible a girl to expect to keep up such a deception and get away with it. You're bound to betray yourself, Miss—what's your name?"

He shot the last question at her with disconcerting suddenness. Jack Brown, from his perch not far from the ceiling, gazed admiringly at this little evidence of LeMar's skill in handling a difficult situation.

But he gained naught by it. The girl stared up at him throughout all his speech with a tired little air about her, but it seemed evident she did not hear a word. Not by the slightest sign did she betray her secret, if she were shamming. There was not a flicker of the eyelids, a tremor of the lines at the mouth, to show that she had been startled by that unexpected question LeMar had hurled at her. She sat placid, pretty, impossible.

Then LeMar had an inspiration. Reaching to the table shelf, he found a pencil and a small pad. He wrote on the top sheet, in plain, bold letters:

"Who are you?"

He passed the pad to the girl. She received it with an abstracted sort of air and gazed upon it without apparent interest. Then she looked up into LeMar's face again and slowly shook her head. The pad dropped from her fingers to the floor.

"She means she can't read, by Juniper!" cried Jack Brown, with a surprised little whistle. "Gee, but that's tough luck, Gordon. What in the name of sacred mackerel are you going to do about it?"

The question seemed to arouse the magician, who had passed his hands wearily across his eyes, as if utterly astounded and bewildered. Now he was rigid, erect, with much of his old assurance.

"The first thing to do is to dismiss this audience at once," he decided.

Jack Brown landed on the floor in a heap.

"What!" he cried. "Dismiss that perfectly good audience and ruin our whole season, right when you're cleaning up? Where's your nerve, man? If this girl could do the 'levi' she can do the rest of the show, and I don't care a Mohammedan damn where and how she learned to do it. Come on. Get ready for your second part."

But LeMar had already sent a boy scurrying out through the private boxes for the house manager.

"The audience will be dismissed at once," he reiterated decidedly. "The fact is that a girl has disappeared. While we are finishing the performance, heaven knows what may be happening to her. We've got to get busy and find her now. All my life, Jack Brown, I've looked for mysteries, and never could find them. I had to make my own mysteries to invent illusions for my performance. Three years I spent in India, and not a thing did they show me but some childish toys for tricks. I've prayed for a baffling mystery, and here it is. And I'm going to solve it!"

"Then you're going to be a detective?" queried Jack Brown, with a queer little smile.

"I'm going to be a detective," defied LeMar, "until Rose Kellar is found!"

"Then I'll be your Watson, Sherlock!" cried Jack Brown, and the two men clasped hands.

They were still clasping hands when the house manager opened the door. He saw a strange sight. There were two men shaking hands, and beside them, in a chair, a girl in costume, fast asleep.

CHAPTER FOUR
THE MAGICIAN DETECTIVE SETS TO WORK

LEMAR DID NOT WASTE TIME MAKING LONG EXPLANATIONS to the house manager.

"There has been an accident, Mr. Ford," he said quickly. "I will thank you to make a little announcement to the audience. Say to them that the money will be returned at the box-office immediately. Mr. Brown will see you later and adjust the matter."

"But, Mr. Le—"

"I beg your pardon, Mr. Ford. Our own business just now is urgent."

With a face helplessly, almost comically, bewildered, the fat little house manager backed out of the room. As the door was closing upon him, he managed to venture one question.

"Is the engagement closed?" he asked.

"That depends entirely upon circumstances," replied LeMar.

He stepped over beside the strange girl, who now sat back limply in her chair, her head drooping, her eyes closed. Jack Brown held her wrist, with a serious, professional air that at any other time would have aroused the magician's amusement, for Jack knew nothing whatever of the pulse and its indications.

"She has fainted!" he announced, with the air of an oracle.

LeMar shook his head in decided disagreement.

"I do not believe she has fainted," he said. "Her manner was far too collected for her to be seized with a fainting spell so suddenly. Moreover, her hands are warm. She is not in a faint."

"Then she is sleeping," declared Jack.

"She is not sleeping. It is contrary to all human experience for a girl to go to sleep under such extraordinary circumstances."

Jack Brown clapped his hands together emphatically and retorted:

"Yes, Gordon, my boy, so it is. But it is also contrary to human experience for a beautiful girl assistant suddenly to disappear, and another girl, almost as pretty, but self-confessedly deaf and dumb, to appear in her place. It is contrary to all human experience for such a girl to be able to perform so exactly the difficult part of the princess in your levitation illusion. There are other things about this affair that are contrary to human experience, therefore, why shouldn't she do another contrary thing and go to sleep?"

In reply LeMar lifted the girl's eyelids, so that the staring eyeballs were revealed. The distorted face jarred somehow on the debonair business manager.

"Look at her," insisted LeMar. "Note the breathing; observe that she does not stir, now that I throw back her eyelids and stroke her forehead, which is damp. If she were sleeping, this would disturb her. She would stir restlessly; she possibly would awaken. But she does not mind. No! This is not the sleep of one entirely exhausted. People who have been working under a long, terrible strain may sometimes fall asleep, even in such a trying situation as this. But this is not one of the times."

"Then what has happened to her?" asked Jack in awestruck tones.

"It is very plain. She has been drugged or hypnotized."

Jack Brown stared at the conjurer with unbelieving eyes. He looked at the girl again, and then his eyes traveled back to the set, stern, but anxious face of LeMar. The business manager whistled long and softly.

"Jumping Hali—holy smoke!" he ejaculated. "What does all this mean?"

"That's just it, Jack," answered LeMar. "That's what we've got to find out. We've got to know what all this means. I wish you would tell them to hurry the doorman in."

A few moments later the guardian of the Globe Theater's stage entrance was trying to answer LeMar's questions, and still stare at the beautiful figure of the unconscious girl in the chair at his side. The examination gave LeMar no information whatever. The doorman was impressively honest when he stated that he had not left his post since seven-thirty that evening; that in that time Miss Rose had certainly not passed him, and that the only two strangers who had gained admission were an aged couple, a man and woman, the former of whom had carried a cane.

"Who were they?" demanded Jack Brown eagerly.

LeMar interrupted to tell him what he understood about this old couple, and that he would explain it when they had more time, as he did not consider it important to the problem in which they were engaged.

"One thing I would like to know, however," continued LeMar, again addressing the doorman. "On what pretext did that old man and woman get by you and get on the stage?"

The doorman's reply was unhesitating.

"They told me you were expecting them," he answered glibly. "They said they had urgent business with you."

"I see," said LeMar thoughtfully. He looked the doorman squarely in the eye for a moment, but the latter bore his gaze without flinching. Then the magician put a final question.

"Did you refuse admittance to any one at the stage-door to-night? That is, did any one else try to get behind the scenes?" he asked.

The doorman scratched his head, as if that were a powerful incentive to the processes of memory.

"There was a man come there," he finally recollected, "and gave me a note which he said was meant for the leading lady—the one who figured in all your tricks."

LeMar and Jack Brown exchanged quick, significant glances.

"Did you deliver the note?" inquired LeMar.

"Yes, sir. It was just about five minutes after the lady got here. She got awful white as she saw the writing."

LeMar got up and put a heavy hand on the man's shoulder.

"How do you make that out? How do you know, when you never left the stage-door, and she had been in her dressing-room five minutes?" LeMar demanded.

This poser did not disturb the impromptu witness to any appreciable degree. He grinned a little and admitted that he *had* left the door long enough to deliver the note. On further prodding he also admitted that he had received a dollar bill for doing so.

"What kind of a man was your generous friend?" asked LeMar with just the suggestion of a snarl in his voice. Inwardly he was raging, and ready to shake the fellow before him. "What sort of looking man was he?"

The doorman's answer struck a sudden chill to his heart.

"He was a tall man," he replied. "A very big man, with a long slash of a scar on his right cheek!"

CHAPTER FIVE
DOCTOR NECK AND HIS SISTER

PRINCESS ROSE WAS NOT IN THE GLOBE THEATER.

When LeMar had dismissed the doorman, and gathered the reports of those whom he had despatched to search the house, he learned to his bitter discouragement that there was not a sign of her in the building, and that she had not returned to the apartment hotel she had been quartered in for the last ten days.

Having thus exhausted every immediate means at disposal, he at once began operations on a line of campaign which was sketching itself subconsciously during the last half an hour.

While he was receiving the reports of Carey and the others of his organization, he sent Jack Brown to the telephone, and in a short time an ambulance drove up the alley in the rear of the theater. There was a door at the back, through which the scenery was carried to the stage from drays. This door was now opened, and the lovely silent and slumbering girl was carried in Jack Brown's arms to the stretcher in the ambulance. Presently LeMar joined his business manager, and the two climbed into the conveyance.

The ambulance driver immediately started up.

As they passed down the avenue on which the Globe Theater fronted and speeded northward to a private sanitarium with which LeMar was familiar, the magician began to unfold his plan of attack.

"To understand what I have in mind," he began, "you must know all that I know."

Here the young conjurer related all that had transpired during the half-hour immediately preceding the rise of the curtain, little more than an hour before. He gave an impressive recital of the brief but startling interview with the old medium and his companion; of the terror that he had noticed on the face of Rose Kellar, when the old man had lifted his cane and told her to beware of the man with the scar on his cheek.

"Jerusalem cats!" exploded Jack, when he heard this. "The doorman said a man with a—"

"Exactly! That is why I am trying to get to work at once. I am going to place this girl where she will be under the most careful observation, and where, at the same time, she will receive the most careful medical attention. We can return to her later, for, however exasperating her coma, her deafness and her lack of speech may be, she will nevertheless be a valuable clue, and there will be some means by which we can use that clue. Meanwhile, as soon as we are certain that she has been taken care of, we will hunt up that abominable old man and his wife and have it out with them."

Jack was tapping the toe of his shoe with his light little cane.

"What are their names?" he asked, almost abstractedly.

LeMar's heart sank at the question. Suddenly, a new phase of his predicament dawned upon him. The old man and woman had not sent in any cards, neither had they been announced. They had not given him their names, or any clue to their identity. How, in a city of a million, was he to reach out and find them?

The light of a street lamp, as they passed it, revealed his troubled face to Jack Brown, and when the latter asked if there was anything especially wrong, LeMar confessed that he was balked at the start.

"Go on!" derided Jack. "You're kidding me. You're a fine magician-detective if you can't do better than that."

As a matter of fact LeMar had already done better. Facing the immediate problem of establishing the names and addresses of his singular visitors, he decided on a plan almost before his doubts had left his lips. As the idea flashed across his mind, the ambulance stopped at the entrance of the Hillman Sanitarium, and the still senseless girl was carried up the broad stone steps and into the quietly lighted hall. A nurse and an orderly in white stepped forward.

LeMar and Jack met the superintendent, Doctor Wild, to whom they communicated a modified version of their difficulties. They did not tell him all that had occurred, but related enough for him to understand the necessity of discretion, and the careful watching which they wished the queer patient to receive. Before leaving the hospital they had the satisfaction of having the interested physician's promise of all that they asked. Being something of a psychologist, the doctor was intensely interested in what they had told him, and they felt assured he would serve them well.

Down the parked street they walked on leaving the place in complete silence. The usually irrepressible Jack Brown seemed to understand that his friend wanted to be quiet, and did not attempt conversation. At a garishly illuminated drug-store at the corner they halted, and LeMar went inside. Jack Brown saw him enter a telephone booth and deposit a nickel. He could not help wondering who the magician was calling.

But he was more than surprised when LeMar emerged soon afterward, smiling a little triumphantly, and announced that he had found what he sought.

"The lady and gentleman," he said sarcastically, "whom we are seeking live at 247 Willow Grove avenue, and their names are Doctor Ezekiah and Sister Rebecca Neck respectively. At least that's what the police told me when I described the pair."

"How far are they from here?" asked Jack, with an eye to the windward for a taxi.

"Just around the corner," answered LeMar jauntily. "We're in luck!"

At a fast clip the two adventurers turned the corner of Willow Grove avenue and began studying the dimly revealed numbers over the vestibules. It was a difficult business deciphering the half-faded gilt figures, but after a few moments they found they had another block to traverse before they reached their destination. This last block they covered almost at breakneck walking.

They found No. 247 Willow Grove avenue without much difficulty. Indeed, it could hardly be missed. It had evidently been built a great while ago, when the surrounding neighborhood was not then a suburb. It was a frame affair, rather shaky in the knees, decrepit, ugly and faded, much like

Doctor Ezekiah and Sister Neck respectively, There was a forgotten garden in front of it, and a drunken paling fence in doddering guard of the premises. On the gate was a sign, which the two men bent low to read:

> YOUR PAST, YOUR PRESENT AND YOUR FUTURE.
> ASK SISTER NECK. SHE TELLS.

Such was the legend of the faded signboard. They thrust back the gate and mounted the shaky, rotting steps. All around was darkness. There was no sign of life, no glimmer of light, no noise of moving things in that silent, menacing, eerie old house. One might almost fancy it to be a gathering-place of ghosts, among whom Doctor Neck and his chuckling sister might well take an honored place.

LeMar knocked at the door, and the sounds of the knocking ran trembling and echoing through the rooms and corridors behind it. He pounded again and again, rattled the knob and shook the shutters. The knob came off in his hand, and one of the shutters collapsed. They half expected to see the two gnarled old figures standing at the window when the shutter fell. But only a black and barren mass of shadows was there.

Then they heard a step behind them and turned quickly. A little girl was looking at them inquisitively.

"Be you lookin' for the Necks?" she asked boldly.

They both nodded, and a silver coin glittered in LeMar's hand.

"They're gone!" the child answered, grabbing at the coin. "They took suitcases and left about—oh, just a little while ago. They told my mother they was going for good, and they didn't say where they was goin', neither."

CHAPTER SIX
A SINGULAR PLEA

IF EVER HE FELT BAFFLED, HOPELESS, DEFEATED, LeMar felt it in that moment.

The one clue on which he had depended for some enlightenment, the sole tangible thing given to work on, had suddenly eluded him. As quickly, as silently, as mysteriously as the spirits with which they affected to commune, old Doctor Neck and his ugly sister had vanished. The sighing night wind seemed to carry on its crest the low, diabolical chuckle of old Sister Neck, taunting the anxious magician and his friend.

Meanwhile, the child, grabbing at the dime which LeMar had offered her, was eager to be off, but Jack Brown, with unusual thoughtfulness, stayed her. Smiling with the winsome way that made Jack such a likable fellow, and always endeared him to children, he asked where she lived.

"Right down the street," the little girl answered readily. "No. 6 Willow

A little girl was looking at them inquisitively. "Be you looking for the Necks?" she asked boldly.

Grove avenue, three doors from the corner, right in front of the lamp-post, and the number's on the door. Me father's name's O'Brien; he works for the city."

In spite of their worry and concern LeMar and Brown smiled together at her free, friendly chatter.

"Never mind, Miss O'Brien," answered LeMar. "We have no immediate need for your personal biography, but we might want to make some inquiries later along other lines. We are real estate agents, and we wanted to talk about the property. Thank you very much!"

With a mischievous smile the little wisp of humanity who had given them such startling and disturbing intelligence darted away in the gloom. There, on the rickety steps of the deserted house of the mediums, LeMar faced his business manager with a face that betrayed his anxiety.

"It's a mess, Jack, old man," he said sternly. "Rose Kellar has been stolen from us. A strange girl has taken her place, and now she is unconscious. And the only sensible clue that I have been able to pick up has completely eluded me. I don't see where I can make another move."

There was a world of sympathy in Jack Brown's eyes, but not a solitary gleam of inspiration to aid in the crisis they now faced. He would like to help, but not being of the resourceful type, he was hopelessly baffled. He knew he would merely blunder and make matters worse if he tried to suggest anything. So he sensibly kept quiet, as he had done on many another occasion, and allowed LeMar to think in silence. He felt sure LeMar would think of a plan. And that was exactly what the tall, hawk-faced mystic was trying to do.

In fact, the magician stood there on the steps in silent absorption so long that Jack began to worry. He feared they would attract the attention of passers-by, and that they might find themselves surrounded by a curious neighborhood crowd. Before this happened, however, LeMar came back to himself with a sudden little exclamation, as if a decision had been reached in his mind.

"The thing is simply this, Jack," he resumed. "These mediums have almost confessed their complicity, if not their actual guilt, by their actual flight. They had a motive, understand, for kidnapping that girl. They knew it would halt my performance, and the very object of their visit was to do that thing, in self-protection. They have fled and taken Rose with them for revenge. But I think I have hit on another clue."

Jack was all earnestness and attention.

"The very mention of a man with a scar on his cheek was sufficient to bring terror into Rose Kellar's face," went on the conjurer. "Now, these mediums knew about him, evidently knew the effect the mention of his name would create, and warned the girl against him in my presence. I believe, Jack, old man, we might look for that man with the red scar among the mediums!"

It did seem feasible. At least, it offered some prospect for action, some hope of getting somewhere. And indeed the situation needed action. The deadly silence all about the disappearance was already having its effect, and both men longed for something tangible. Either one of them would have welcomed a set-to with a gang of desperate ruffians, in order to rescue Rose Kellar. But the irritating fact that the girl was gone, and the mediums gone, and that they had no way in which to track either one of them, was becoming oppressive. So Jack Brown hailed this new theory with delight. They would try to find a medium with a scar on his left cheek.

LeMar, once his mind was made up, always got to work immediately, whatever the nature of the task.

"We will walk from here to police headquarters," he decided. "It is only a matter of a few blocks or so. When we get there, we will telephone the Hillman Sanitarium and find out if our strange lady friend, who is deaf and dumb and unconscious, has had anything else overtake her in our absence. Then we'll put this thing squarely up to the detectives, this question about the medium with the scar on his face, without telling him why we want to find out. I don't want to make a public scandal of this by reporting it to the police until I have to. Before I go, though, Jack, I would like to take another look around these premises."

Mounting again the shaking steps, LeMar stepped across to the shutters and tried them. They were locked, though he felt sure if he had exerted his strength he could easily have torn them bodily from their rusty, ancient hinges.

Next, being of a neat and orderly nature, LeMar picked up the fallen handle of the door and carefully replaced it on the end of the iron rod which projected through the opening. Almost mechanically he turned the knob and, to his utter surprise, the door gave beneath the pressure of his hand.

"Jack!" he called softly. "This door is open!"

The *blasé* young manager did not appear startled at the information.

"What about it?" he asked.

"Simply this," answered LeMar impatiently. "I tried this door not fifteen minutes ago, and *it was locked then*."

Jack Brown was at his side in an instant.

"Come on, Gordon!" he cried. "Let's go in and find the spooks!"

CHAPTER SEVEN
MARKED "PERSONAL"

IN ANOTHER MOMENT THE MAGICIAN and his manager had pushed back the door. They found themselves in a narrow, dark hallway, smelling vilely of musty carpets, dust and stale onions, mingled with another and peculiar odor which they could not give a name to, but which was more penetrating than all the others put together. Moreover, they were in total darkness.

Neither had a means of defense, and neither had any doubt that the old people who had dwelt in this ramshackle old barn, while not physically dangerous themselves, would not hesitate at any means to strike back at their enemies. And they regarded Gordon LeMar and all his kind as their worst foes. Therefore they went forward with considerable caution.

Feeling in pocket after pocket, LeMar at last found his matches and struck a light. The flaring little flame gave them but a feeble illumination, but by its light they managed to get some idea of their bearings.

Evidently the place was meanly if not miserably finished, and there were evidences of very hasty departure, such as tumbled-over boxes and knocked-down wearing apparel. Before the light went out they had found the door of the parlor to the right, and through this they passed, LeMar meanwhile striking another match.

The parlor plainly had been the room in which the séances at fifty cents a head for the faithful had been held. There were old-fashioned kitchen chairs arranged in rows, with a sort of platform and table at the farther end. Here Sister Neck had been wont to get her psychic impressions and pass them on to her dupes. Gordon LeMar, who was keenly interested in the scientific side of spiritualism, and who believed in all genuine phenomena, could not help sighing at the empty trumpery and shallow trickery here indicated. He felt the deeper convinced that Doctor Neck had acted desperately, but has acted to save himself and his kind of fakirs.

The most profound stillness prevailed throughout the house—a hollow silence so hauntingly eerie that the two men, when they did speak, conversed in whispers. It was almost as if they were hushed in the presence of the dead. But they feared more practical things than ghosts. Both of them felt there might be enemies lurking in the shadow, and were ready for a fight, if one should come.

But they were not molested. They passed through the dining-room into the damp and ill-smelling kitchen, but found no one. LeMar opened the kitchen door and peered into the small back yard, piled high with rubbish and junk of every description, on which the moon gazed disconsolately. A black cat scurried across the fence and disappeared down the alley shadows. Rats darted in and out, with frightened, angry little squeals. LeMar shut the door and, lighting another match, peered about him.

A door, across from him, opened on a steep stairway that led up to the rear of the second floor. Determined to find if any one were eluding him, to place his hands on any friends of the Necks, if they still remained in their queer place, LeMar led the way up these dark, narrow stairs, with Jack Brown following in stolid silence. Arrived at the head of the stairs, they stopped and listened intently.

In such a situation it is strange how one fancies things. The slightest noise takes on a sudden and momentous significance. Small, cracking noises in the wall that ordinarily possess no significance at all assumed a new meaning. LeMar could hear his own heartbeats; he could hear the tiniest sounds, and Jack Brown's hearing was extraordinarily acute.

"Jack!"

LeMar's mouth was at the ear of his friend; the name had been spoken so carefully, in so low a tone, that it was like the ghost of a whisper. Jack answered in a voice almost equally difficult to detect, if there were any near to listen. Then LeMar spoke again, slowly, distinctly, so that not a word would be lost. It was a moment of crisis that had come suddenly, but they were meeting it well.

"I fancied I heard the chuckle of old Sister Neck just now. It seemed almost at my elbow!"

A revulsion of feeling came over Jack Brown. The remark struck him as utterly absurd, preposterous—almost superstitious. The thing was not within reason. How could that old woman be anywhere about? Had not they been seen to depart by the neighbors? The impatient young business manager could not altogether control his feelings.

"Don't throw a scare into me like that again!" he whispered, with less caution. "Jerusalem cats! You know that old hag isn't anywhere near here. Cut it out, Gordon; this thing is getting on your nerves!"

The magician again came closer with his lips to the ear of his friend.

"I heard it again!" he murmured, and there was a challenging note in that soft, delicately spoken sentence. "I tell you, old Sister Neck or some one else is near by. I know."

Some sharp reply was hanging on the tongue of Jack Brown, but it was never spoken. Before he could open his mouth something clammy and cold, with a cool little breeze around it, rushed by his face. He darted back, with the chills racing down his spine. Then he heard a stifled exclamation from Gordon LeMar.

"Catch it!" shouted LeMar. "Get it quick. Don't let it get away. Where's your matches, Jack?"

Desperately, in an agony of suspense, Jack Brown fumbled with his matches, shaking hands dropping matches as he tried to light them. Then a little flicker spluttered up in front of him and he saw the angular figure of the magician holding aloft a match.

"She's gone!" cried LeMar, and his voice was like a groan. "She's gone!"

The match was flickering low, and he lit another, moving it about and trying to pierce the inky darkness with its tiny glow.

"What happened?" blurted out Jack.

"A cold hand touched my wrist," replied LeMar, as if he were relating some common-place thing. His voice sounded dazed, as if he had passed through some horrible experience, and was not yet quite certain as to what had actually happened. "Then it pressed something into my hand. It was this!"

He held up a small, white envelope, from which a perfume exhaled—a faint, delicious aroma. They bent low over it as LeMar lit his last match.

It was addressed to "Mr. Gordon LeMar," and in the lower left-hand corner of the envelope was marked "Personal."

"Do you know who wrote that?" asked Jack.

"I do," was the magician's astonishing response. "I have seen the handwriting many times. This note is from Rose Kellar!"

CHAPTER EIGHT
AN UNFINISHED SENTENCE

SHOCKED AND AMAZED, and not free from the eerie suggestion of this place, the two friends came closer together in the darkness. They braced themselves for whatever the gloom might hold. Moment after moment they waited.

Out in the street they could hear noisy children shouting nursery rhymes. The distant roar of the elevated came to their ears, and every now and then the hoarse warning of automobile horns. All these sounds of ordinary city life gave an extraordinary accent to the strange situation in which they found themselves. It was the haunted silence of the house all the more sinister; it made the darkness about them the more menacing, the uncertainty all the more unbearable.

But as time crawled on there was no further sign. There was not even the sound of a mouse scrambling behind the wall paper, nor the flapping of a shutter. All was quiet; as fearfully quiet as a specter-tormented tomb. It was a creepy, crawling kind of stillness; the silence that breaks the nerves of strong men.

Its effect was soon manifest upon LeMar and Jack Brown. With one accord they rushed forward into the dark bedroom at the end of the hall. They dashed to the windows, threw up the curtains and the windows, and thrust out the shutters. The light of the swinging arc lamps of the street flooded the place.

Certainly, save for themselves, this room was empty. The illumination was ample to show them the old-fashioned wooden bed, with its heaped-up coverlets, as if it had only recently been slept in; the time-shaken chairs, and the antique black walnut bureau with the marble trimmings in the corner under the gas-jet. The curious Jack was making a quick exploration, and presently he gave a triumphant little chortle, as he held something aloft in his hand.

"Matches!" he exulted. "I've found a box of 'em!"

It was but the work of a moment for him to light the gas and still farther brighten the sleeping chamber that had evidently belonged to Sister Neck, of occult reputation. They saw in its ill-kept appearance, its dust, its carelessly thrown old garments in the corners, and the all-pervading air of carelessness and dirt a true portrait of the character of the old woman with the diabolic chuckle.

There was not much time, then, however, for them to make an examination of the domestic habits of the Neck family. Some one, or something, had been under this roof with them, had given them physical, tangible evidence of its presence, not five minutes before. Whoever or whatever it had been, most certainly its activities concerned them vitally; motive was evident in the note which had been thrust into LeMar's hand, and it behooved them to act with all decision and despatch.

"Shall we read the note, or go on searching?" asked Jack.

LeMar's actions were all the reply that was needed. He thrust the note into his wallet and placed it again in his pocket. Then he strode toward a cupboard door that was standing just a little ajar. He drew this back quickly, but faced nothing but a job lot collection of clothing left behind in the hurried departure of Sister Neck. Jack, meanwhile, was lending all his aid, though all the things he did could not be described as of the highest importance in solving the case on which they were bent. He looked under the bed, which was practical; but he also drew out all the bureau drawers and poked around in every sort of odd corner, moving with the greatest haste and enjoying every minute of it.

The net result of this, and a subsequent investigation of every nook and cranny in the house, was a complete failure.

They threw caution to the winds. They lighted every gas-jet in the house to aid them in their search; they explored the cellar, they prowled around in the rubbish of the backyard, they tried to find some means of egress to the roof, in order to account for the escape of the person or creature who had left that note in LeMar's hand.

"I'm beginning to believe it was a real ghost!" said Jack, with a gleam of superstition in his eyes. Jack was from Irish stock, and there was a vein of the dread of unknown things in him, inherited direct from his Celtic forbearers.

LeMar gave an impatient little snort in reply.

"Nonsense!" he declared. "It merely confirms the fact that old man Neck and his sister are implicated in this thing, and that Rose Kellar is in their clutches. Perhaps the note may tell us something. Certainly, there's no use looking around in this house any more—I'll swear there's no one in here now."

Removing the note from his wallet, LeMar broke the seal and drew forth a small sheet of paper, folded once. Standing beneath the old chandelier, lighted now, probably for the first time in many years, LeMar spread it out, as Jack Brown bent over his shoulder eagerly.

This is what they read:

MY DEAR FRIEND: You are making a dreadful mistake. The old man and his sister have not harmed me. They have had nothing to do with my disappearance from the theater this evening. You are on the wrong track, and the best service you can do me, as a kind, good and sincere friend, is to drop your personal investigation of the matter at once. Dear Mr. LeMar, you will never see me again. The little Princess Rose, who was to be the disappearing lady in your illusions, has really vanished at last. You must not hope, you must not try to call her back. It is wiser for her to go. There are so many things I wish I could explain to you, but I can't. It's all so hard. Try to forget all about me, you good man. The little girl who took my place can serve you well. She will be very valuable to you. Just try her and see. Good-by. The best of everything should be yours. R.K.

P.S. Because I know that we shall never meet again, there are two truths I can safely say to you. One is that I know, for I am a woman and I am not blind, you are in love with me. The other is that I love you. It may be that—

And there, as if the hand of the writer had been seized, the writing ended in an abrupt, sudden jerk. There was nothing to suggest what the thought of that unfinished sentence might have been.

CHAPTER NINE
ONE GLIMPSE OF TERROR

INTO THE EYES OF EACH OTHER THEY GAZED, those two warm, true friends. And each read a true, plain story. LeMar was suffering, but he was glad in his pain. And as he looked at his friend, the worldly, careless, always jesting and often shallow man of the world, the magician saw the comradeship that best expresses itself in inarticulate sympathy. At such a time there was not a word Jack Brown could have uttered that would have been as eloquent as the unspoken message of his eyes, the tender reassurance of his hand resting on LeMar's shoulder.

The magician folded the note again, replaced it in its envelope, and tucked the missive away in his pocketbook. Then he cleared his throat, as if it were not easy to speak.

"Come on, Jack!" he said.

"Where?" asked the business manager, with genuine curiosity in his voice.

"Home!" answered the magician laconically.

That was a stunner for Jack.

"Home!" he repeated in indignant ejaculation. "Holy skipping mackerel, what are you going home for? Are you ready to give up as soon as this?"

The intention of this was obvious, but altogether unnecessary. It did not draw the fire from LeMar that Jack had expected.

"We can do nothing here," responded the magician, "and the more I think of the police plan the less I like it. I want to keep away from the police. I want to avoid publicity, scandal, pictures in the paper, and the rest of it. Besides, I want to win out on this thing myself. I have made up my mind to solve this mystery, and that note has only strengthened my determination. I believe in the quiet of our room we can think better. We can do nothing here now that I can think of. We must examine into this thing and map out our plans well. So we're going home."

By home LeMar meant the hotel where they were quartered. It was miles away, but the street cars were not distant, and they set off in silence to reach it. Jack had acquiesced without a word to LeMar's idea. But Fate was not so obliging.

They had reached the corner, with the car line but two blocks distant, when a stream of passing automobiles caused them to halt momentarily just in front of the curbing, while they awaited an opportunity to cross. As they stood there they noticed a large, dark-red automobile speed down Willow Grove avenue and come to a stop within a few feet of them. It had come from the direction of the deserted house of the Necks which they had just quit.

In itself this was nothing remarkable, and probably the big red automobile would have found an opportunity to turn into the busy thoroughfare southward without attracting the particular attention of either LeMar or Jack, but for one trivial, apparently inconsequential, thing. It was the fact that the irrepressible Jack Brown began to whistle. He always whistled when he had nothing else to do. And it chanced that at this particular moment he was whistling that hauntingly sad, sweet melody which accompanied Gordon LeMar during his handkerchief manipulations; an Eastern waltz melody that had not yet become popular and was therefore not familiar to most people.

Its effect was almost instantaneous. He had scarcely whistled more than half a dozen bars of the music when there was a commotion evident inside the limousine. Both LeMar and Jack heard the unmistakable noises of a struggle, the quick thumping against the sides, the quick sound of feet, and then a volume of profanity in a hoarse and angry tone.

This attracted their attention, but it did not arouse their suspicions. It will readily be surmised that neither dreamed the struggle, whatever its nature, had been precipitated by the harmless whistling of an almost unknown composition. Indeed, that connection was not established in their minds until long afterward.

But they learned suddenly and quickly enough the truth, or at least a big and vital part of it. The door of the great red car was suddenly hurled back with the violence of a furious struggle. As they stepped closer to see what was happening, an amazing situation confronted them.

There was a huge man, his face scratched and covered with blood, his lips parted, his breath coming in terrific gasps, struggling to hold back a white-faced, horror-eyed girl seeking to gather strength to scream. She saw LeMar and Jack, and her face was transfigured with wild, unbelieving, sudden joy. In that same instant they recognized her. She was Rose Kellar.

"Save me!" she sobbed.

As she spoke the man clapped his hands over her mouth and hurled her back into the darkness of the car. The chauffeur threw on the power, and like a rocket the automobile dashed away.

But not too quick for the magician to recognize the man in the machine. He had seen him too well ever to forget him or the red scar slashed across his cheek.

CHAPTER TEN
THE MAN WITH THE RED SCAR

"WHAT ARE WE GOING TO DO?"

There was genuine anguish in Jack's voice as he turned to LeMar for guidance. But the magician had no need to tell him. Already he was off. Before the machine had rounded the corner, before the echo of Rose's voice had been drowned by the honking of the auto horns, the chugging of many motors, and the shouts of the drivers in that sea of late uptown traffic, he had acted. Out into the street he rushed, and Jack was right behind him.

The situation was not so difficult as at first appeared. For the first time that night the gods of chance were smiling on them. So congested was this busy corner that it was impossible for the driver of the big red car to make any speed. At any moment, of course, he might extricate himself from the tangle of automobiles and rush off down the avenue and away. If that happened, pursuit would be impossible. There was no time to hire a taxi, even if one were near, but if they did succeed in getting one, its small power would soon be outdistanced by the powerful engines of the fleeing machine.

LeMar knew all this; it all flashed through his mind as he darted into that whirling maze of moving machines, with their glaring headlights, and chauffeurs hurling curses and maledictions on his head. Every moment the lives of the conjurer and his friend were in danger from the cars, but they rushed on, scrambling in and out with the agility of men who know that time is precious and life and death hangs upon them.

As they reached the middle of the thoroughfare, an astonished policeman grabbed after them, roaring a warning, but they heeded him not. Before them was the red automobile, proceeding slowly, perforce, because in front of it, behind it, and all around it were other automobiles. Its way was blocked; until it was out of this maelstrom it could only creep along. In their hearts the panting LeMar and Jack Brown already exulted. They were not too late. The red automobile, containing Rose Kellar and the man with the red scar, could not get away. Another moment would tell the tale.

Panting and eager, they drew close on the fleeing machine. They almost stumbled over its huge tires, and they noticed that no license tag dangled from behind. Evidently the man with the red scar was determined to play safe.

As they reached the door of the car there was a sudden and complete halt. The machine stopped, as did all the others near it. Something had happened in the jam of cars some yards ahead, and for that instant movement was paralyzed. The red automobile, its horn tooting frantically, was still, immovable, at their side.

They had not been noticed. The chauffeur, a small, wiry man with a far, wild look in his eyes, that even then struck them as extraordinarily familiar, was staring straight ahead, feet and hands ready to dash off at the first break in the line. It was practically certain they had not been seen by the man inside the car. They would take him by surprise.

LeMar reached up and clutched the handle of the door. He turned it and pounced into the machine, with Jack right behind him. The business manager closed the door, so that their little affair might not be witnessed and interrupted.

They were entirely unprepared for the scene that met their gaze.

Lolling back on the large, richly furnished cushions, puffing coolly on a big cigar and affecting the most shocked surprise at their entrance, was the man with the red scar. They saw no traces of blood upon his face, nor emotion or excitement in his manner. He was merely amazed at the audacity of the two men who had thus summarily intruded the privacy of his automobile.

"What in the devil does this mean?" he asked, in well-bred anger.

LeMar gave him no answer, and Jack was too astonished for speech. Surely they had cause to be. This was undoubtedly the car in which they had just witnessed the struggle of Rose Kellar with this man, yet where was Rose Kellar now? Where was this man's anger, his raging excitement now? Where was all the wild intensity of the scene they had witnessed not five minutes before?

For the man with the red scar was alone. He sat up very straight now and looked them squarely in the eye, and repeated his demand as to who they were, and what was their business.

"Are you gunmen? I haven't got but twenty-five dollars on me," he wound up aggressively.

With a sinking, foolish feeling, LeMar and Jack sat down and faced him, still not knowing how to attack him. This was so utterly unexpected. As the whole situation danced before his excited mental vision, LeMar told himself it could not be. It was another of those impossible things; as impossible and yet as real as had been the transformation of the girl he floated in the air from Rose Kellar to a strange deaf mute. Rage filled him, and resentment at being duped and tricked; hot anger at not knowing how. For the machine had always been in sight, and there had apparently been no opportunity for the girl to have left the car unobserved. The whole thing was preposterous, and yet bewilderingly, hopelessly true. For there were but three men in the car, and no girl to be seen.

"Where is Rose Kellar?" demanded LeMar hoarsely.

The man with the red scar lifted his eyebrows questioningly, and drew a long puff on his cigar, as if anxious to steady his nerves.

"I beg your pardon?" he asked, with an inquiring inflection. "You see, gentlemen, you have me at a disadvantage. I do not know who you are. I do not know from whence you came. I do not know what you want. I do not know what you are talking about. Forgive me, please, if I seem dull or stupid. Will you smoke?"

He drew forth a silver cigar case and offered it. LeMar and Jack ignored it, as if his hand were not in the world at all.

"Where is Rose Kellar?" repeated LeMar with inexorable sternness. "What have you done with her? If you want to keep healthy, I advise you to open up now, for I'm here on business!"

The man with the red scar gazed about him uncomfortably.

"Mad! Quite mad!" he muttered to himself, with a sidelong glance of anxiety at LeMar. "Who are you, anyway?" he asked petulantly. "It seems to me I have seen you somewhere before. Hasn't your face been around on the billboards, or street car signs, or something like that? Perhaps you endorsed a soup, or a new brand of cigars, or maybe you—anyway, what do you want?"

He settled back as if he were no longer fearful of his visitors, and was getting mildly curious. He was exasperatingly superior.

"You are responsible for the disappearance of Rose Kellar from the Globe Theater this evening," said LeMar coldly. "I know your connection with the case. I know that you were at the stage-door this evening. I know some other things about your movements since then—quite enough to hold you until further evidence can be obtained," he lied to strengthen his words. "You had better meet me now, when I am inclined to be merciful, for I've got the goods on you!"

The man with the red scar smiled in tolerant amusement.

"You are a liar!" he replied.

LeMar sprang up as if to attack him, but he got no farther. He had failed to notice in his excitement that the machine had stopped. Now something came down on him, out of the nowhere it seemed; a sudden, stunning sensation, as if all had grown suddenly black, chaotic—and then nothing at all.

CHAPTER ELEVEN
MAGIC AGAINST MAGIC

ONE HOUR LATER GORDON LEMAR OPENED HIS EYES.

It was a little difficult for him to get his bearings at first. There was an uncomfortable feeling about his head, and as his sensations grew clearer he realized that this uncomfortable feeling was really a throbbing, merciless pain. Then he felt about and his fingers played over the roughness of a spread. He gradually began to take in his surroundings, and eventually it dawned upon him that he was in his own room at the Hotel Garrison.

He was in his pajamas, he noticed next. The room was lit brilliantly; his clothes were hanging neatly in their places. All was as it should be. Could it be possible that all he had gone through had been only a dream? Had Rose Kellar not disappeared after all? Had he really experienced that ghostly adventure in the deserted house of the Necks? The automobile, the cry of his vanished assistant, the encounter in the machine with the suave man of the red scar—was all this dreaming, nightmare stuff of one's uneasy sleep?

Instinctively his hand went up to his head. No! It had not been a dream. His head was neatly bandaged, as if it had been given careful attention. He had been hit then. Ah, yes! Certainly he had been hit. He had been talking with that beast in the red auto, and the beast had called him a liar, and he— some one had felled him then. How and who? LeMar settled back weakly, with a sigh. Those questions were too difficult at that moment. They must wait until his head stopped throbbing that way.

But thoughts of Rose would not leave him, and as they came they brought with them new vigor and determination. Though all around him was still a little hazy, he sat bolt upright, his mind made up to lose no time. He judged he had not been unconscious so very long. It must be about two or three o'clock in the morning. Where was Jack? And how had he reached home?

Jack was not in the room; in fact, no one was in the room, as LeMar verified by a quick survey. His eyes were growing clearer now, and he felt more himself. He was filled with an abiding curiosity to know what had happened during the time that he had been unconscious to what passed around him. He reached for the bell button to summon a boy and make inquiries.

Pinned to the button was a note. It was in an envelope on which the monogram of the Garrison Hotel was printed, and it had evidently been written at his own secretary desk over there in the other corner of the room. Consumed with eagerness, and altogether forgetful of his aching head, LeMar tore it from its fastenings and ripped up the flap. There were two sheets of hotel stationery folded inside, and with trembling hands the magician spread them out before him and read:

MY MOST ESTEEMED PROFESSOR LEMAR:

As a wizard you are a wonder, my dear fellow, but really you will never make a success as a detective. Your methods are too direct, far too crude to show any possibilities of improvement with study, research and painstaking effort. Stick to your stage mysteries, my friend, and leave the real ones, and particularly this one, severely alone. It will be better for all concerned, and especially for Miss Rose Kellar, in whom you display such a profound and suspicious interest. I do not mind admitting, professor, that I enjoy seeing you behind the footlights. But I must insist that you stay there and not meddle in affairs that do not in the least concern you.

I am quite aware that you wish to know, naturally, what has taken place since you entered the machine which I had hired for the occasion. And, by the way, it will do you no good to try to trace me in that way, as another person hired it for me, without knowing for whom it was intended, so that trail would lead you only up a blind alley.

I have a little portable device—simply a little electric affair, which I invented, attachable to any electrically equipped automobile—by which my chauffeur and I can remain in constant though silent communication. I do not mind telling you that my chauffeur and I are inseparable friends, and that he is a very clever and a very daring man. If he were not, he could not remain in my confidence, which means that he could not remain on earth, as he would then be dangerous.

Well! By means of this portable device, one end of which is connected with my pocket, the other to my chauffeur's ear, I ticked off, by telegraph, a full explanation of my predicament. I was captured! And he got rid of you and your well-dressed friend by the simple—and rather disgustingly elemental—fashion of black-jacking you. He stopped the machine, hit you both on your heads, and over you fell into our tender hands.

Now note how graciously kind we have been to you. We could have thrown you out in the street, we could have dropped you overboard, we could have done worse. But we did nothing of the kind. First, I managed, with the aid of some material purchased at a near by drug-store, to attend your wounds. I had five years in medicine and surgery—one year post-graduate at Johns Hopkins—and so I did a fairly neat job, I think. Then I bundled you up nicely and brought you, of all places in the world, to your own hotel.

There is one point about which I must really ask your forgiveness. It was necessary, in order to avoid an embracing colloquy, to offer some kind of logical, reasonable and simple explanation to the hotel clerk. I adopted the simple expedient of informing them that you and your friend were intoxicated, and had been injured in a drunken brawl.

Your friend is in his room, next to you. I did not write him a note, as I fear his intelligence would not appreciate the finer points which

I insist enter into all my correspondence. You may tell him about it, and tell him I am sorry a little blood got on the braided cord of his spectacles. I left one dollar on his bureau which will buy him a new one.

Just one other thing. I am not going to tell you how I managed the sudden disappearance of the young lady. As an illusionist, you might be able to figure that out, as I had to do. But you may rest assured that unless the young lady complies with my wishes she will die a most horrible death at my hands. And you may rest assured, my charming young friend, that your life will go out like the flame of a candle in the draft if you get in my way. You have never heard of me before. Leave me to my delicate little whim and fancies, and my artistic pursuits, and you can go ahead and do anything else you like, with no interference from me. But raise one finger to oppose me and your last hour is set. God bless you!

RAVEN.

Chapter Twelve
A REAL CLUE

WHEN JACK BROWN, IN SOME CONSTERNATION, entered LeMar's room, not half an hour later, he found the magician still sitting erect in the bed, staring very hard at his own rather bedraggled image in the mirror. He had no inkling of what had transpired, but had rushed to LeMar's room as soon as he had regained his senses. LeMar could not restrain a smile at the unkempt bewilderment of his friend, who stood regarding him in the doorway with an air of wearied astonishment.

But the situation called neither for smiles nor wasted wonder, but for action. No one knew that better than LeMar. Silently he offered the self-explanatory note to Jack Brown, while he knitted his brows again and tried to reconcentrate his scattered mental forces. Stirring back in the dim recesses of the conjurer's memory was a clue, and he was doing his best now to rescue it. It was elusive, intangible, tantalizing and obscure, and the hazy condition of his mind now, as a result of the blow on his head, made thinking a labor of thrice-fold difficulty. But LeMar was a man who never balked at difficulty, and he was never willing to admit defeat. He told himself doggedly that he had just begun to fight. Even in his present battered condition he felt the tang of real sport in matching his courage, his skill and his audacity against such a merciless, conscienceless man as the writer of that note had proclaimed himself to be. And still that lurking suspicion that refused to define kept dancing like an elfin thing in his mind, always escaping capture.

He reached over to the little table beside his bed and secured the telephone. Jack was still immersed in an excited perusal of the note from the man who had signed himself "Raven." LeMar ordered a neat little supper with a bottle of wine to be brought to his room immediately, an order which quite upset the decidedly *blasé* phone clerk at the desk. When he hung up the receiver, Jack had finished reading Raven's message.

"Whew!" exclaimed the business manager as he threw himself in a chair. "We're up against a bear-cat!"

His brows still contracted, LeMar looked his friend squarely in the eye.

"I'm going to know something in a minute, Jack," he said.

Jack only stared. For once the loquacious fellow was silenced. The events of the night had robbed him of all his picturesque expletives and explosives. He did not know what to say. He was losing his capacity to be surprised. He merely waited for LeMar to explain himself.

"That cruel note there," continued the magician, "is a blessing in disguise. It has given us a starting-point which we lacked before. We know now where we stand."

"How?" inquired Jack.

"Before that note was left for me we did not know what to think. Now we know something. We know that Rose Kellar has been kidnapped for a purpose. We know she has been kidnapped by an unscrupulous, self-confessed murderer, who desires her to do something, the nature of which we do not now comprehend. Our line of action must now be to find that man. *And I think I know who he is!*"

"You mean you think you know the identity of Raven?"

"Exactly. Or, at least, I know how to find out. Ever since that moment that I saw Rose in his clutches, in that wild moment when the opened automobile slid past us, my mind has been busy trying to dig up from past memories the name of that man. I am certain I have seen him before. I am certain that I shall soon remember—Eureka!"

The last word the magician shot out like a vocal explosion. He leaped out of bed in his sudden excitement.

"It must be true!" he said, after a tense pause. "He has been missing from America for years!"

"Who?" asked Jack in exasperated impatience.

"Wait!" bade the magician, as he paced the floor. "We must be certain about it. We must see Nagen about it. Nagen will tell us. Nagen knows everything about everybody, and Nagen never forgets. We must get Nagen out of bed!"

"Who is Nagen?" persisted Jack.

"Never mind! I'll introduce him to you before another hour is over. We shall not rest, Jack, old boy, until this thing is settled, one way or the other. We do not know why Raven has kidnapped Rose, but we're going to get her back before he gets a chance to put his hands on her again."

A rap came at the door, and a waiter came in with a tray, on which a tempting little meal had been prepared. It warmed their hearts to gaze on it. Though both were distressed at the peril of the missing girl, and eager to be at the search, they already felt the need of stimulating themselves for the trials they felt sure lay ahead of them. It did occur to Jack that they ought to be moving without pausing for a meal, but he had naturally accepted the self-imposed leadership of LeMar and so he did not question what he had ordered. They fell to on the viands and the wine without loss of time, and fifteen minutes later felt renewed and refreshed for whatever might befall.

Only once did they pause during the meal. That was when LeMar became suddenly but laconically communicative.

"I told you!" he said, with a glass of wine half-lifted to his lips. "I told you once, Jack, that a magician would make an ideal detective. I tell you now that a magician is the only person who can solve this strange puzzle."

Jack was munching, but he shook his head to indicate that he wanted to know why.

"Because," replied LeMar, "it was by magic that Rose Kellar vanished for the second time to-night. I was a fool not to have guessed it. I was a fool not to have denounced that scoundrel then and there. He is turning our own art against us, Jack. He used a principle of stage magic to vanish that girl under our very eyes, and I was taken in by it. And I can see now that it will be by using magic against him that I shall win her back."

"You mean," spluttered Jack, himself vanishing a big mouthful in the same instant, "that you will use magic in your detective work? You mean that by magic you will recover Rose Kellar?"

"By magic!" answered LeMar, but he refused to explain another word. All Jack's attempts at conversation from that moment on were fruitless. The magician was planning his course now, and his dancing eyes showed that he was not engaged on a hopeless task. There was a scheme in his head which promised well. Any one could see that, who noted the gleam of eager interest in his eyes, and the way that his fingers were beating a devil taps on the table. Jack noticed that as he dressed he stowed some arrangement under his coat, but he could not guess what it was.

A few moments later they were in a taxi cab, rolling under the giant L structure on the East Side. Nagen, LeMar had explained, lived on Third avenue, not far from Eighty-second street. He would not mind being called out of bed, for Nagen was a good fellow, under any and all circumstances.

The magician and his friend left the taxicab at the corner and walked to the center of the block. The dwelling-place of this mysterious friend of the magician was on the third floor of the place, the lower floor being given over to a store. At the entrance to the left there were three bells, and beside this, on a small plate, was the name "Nagen." They read it with difficulty by the light of the street lamps near by.

LeMar pressed the button, without relaxing the pressure of his thumb, for several minutes. Again and again he rang it, until at last there came a little clicking noise at the door and it fell back a little, the latch having been released. The two partners of the night stepped into the narrow hallway and began the ascent of the stairs. They were half-way up when they discovered a figure on the first landing. It was a very small man, with tousled hair and a sandy mustache, holding a candle, and staring with unmitigated curiosity at the two men mounting the steps.

"Hello, Charley!" called out LeMar. "Don't you know me?"

"LeMar!" cried Nagen, in a transport of delight. "Nobody I'd sooner have get me out of bed than you. Come right up. But what's the big idea?"

LeMar waited until they were in the neatly furnished reception-room at the front of the little flat. Nagen lit the gas, and then turned again inquiringly to his visitors.

"Nagen," began LeMar abruptly. "Charley Nagen, you're supposed to have the greatest collection of old books, photographs, programs and other magical relics among all the amateur magicians in America. Is that right?"

"Outside of Houdini and Ellison," admitted Nagen with great honesty.

"Well! You showed me a scrapbook you had once, with photographs in it of famous magicians then appearing before the public—I think it was dated in 1915. I'd like to see that scrapbook now."

Nagen darted a quick little glance at LeMar, as if the question of his sanity or his sobriety had just occurred to him. Without a word he shuffled over to a little bookcase, which he opened reverently and rummaged around for a moment or two. Then he drew forth a bulky volume and spread it on the top of the old-fashioned square piano which occupied one portion of the room.

"Come here, Jack," said LeMar, and there was a thrilling little note in his voice, as if he felt himself on the trail of something vital and startlingly important. Nagen stood back, while the two bent over the scrapbook, and LeMar quickly turned the leaves. About the middle of the book he paused, and drew back the book quickly, so that Jack did not see.

"Charley," said LeMar, "who is this man?"

Nagen came closer and gave one glance at the portrait which he himself had pasted in the book a few years before.

"That is Doctor Grim!" he said decidedly. "Very few people remember him now. He was only here one season. He came from Australia with a big magic show and toured the country. Then all at once he disappeared. There were queer stories circulated about him; I've got some notes of him there in my scrapbook of biographies. He was one of the best magicians who ever came to this country—it was a loss to the stage when he left. Why?"

LeMar made him no reply. Instead, he passed the book silently to Jack. And the business manager recognized the picture as Raven, the man with the red scar.

CHAPTER THIRTEEN
DOCTOR GRIM

AT A WORD FROM LEMAR, the obliging Nagen passed into another room, where more of his treasures were kept, and presently reappeared bearing another scrapbook. This he laid beside the other on the piano, and hastily ran his fingers over the pages. He stopped at a place where a sheet of typewritten notations had been carefully pasted in.

"I got 'em all, Mr. LeMar," he said, with a broad smile. "There ain't no man in the magic business I ain't got the dots on. They say, some of the professionals, that the magical amateurs are pests, but they know where to come when they want something!"

Ignoring this, LeMar bent over the opened page, with Jack close beside him. Together they read this surprising entry:

> GRIM. Dr. Raven Grim. Supposedly born in Australia. Came to America with a magic show in 1915, and toured America for one season, playing the popular priced houses. Was quite successful, and his subsequent disappearance created some talk in the theatrical world. Wild rumors were circulated concerning him. He was reported to have led, at one time, the life of a bush ranger and an outlaw in the wilder portions of Australia. Notorious for his bold nature, and his uncompromising attitude on everything in which he was engaged. Those who played in his company were said to have lived in terror of him. Many were heard to wonder why he had taken to the profession of conjuring. Was always experimenting with scientific effects, to produce new illusions for his show. Was also said to have enormous financial resources, the results of his bushwhacking days. Many vain attempts were said to have been made by the Australian police to find the hiding-place of his ill-gotten gains, but never with success.

LeMar and Jack Brown exchanged quick looks of understanding. Certainly this corresponded well with what they knew of Raven. The name Raven Grim, too, seemed conclusive. And while this brought them no nearer the solution of the mystery on which they were bent, it at least cleared the way for the work they had in hand. Nagen, meanwhile, was getting restless from curiosity.

"Would you mind telling me why you wanted to get this information at this hour in the morning?" he asked LeMar. "It looks sort of funny."

His ingenuous manner brought a smile to the face of the conjurer, but he shook his head.

"Are you still the New York correspondent for the *Sphinx*?" asked the magician, apparently irrelevantly, and naming a magazine devoted to the interests of magic and magicians. Nagen shook his head in the affirmative.

"Then," replied LeMar, "I can only say that you will have a first-class story to send the editor if we get what we are going after. Beyond that I cannot say a word now. Good-night, and many thanks, Charley!"

The puzzled collector was forced to be content, and led them to the stairway, where he lighted them down with his candle. Once more on the street, Jack faced LeMar with something like severity.

"Now, what on earth can we do next?" he asked.

LeMar smiled, with a suggestion of a superior air that nettled Jack just a little. The business manager felt that he was no longer altogether in the confidence of the magician, and he resented the fact just a little. He would prefer to think that he knew all the cards in the hand of his friend, but evidently the latter was not ready at that moment to play the game in that way.

"We shall see what we shall see," murmured the magician, and not another word passed between the two friends for the next five minutes. But things were happening which bore an important relation to the situation. LeMar stepped up to the taxi driver, paid him and dismissed him. Then the two set off down deserted Third avenue, which at that hour was very dark and lonesome. The fall of their feet echoed across the empty street, drowned only once by the savage, roaring rush over their heads of a belated elevated train.

Down Third avenue they continued until they reached a dark street in the upper Seventies. Into this they turned quickly, LeMar seizing Jack's arm and almost dragging him with one mighty effort around the corner. Of course, Jack was surprised, but he was getting used to unexpected tactics by this time and soon recovered his balance. He gave himself up to LeMar's leadership absolutely, which was well. The magician skipped into a dark doorway, with Jack right in back of him. LeMar put his finger to his lips and they crouched back in the shadows.

Suddenly they heard a sound. Some one else had turned the corner and had suddenly hastened his stride into an energetic walk. The footsteps were coming nearer.

In a flash Jack understood, LeMar had guessed they were being followed. He had not regarded that as a calamity, but had welcomed it as an opportunity. They had eluded their shadow, and Jack could foresee their next step. They would follow the man who had set out to follow them.

Meanwhile, the footsteps came closer.

CHAPTER FOURTEEN
TO THE RAVEN'S HIDING-PLACE

WHEN THE MAN WHO HAD BEEN TRAILING THEM turned the corner he evidently saw at once that he had been tricked. LeMar guessed rightly that he had believed himself secure from detection, and felt sure that by keeping about half a square behind them he could follow them throughout the night without himself being observed. Accordingly, when he came around the bend and saw his men had vanished, he hastened his pace in the hope of passing them as they were entering some house on the block. His job then would be to wait until they came out.

As LeMar heard him coming closer, the danger of this suddenly suggested itself. Instead of going back to his superior, this shadow might remain on guard until daybreak. Moreover, they themselves might be ousted from their hiding-place at any moment. Some one emerging through the door of the vestibule in which they were sheltered would discover them immediately. Explanations would then be in order, and however they might bluff, the end was fairly certain. They would be forced into the street again, and while they might manage to shake their shadow, they would surely have no further opportunity to trail him.

These reflections were speedier than a flash of lightning. In less than two minutes the man would be opposite them. He would pass them, go to the end of the block, and probably return. They must do something. LeMar fidgeted behind the door, racking his brain for some expedient that would serve them in this latest emergency.

"Good Lord! I'm getting sleepy!" whispered Jack.

At any other time the remark would have irritated LeMar to exasperation. He knew Jack didn't mean it. The business manager was simply irrepressible; he had to be saying something, and having nothing better to say at the time, he observed that he was sleepy. To a man of LeMar's temperament, under such circumstances, such a jest could hardly prove otherwise than annoying. But in that time of uncertainty it brought with it a happy inspiration that solved the problem.

"Jack," whispered the magician hurriedly, "you've solved it. This fellow is liable to wait for us to show ourselves and stay here all night. He thinks we've gone in some house on this block with some important object, and he'll never leave us. *Sh!* Wait a minute!"

The wizard's eye was at the crack formed by the hinges of the door. The man they believed had followed them was about to pass. They could hear the beating of their hearts as they waited.

He was walking very rapidly as he came suddenly into their line of vision. Like a shadow picture on a screen he darted past, visible to them only for a second. They strained their eyes to see him, fearful that he would go by too quickly. But it was enough. They both saw and recognized him. He was the chauffeur who had driven the car in which Rose Kellar had been a prisoner.

LeMar's fingers closed around Jack's wrist, impelling silence; he waited until the sound of retreating footsteps told him the chauffeur was out of earshot. Even then he whispered his plan.

"Say good-night loudly," the magician said quickly. "Remark that you will meet me in the morning, and that everything will come out all right. Do it naturally. Tell me to stay here and get a good night's sleep. Then go to the next L station, go up and jump on a car, and go back to the hotel. Go to bed and wait until I show up. I will let you hear from me."

Then LeMar had an incipient riot on his hands. In profane whispers and elaborate gestures, with vigorous shakings of his head and gritting of his teeth, Jack Brown declared his complete animosity to such a plan. He refused to listen to LeMar's entreaties. He was a partner in the night's adventure, and he intended to stick.

But LeMar refused to be budged from his intention.

"Can the argument!" he said, not unkindly, and his slangy words had the air of *camaraderie* in them. "It's just got to be, old fellow, and it's got to be quick. We've got to fool that fellow, and fool him now. He'll be back presently. Go on and do what I tell you. Remember, we're not out on a lark. Rose Kellar's life is in danger!"

Obediently, but very unwillingly, Jack prepared to leave. Having been graduated from the stage into the front of the house, he was sure to give a good account of himself in the little comedy which LeMar had outlined, and the conjurer waited with entire assurance that Jack would carry it off well.

The business manager stepped carefully from behind the door and then began to speak. He did not raise his voice too high, but he made his words clear enough for the man down the street to hear.

"Good-night, LeMar!" he said. "Don't come back to the hotel to-morrow. It isn't wise. You stay here and let me handle matters as you directed. Try to get some sleep now. Everything will come out all right, you can bank on that. Good-night!"

Then, to the surprise of LeMar, he deliberately raised his foot and gave a strong kick against the door. It was expertly done, the result of inspiration. On the silence of the night it sounded exactly as if a door had been closed. But LeMar trembled for himself. That kick against the door was loud enough to wake up any one in the house; he felt his own position would soon become untenable.

Jack, meanwhile, sauntered down the steps and gazed carelessly up and down. LeMar wondered what he saw. With a buoyant little whistle—for Jack was an inveterate whistler—he descended to the pavement and set off briskly in the direction of the Third avenue L, which was less than half a square distant. The nearest station was three blocks away.

From his hidden post of observation LeMar watched eagerly. He heard Jack's whistle, as it grew fainter and fainter in the distance. Then along came a north-bound elevated train, with a crashing, roaring rush that drowned out every sound, and the anxious magician could not tell whether the man had swallowed the bait or not.

He was not kept long in doubt. Before the noise of the train had died out the chauffeur of Raven came suddenly into view. He made straight for the steps which Jack Brown had vacated not two minutes before.

LeMar braced himself for a struggle. The chauffeur was slenderly built, and the wizard had no fear in a fair fight.

The man entered the vestibule stealthily and quickly, moving with a cat-like noiselessness, after having glanced rapidly all around him to see if he were observed. Once within the vestibule the object of his mission became apparent. He was not there searching for LeMar. He had another purpose.

In his hand was a small flashlight, which he turned on and played the tiny stream of light over the mail-boxes, each with its little card bearing the names of those who occupied the apartments. The man studied each name rapidly but carefully. Evidently he was prepared to give a full report to his employer.

Then, replacing his flashlight in his pocket, he darted out of the vestibule and rushed off on a silent run for Third avenue. One important piece of information gained, he evidently was now hot on the trail of Jack Brown, believing he might learn something from that young gentleman's movements after all.

Hope once more in his heart, LeMar, too, emerged to the street. But not before he had gazed carefully around the edge of the doorway and assured himself that the chauffeur had himself rounded Third avenue. He blessed the fates which had kept the policeman on the beat out of the way, for such suspicious actions would undoubtedly have drawn him down upon them had he seen them.

The magician set off, sure in his conviction that the man he was trailing would lead him to Rose Kellar.

CHAPTER FIFTEEN
THE HOUSE OF MURMURS

IN THE BEGINNING THINGS HAPPENED exactly as LeMar had hoped and planned for.

The chauffeur of Dr. Raven Grim had caught sight of Jack as soon as he rounded the corner. LeMar's business manager purposely had sauntered, so that he should not be lost in the dark shadows beneath the elevated structure. And Jack was whistling so merrily and so jauntily that the trailer, LeMar felt sure, was completely deceived.

Thus, when the magician rounded the corner, there was a little procession of three, strung out in less than two blocks. Jack was making his way unconcernedly to the steps leading to the L station not far away. The chauffeur of Doctor Grim was tracking him silently, loitering as Jack loitered, and hastening his steps whenever Jack took it in his head to hurry. Behind these two came LeMar, determined to play the game out to the finish, to stake his all for the prize which he held so dear.

He hoped that the man ahead would give up his pursuit as soon as he saw Jack safely on the L train. LeMar had adopted one always valuable trick of the detective. It had come to him naturally—the knack of putting himself automatically into the shoes of his antagonist, and striving to understand his psychology, to get his viewpoint, so that he might anticipate what he might do before he did it. These were the tactics he had employed in the present crisis. All the schemes buzzing in his head for the rescue of Rose Kellar, and the capture of the relentless Doctor Grim, depended on his success in inducing this chauffeur to lead him to the bandit's hiding-place.

"Just give me the chance!" cried LeMar, in a little whisper, addressing the moving shadow of the chauffeur, half a block away. "I dare you! A magical detective matched against a magical criminal! Well, Doctor Grim, from Australia, or from wherever else you may be, I'm ready for you. My magic is greater than your diabolic capacity for crime, and here is where white witchcraft will triumph over black art!"

With these things in his mind he continued the little game of hide and seek in which they were engaged with fresh enthusiasm. Matters were going well, and the crucial test was almost before them. They had crossed the last street—Jack and the man behind him—and were almost at the steps leading up to the platform. The chauffeur halted and instinctively LeMar stepped into a doorway. There he was invisible, but he realized that if the man he was following were to turn and retrace his steps, he must face discovery and total failure. That was a chance which must be met. LeMar could only watch and wait prayerfully.

The chauffeur stepped out into the street, where, masked by the darkness near a great steel girder, he was almost obliterated. Plainly he was sure he was safe from observation. He watched Jack climb the long flight of steps, and waited until, a little while later, a south-bound train rumbled up, stopped and then rushed off again.

But still the man under the steel girder did not move. He was too crafty to be thus careless of his own business. Certain that the train had gone, he stepped boldly from his hiding-place, and LeMar saw him go up the L steps himself.

For the moment LeMar was nonplussed. Somehow, he had never associated this man with the idea of riding downtown on an L. This will serve to show that, with all the brains and cunning and courage in the world, LeMar was not yet a finished detective. If he were, he would have tried to have looked far enough ahead to foresee any emergency. He had felt so certain that the chauffeur of Doctor Grim would not return downtown on the elevated train that he had not considered what his own course would be if he did.

As it turned out, however, this worry was without cause. The man had not climbed up the steps for the purpose of catching the next train, but, as LeMar surmised on seeing him soon reappear, to assure himself that his quarry had really taken himself home to the hotel. Possibly he had inquired of the guard if the man who mounted those steps had really boarded the train. This was a crafty fellow, this assistant of Dr. Raven Grim; a man who took no chances, possibly because he knew what to expect from his terrible employer if he were to fail.

LeMar's nerves were tingling now. Things were going too well, he told himself with superstitious dread. Without glancing either to the right or the left, the chauffeur set off at a fast pace, and LeMar, letting him put about a block between them, started in pursuit. They were off, and the magician was happier than he had been since the troubles of the night had overtaken him. Unarmed, except with the knowledge that he was up against the most audacious, unscrupulous man with whom he had ever come in contact, and a magical weapon in which he placed such confidence, he set off joyously, eager for the moment when he and Raven Grim again should stand face to face, no matter how unequal the odds. There was no fear in LeMar's heart, any more than there was overconfidence. He fully appreciated the danger that he was soon to run; his experiences earlier in the evening had been ample confirmation of all the threats in the letter from Raven. But he cared not, because he was ready to make any sacrifice in behalf of the imprisoned girl. He was ready to give his all, and thus he had no further reason to be afraid of anything. Indeed, he felt high hopes of being able to effect a rescue, if given half a fighting chance.

He was very cautious, and yet not too much so. That is to say, he did not go slinking along in the shadows of the buildings, like a wary gunman, about to hold up some one. That would have been the surest way of attracting the attention of any one else who was passing. It was exceedingly difficult to manage, because, if he did anything to arouse the suspicions of the man in front, the game would end right then and there. And in the hush of the early morning it is almost as impossible a task to follow a man, perhaps for miles, and not do something to apprise him of that fact.

Luckily for LeMar, it was not necessary to follow the chauffeur far, else it is possible that he would have been detected, and the outcome of this affair might have been altogether different. The man walked down Third avenue for three more blocks and then swung west, covering block after block, until he was approaching the Drive. Behind him, as relentless as his own shadow, crept LeMar, always walking so that his feet made no sound on the pavements, always ready to dart back of some sheltering steps, if his man were to turn quickly.

They were less than a square from the Drive when LeMar knew that his work was at an end. The chauffeur stood at the curb, and suddenly began coughing violently. It was an unusually well-counterfeited cough, but LeMar felt sure that it was counterfeit, and that it was done for a purpose. He believed it was a signal to some one inside one of the houses.

In this view he was presently confirmed by what happened. The man he had followed rang no bell; gave no additional evidence of his desire to enter the house before which he had taken his stand. He simply walked up the steps, and before he had had time to fit a key into the lock, LeMar heard the slamming of a heavy door.

The magician waited for no more. His eyes intent on the house in which he felt sure Rose Kellar was a prisoner of an ex-Australian bandit, he walked forward swiftly, but still silently. The house was one of those large, ornate, five-story brown-stones, and bore an air of the utmost elegance. Its basement windows were guarded with curving, bellying, twisted iron bars of Venetian design, and as his eyes traveled up the front of the place, the magician was surprised to note that bars such as these were in front of all the many windows at the front. It gave him a new insight into the elaborate arrangements which Doctor Grim had made for his mysterious pursuits; it gave him new fear for the fate of Rose Kellar, if he were too late, and new courage to go on.

As he stood there a strange sound arrested his attention. It was a confusion of murmurings, a low shrillness of many excited voices—thrilling, because there was so much wild passion and earnest intensity, such tragedy and such burlesque, in their notes. It was like a low-pitched but hysterical chorus of women's voices coming from somewhere in or near this large, dark house of Dr. Raven Grim. LeMar wondered at it, puzzled over it, with all his soul.

As his eyes rested vacantly on the darkened front, while he struggled to interpret those singular sounds, he saw a heavy brass plate at one side of the door. It glistened from the rays of a street lamp, and he saw it was lettered with a legend. Rather incautiously, he mounted the steps, where he could read the sign. It was a stunning surprise to him when he did read it.

THE RETREAT OF THE RAVENS. NERVOUS CASES A SPECIALTY.

So this was a sanitarium. Those were voices of mad women he had heard.

And his Raven—what new mask was this? LeMar began to believe the problem was even deeper than he had dreamed.

He did not need to reconnoiter the premises to learn that this house was practically impregnable. Already he knew enough of Dr. Raven Grim to be sure of that. But LeMar did not care. He had gotten what he had asked for and he was satisfied; the future now rested with him. In the chase after the Raven chauffeur he had promised the Fates that if he would only be led to the lair of this criminal he would ask no more; that he would then be able to fight his own battles. For LeMar was hugging a strange weapon to his bosom, a weapon which gave him such confidence that he wanted only to be face to face with the abductor.

Therefore, he wasted no time seeking a way in which to steal into the retreat of the Raven. Instead he walked boldly up the steps and rang long and loudly.

The door was opened by the very man LeMar had followed to the house. On the latter's face a slow astonishment spread as he beheld the identity of this early morning visitor.

"Tell Doctor Grim that LeMar is here!" said the magician sternly, and stepped over the threshold.

CHAPTER SIXTEEN
THE LATEST ILLUSION OF DOCTOR GRIM

LEMAR WAS LEFT WAITING in the dimly lighted, luxurious hallway only a very few moments.

The returning man-servant, chauffeur and confidential assistant of Doctor Grim asked him in a low voice to follow him down to a door at the farther end. The fellow's face was as cryptic as the sphinx. LeMar entered this doorway and found himself in a brilliantly illuminated reception room. Not five feet away from him was Dr. Raven Grim.

Faultlessly fitted in full evening dress, his graying hair thrust back adventurously above his high forehead, his unnaturally pale face lighted with condescending welcome, the abductor of Rose Kellar made a dignified bow before the magician. Even in his turbulent, excited state of mind LeMar could not help observing the polished air, the finished deportment of the man. He was a Chesterfield among criminals.

"We meet again, my good LeMar," said Grim unctuously. "Sit down and rest yourself before I kill you!"

"Bring Rose Kellar to me before I kill you!" cried LeMar, and his voice, too, was cool and threatening.

"There's a contradiction of desires," said Grim amiably. "We shall settle it this way: I shall let you see the young lady, and then we shall see who dies!"

He deliberately turned his back upon the magician and strode over easily to a cellaret. His coolness was meant to be disarming. Quickly LeMar looked around him. He was entirely alone with Dr. Raven Grim, and while he did not know how many invisible eyes were watching them, how many invisible hands waiting to interfere, should there be a struggle, he did not much care. For LeMar was holding back a trump card, and though he was playing a lone hand he was beginning to believe more and more that he was going to win. Meanwhile, Doctor Grim set glasses and a decanter on the table.

"Ordinarily," he apologized, "I do not mix my own drinks. Alphonse, my man, whom you followed to-night, is a past master. But there are times when things must be said and done of which even my confidential Alphonse must not know too much. He will never ask a question about you—of that you may be entirely sure. The fact that you and I are alone is all that is necessary for Alphonse, for he knew that was my desire. Now, LeMar, I must entreat you to sit down."

"I prefer to stand," LeMar answered.

"Then pardon me if I do not follow your example," replied Doctor Grim as he threw himself lazily into a comfortable chair, of broad and generous dimensions. His handsome, but cruel face, against the green velvet of the chair cushion, and the light playing full upon it, was a strange study. There was so much of ability there as to deceive even a practiced observer. But, with a key to the man's character, the markings of his character stood out in bold relief—the symbols of genius, prostituted to evil.

Doctor Grim held up his glass, in which the green liquor sparkled and glowed, and studied it musingly.

"For the love of a woman," he said, "many men have done foolish things. Poor old Mark Antony—what an ass he made of himself for that Cleopatra woman! In some of the writings of contemporaneous scribes I have read that Cleopatra was an overwhelmingly fascinating creature. But she was just like any other woman, after all, and there were thousands of others to pick from, to say nothing of Mrs. Mark Antony, who was called Octavia. Yet for the sake of Cleopatra Mark Antony lost everything, and at last, LeMar, life itself.

"Now, you are just as big a fool as Mark Antony. There are thousands of other women in the world, and yet because I happen to need the one who had caught your eye—*pouf!* You make it necessary for me to make away with you. And you know you are a clever fellow, LeMar, a damned clever fellow, and I hate to see you go!"

He lighted a cigar, leisurely, almost lazily, and watched the rings of smoke as they mounted like fragrant incense to the ceiling. Once he stole a quiet, calculating look at LeMar, but if he expected to find any weakening signs there, he was disappointed. Rigid, raging, prevented from springing at his cool monster's throat only by the prompting hope that something would happen, something would turn up that would give him an advantage, the magician stood with folded arms.

"Dr. Raven Grim, you have made a mistake," said LeMar, with a contemptuous smile that did not escape the attention of his smiling enemy. "I shall not be killed by you, now, or at any other time. You are going to the penitentiary, and your journey will soon begin. You will be lucky if you escape the electric chair!"

With a sudden burst of laughter Doctor Grim flung back his head and gave vent to the heartiest amusement. For a moment he paused, sat up and stared impudently at LeMar, then relaxed again into derisive laughter. It was the first crack in the fine veneer of his polished bearing; the first showing through of his bushwhacking, primitive, lack of those qualities which make a real gentleman.

"My dear LeMar," he cried, wiping away his tears. "Don't be absurd now. Do you know what you are, so far as the law and the prophets are concerned? You are a lunatic! This is a lunatic asylum. I am a lunatic doctor. I have been established here for years. What chance would you have, if you went to one of my windows and called for help? The passers by, even the policeman on the beat, would say that one of my patients was getting unruly. That thing has happened a good many times already—it would not be unusual. The police would remember it in all the years I have been here."

"Yes. You have been here since 1915," shot back LeMar with savage meaning.

The insinuation did not miss its mark. Master of himself always, even Grim could not conceal the fact that he was startled. He did not know that LeMar knew anything of his past. He turned toward the magician with a new glint in his eyes. "You seem well posted," he sneered, as he flecked the ashes from his cigar.

"So well posted," replied LeMar, "that I have taken the trouble to glance over some Australian memoranda!"

He was playing his few cards as best he dared. If he could trick Grim into believing he knew more of him than he really did he might be able to intimidate him into delaying matters for a little; he might gain time; at least, he might help himself in some way.

But Doctor Grim was far too shrewd to betray any further immediate interest in the subject. Only a taunting laugh greeted LeMar's last thrust, and Doctor Grim mixed himself another decoction. This he drained with the air of a connoisseur, remarking in a polite little aside that his guest's continued refusal of his wine was a distinct disappointment.

Finally he arose with a decisive air and stood facing LeMar in an elegant attitude, and with a devilish little smile curling his lips. LeMar knew that something more than ordinarily fiendish was about to develop, and mentally he made ready for whatever shock might be coming.

"Before you die," resumed Grim, renewing the unpleasant emphasis he placed on that phrase each time he used it, "I am going to show you some surprise. I was not aware that you knew anything of my past, but since you do, I suppose that you know I was once quite interested in the art by which you have gained such a professional reputation. It is too bad! The stage is to lose in you one of its very brightest and most promising entertainers. Remember that I say this to you—it shows you I cherish no professional or artistic jealousies. I have some new illusions in this house. They were designed for my patients—the mad people and the people the world and his wife choose to call mad—and some of them are ingenious. If you will come with me, now, into this next room, I shall show you the first of a series of such deceptions. As I have to be rid of you within an hour, I shall show you only this one, I fancy, but you may rest assured this is the chef d'œuvre. What the French call the *mise en scène* is most artistically developed. The atrocities reported to have been committed by the Kaiser's soldiers in Belgium and France first suggested the idea to me, and I have given it what I consider to be a most appropriate title—'Kultur'!"

"I am not interested in your illusions," snarled LeMar. "I have heard you too long. My patience is at an end. I warn you that I have not come here unprepared. I demand to see Miss Kellar instantly, and I shall not leave this house until she goes with me!"

Doctor Grim spread wide both hands and bowed in apologizing pantomime.

"I have been frank enough to inform you that I intend to remove you from your mundane activities," he said sweetly. "Now trust my frankness when I tell you that Miss Kellar is just now the subject of this new illusion—this 'Kultur'—and you cannot see her without seeing the illusion. Won't you pass in?"

LeMar studied his face for a moment. He wondered if he were walking into a trap. Certainly, everything pointed that way. Yet, there was something honest in this fiend's calm admission of his own evil; something so honest that LeMar was prompted from within to trust him now.

"Where is this thing?" he asked.

"It is in the next room. Let me be entirely frank with you. I shall give you one hour to watch it. At the end of that time you will be an entirely different man from what you are now. On my honor—and I am jealous of my honor, LeMar—I promise you no harm will come to you until you return to me in this room. I promise that you shall have one hour with Miss Kellar in that room, and that you will not be molested. At the end of that time you will be brought back into this room, and I shall see to it that you trouble me no more. But you will return here exactly as you are now, as free as you are now to work me injury. The only difference will be that you will hate me more than ever. If you have any hopes of overpowering me—but I warn you I am invulnerable—you will have as fair a chance then as now. But I think your presence in the next room will have a distinct psychological effect upon the young lady which will aid me in a very difficult and important matter."

LeMar was certain now that, in this, at least, Grim was not lying. It is a curious situation, when one enemy is ready implicitly to believe another in what may prove such a vital matter as this. Yet the magician could not escape the conviction that it would be better, if he were to go through that door, come what may; even if he were tricked, he might escape and find himself better able than ever to cope with the situation. And, it must not be forgotten, LeMar held a trump card of which Doctor Grim did not dream, and thus he felt secure against even the unknown mysteries of the room into which his host was so anxious that he enter.

And he had promised him an hour alone with Rose Kellar! In one breath the prospect looked hopeless and then filled with boundless possibilities.

An hour! One hour in which to defeat this man in his own fortress, to outwit him, his man Alphonse, and all their crew, to find Rose Kellar and to take her to freedom. The task, indeed, looked hopeless. As Grim stepped to the broad mahogany door at the other end of the room, LeMar watched him with eyes that saw not. Instead, he was thinking as drowning men are said to think, only the magician's mind did not conjure up any visions of his past. No pictures of his boyhood, his family or his early friends came to him now. Only the baffling puzzles of this strange business came to his thoughts. He saw again the accusing face of old man Neck, he heard again the devilish chuckle of his sister, he lived over again the dark uncertainty of those moments in the house of the medium, and the rest of the night flooded over his consciousness and dismayed him. He wondered what Jack would think.

The door swung inward ponderously. Like a courtier, Grim stood at one side, and with a hand put slightly forward, indicated to LeMar that he was to pass through.

"Go in and enjoy yourself," said Grim, with an ingratiating smile.

LeMar stepped across the threshold and the door closed behind him. Grim had not come with him. The room was dark—so dark that he could not see.

CHAPTER SEVENTEEN
"KULTUR!"

LEMAR WAS CERTAIN THE DOOR HAD CLOSED BEHIND HIM. He felt in back of him and his fingers closed over the knob. He turned the knob and pressed with all his might, but he knew before he had tried it that the door would not give. He was locked in.

It was, therefore, an acute shock, when a hand was suddenly placed on his shoulder, *from behind*. The door was closed, there was scarcely two inches of space between its heavy panels and his shoulders, and yet a hand came out of the rear and grasped him with a clenching firmness that betokened great strength. He was pushed downward with impatient force, and to his amazement found that he had simply been hurled violently into a chair. For some mysterious reason it was desired that he sit down, and so specter-like hands placed him, unresisting, in a sitting position.

At first, the magician did not understand this, but he was not long kept in doubt. The chair, which had been immediately in front of him, but invisible because of the darkness, was a massive, wooden affair, and evidently contrived with devilish ingenuity. LeMar rested his hands on the arms and suddenly felt himself caught in a clamp which had risen automatically to bind him. It was as if two other iron arms had closed over his own and gripped him to the chair. At the same moment two bars of steel closed around his waist and locked. He was again a helpless prisoner, secured to this chair, at the will and the scant mercy of Dr. Raven Grim.

LeMar then resigned hope. He was confident the chair in which he sat was some electric invention of the mind of Grim, and that in this he was to be executed without delay. But in this he forgot the promise of Doctor Grim that he was to witness his best and latest illusion—and LeMar did not know that Doctor Grim never broke a promise, except when it was expedient.

As he stared into the darkness the magician suddenly became aware that something was transpiring before his gaze. There was a light growing. Things were becoming more distinct, as if black mists were parting. Indefinite objects were taking form and substance, as the strange light grew more softly beautiful. At last the full setting for Doctor Grim's illusion was displayed.

There were two shining swords, crossed in mid-air, and suspended as if without support. Resting on their broad curved blades was the head of Rose Kellar. Below it, above it and all around it was nothing but space, which momentarily was growing brighter, from the illumination of soft lights which could not be seen.

The face of the girl was drawn, as if with intense suffering. The eyes were closed, the mouth drawn tightly down, as if her pain were great. There was nothing visible but her head, resting on the edges of the swords. To all intents and purposes, she had been decapitated. But the head was alive.

Fascinated at the dreadful horror of the picture which Doctor Grim had prepared for his entertainment, the magician could not, for the first few moments, speak. He watched in dumb wonder the eyes slowly open, and the girl gaze around her in startled fear. Then he found speech.

"Rose!" he cried. "It's I, LeMar!"

His voice echoed with eerie distinctness through the room. It reached her, though he fancied it seemed very faintly. She turned quickly and glanced all around, seeking him out, but not seeing him. Then he realized that he could see her, but that to her he was invisible.

"I am sitting just in front of you—not five feet away," he told her.

"Is it really you—or another torturer?"

It was Rose Kellar speaking, but LeMar would not have known if he had not seen her before him. So changed those sweet tones that had pleased him so well. They were hoarse and shaken now, as if they reflected the broken spirit which sent them forth. It shocked him.

"Really, it is I, little Rose," he hastened to assure her. "And I am here to save you. Take heart!"

"No!" she answered. "You cannot save me. You cannot fight against that unspeakable monster. Be careful what you say. He is listening, and he is so cruel that he will make you pay in suffering for everything you say against him—as he is making me pay now. Try to save yourself, and leave me to fight it out alone."

"Fight out what alone?" cried LeMar.

But she only closed her eyes wearily and was still. LeMar sat there in the dark, determined the situation could be solved, yet seeing no hope of solving it. If she could only tell him what she knew! If he could really have an hour with her, alone—utterly alone—with no listening master criminal to stop her, when she had gone too far. Surely she could help him save her, if she could but speak to him unheard.

But only a miracle could make that possible. He was bound hand and foot to a chair, and she was—well, only God and the devil knew what she was bearing. Only a miracle! Then why not a miracle?

The question answered itself. It came as a holy inspiration in that hour of despair, and it filled with exultation the heart of the harassed magician.

"Rose!" he cried sharply, "before you left the theater did you water the geraniums?"

There was a moment of dreadful silence. He wondered if she could understand. The seconds seemed hours, until her answer came:

"No, I did not, because I was too busy answering the correspondence."

"Did you have two lumps of sugar in your coffee at supper, as you insisted you would?"

"Yes, but I did not like the waiter. His mustache was too black!"

LeMar was happy. His hidden-meaning language had succeeded. He almost felt like shouting hurrah! Let Grim and his men listen all they cared to—the hour was young yet.

"The lobby was rather crowded when I came up tonight," he continued. "And did you notice that man with a crutch at the box office?"

"He looked like a German spy," answered the girl solemnly.

They talked incessantly. Moment after moment passed, without a pause, without a break, in that long, apparently purposeless, useless, utterly trivial conversation. They talked of everything, as if they were chatting over a dinner-table. They actually laughed. But always they talked; they did not pause, even to catch their breath. They used their hour well.

They had talked of all subjects; they had said nothing to inform the sensitive ears of Doctor Grim and his man Alphonse. Yet when presently the dark mists came again and hid his beloved one from his view; when strange hands came from the darkness and released the irons that bound him to the chair; when he was drawn back to the waiting Doctor Grim, all the mysteries of the night were lifted from his mind.

LeMar *knew* at last. And, knowing, he was all the readier for the battle.

CHAPTER EIGHTEEN
AGAIN—MAGIC AGAINST MAGIC

DR. RAVEN GRIM WAS STANDING IN THE CENTER OF THE ROOM, his arms folded, a smile of settled triumph on his face. He fairly gloated over the erect, sturdy figure of LeMar, who, released from the scene he had witnessed in the other room, had returned, as Grim had predicted, hating him more than ever.

"We shall parley no more," said Doctor Grim sternly. "By this time your inamorata has been told that you are to die. She believes that if she will break her long silence, a silence we have tried to shatter with the most exquisite tortures, only to fail, that I shall spare your life. In that case I may yet cause her to speak. But that, LeMar, will rest with the future—my immediate business now is with you, and I cannot longer delay. I am going to give you what you most certainly will appreciate—a magical execution!"

"Dr. Raven Grim," LeMar returned, "I beg of you to remember one or two things. Remember that until I saw you in the automobile to-night, the man with the red scar was a total stranger to me, except as I had pictured him in my imagination. Yet I tracked you here. I found you out, despite the best precautions you and your man could take. I have done other things against you, which I do not believe you know.

"Now I warn you! Bring Rose Kellar here to me; send us out into the night unharmed, now, without delay, or the death with which you have so vauntingly threatened me since I came here will overtake you before you are aware. I am not bluffing. This is your last chance."

The blazing fury of the magician's tones, the challenging note in his voice, the undaunted light on his face, his own sureness of himself, nearly stunned the amazed Grim.

"I really believe you think you can accomplish that," he sneered.

But his taunts failed to spur LeMar into losing that coolness, which was now his best weapon.

"It's magic against magic, Doctor Grim," he retorted slowly. "You tell me you have prepared for me a magical execution. I tell you that you shall die by magic, or be overpowered by magic—that you will be subject to my will—within five minutes if you do not accede to my demands!"

With an impatient gesture Doctor Grim turned on his heel and walked to the other side of the room. From out of a corner he wheeled a ponderous wooden cabinet, set on casters. He wheeled this to the center of the room, with that exact professional air assumed by an illusionist in exhibiting one of the famous stage cabinet feats.

"You are going into this cabinet," Grim assured him, as if he were explaining to an audience what was about to happen. "And you are going to disappear. I shall close that cabinet door upon you, and you will never be seen or heard from again. It is a remarkable invention, which you will have ample leisure to study during the process of shuffling off this mortal coil. And I promise you it shall be a painless affair!"

"You fiend!"

"Get in the cabinet," ordered Doctor Grim. His voice had lost its silken texture now; he spoke with the arrogance of a Hun.

"I shall not get in that cabinet. I am waiting for you to bring Rose Kellar to me," returned LeMar patiently.

"Choose!"

Doctor Grim had drawn from his pocket a revolver which he leveled directly at LeMar's head. He came nearer to him, his eyes dangerous, his mouth set in evil lines, his head bent forward, the very picture of brutal, merciless rage.

"Die one way or the other—choose quick!" he cried.

But LeMar cared nothing for either choice. He had dallied long enough. He had held off until he had his man where he wanted him. They were at the final grips, and the time for him to strike was at hand. He waited no longer.

As if frightened at the sight of the revolver, the magician threw up his hands, an action which brought a leer of scorn to the face of Doctor Grim. As his enemy came nearer, LeMar stood perfectly still, hoping and praying that he would come closer still. He waited, until Grim had paused, and was about to speak again.

Then an extraordinary thing happened.

Doctor Grim settled back a little on his heels, a look of blank astonishment on his face. A queer, dazed look overspread his face as if he were not certain of his bearings, or as if intoxication had suddenly seized him. He put out one foot to steady himself, and his arms spread out weakly, helplessly, in a vain effort to retain his balance. His eyes were rolling, and presently a little fleck of foam showed at each corner of his mouth. For a brief second his eyes came even with LeMar's, and the look of superstitious dread, of drunken terror in them was startling to behold.

Doctor Grim was reeling. He was clutching madly at the air to regain his balance, he was striving desperately to regain his hold upon himself, but he was losing out as second after second ticked away.

The room was in utter silence. There was no attendant near to watch, to spread the alarm.

Doctor Grim himself had said there were times when it were better that no one else be near. The hopelessness of his gaze, now, as he stood there, rolling and momentarily about to fall, showed how he was struggling to speak, and finding that he had no voice, no power to call, no strength to summon assistance, no—

He fell in a heap to the floor. And then LeMar, who, through all that tense three minutes had stood perfectly erect, hands lifted, as if he were mesmerizing the man who had sworn to destroy him, dropped to his side, his face eager and anxious. He rolled the fallen Doctor Grim over to one side and assured himself that his coma was really complete; that he had really gone off into a sleep of which no one could foretell the hour of awakening. It was the result of LeMar's contrivance concealed in his clothes.

Back upon his feet again, LeMar moved around the room with quick, cat-like motions, searching for ropes, or something that would aid him in binding his prisoner. To his surprise he found something far better—a pair of new handcuffs, in a cabinet drawer, and a set of heavy leg irons. Probably they had been used, at times, in keeping the inmates of this place quiet, for it must not be forgotten that this was a retreat for the insane.

In less time than it takes to tell, LeMar had these fetters firmly on the wrists and ankles of Dr. Raven Grim. Then he stuffed a handkerchief into his mouth, jamming it in chokingly tight, and securing it so tightly that he felt certain Doctor Grim, even if he should regain consciousness, could never work himself free in time to sound the alarm before LeMar and Rose Kellar could get to the street and safety.

But even then, anxious as he was to return to Rose Kellar and set her free, aware as he was that his danger was not yet over, by any means, so long as Grim's servants were near, LeMar was not content to leave him in that position on the floor.

There was the cabinet of death, into which Grim had hoped to place him, still standing, black, gaping, threateningly sinister in the middle of the floor. Why not put him in there? He had said it would mean the end of LeMar, when he was put in there, but that must depend on some hidden spring, some mechanism, which must be touched. Besides, in his present mood, with the memory of what had already been done to Rose Kellar, and what would have been done to him fresh in his heart, LeMar was not inclined to be over-particular in his treatment of Doctor Grim. What he wanted was to secure Doctor Grim in safety until he and Rose Kellar were out into the street, where they could invoke the protection of the law. An instant decided LeMar.

He dragged the heavy, unconscious form across the hardwood floor and lifted it into the cabinet. He did not look to see what was there. He simply threw the body into the cabinet and shut the door. It closed with an ominous crash, and LeMar quickly wheeled the cabinet back to its original resting-place in a far corner.

Then, with the joy of the conqueror in his heart, he bounded across the room and turned the knob of the door through which he had been thrust to witness the illusion called "Kultur." He turned the handle, and it gave beneath his grip. The door swung backward, and he rushed into the darkness where Rose Kellar, he knew, was waiting.

CHAPTER NINETEEN
ALPHONSE—AND ONE OTHER

THE ROOM IN WHICH HE HAD WITNESSED THE ILLUSION called Kultur was as dark as the Stygian cave. LeMar could not see his hand before his face.

He knew the perils of this house. He knew that the diabolical cunning of Doctor Grim might have laid all sorts of pitfalls into which he might tumble while groping about in search of Rose.

"Magic against magic," he repeated to himself grimly. "So far, Doctor Grim, my magic has outwitted yours—and here's where I score again!"

In the darkness, you could not have seen what he did, but if you had been at one of his performances, where this was one of his famous feats, you would not have been any the wiser. In one moment there was total blackness. In the next instant there was flaming light, which lit up the entire room. In LeMar's hand was a bowl, from which a fountain of flames was dancing and leaping, casting a cheerful, warming glow all around. This was the bowl of fire he ordinarily produced in the second part of his entertainment. It had still been hanging from its hiding-place under his coat.

It enabled the magician to see clearly and to gather his bearings. And before him, staring up at him in wide-eyed, dumbfounded amazement, too frightened to cry out, almost too happy to believe, was Rose Kellar. She looked at him as if he were an angel, suddenly come from Heaven. All the apparatus for the illusion which he had been shown had been removed; the room was simply a black dungeon now. Then LeMar saw the real plight of Rose Kellar.

She was seated, with her hands resting on a sort of stock in front of her, with two little sockets, into which her thumbs and had been placed. Clamps had been screwed on these, and it was evident the brave little woman was enduring agonies, but there was no murmur of pain coming between her pale lips. She was happy now; so happy that the tears were streaming down her face at the sight of him.

"I told you I'd come!" he said, as he sat the bowl of fire down on the floor and came over to her. "So this is how they tried to make you tell! Dear little Rose!"

There was a suspicious moisture in his own eyes as he bent low over the viciously fashioned framework, and with strong fingers tugged at the screws and bolts until the cruel clamps were loosened. Then he caught her hands and kissed them, and in that strange scene in the dungeon, with the bowl of magic fire glowing them with strange light, and with phantom shadows dancing all around them, he kissed her, twice, and clasped her close.

"Where is he?" whispered Rose fearfully.

"He's where he will be quiet for a little while longer," answered LeMar, as he put his arm around her. Then, releasing her for a second, he stooped and lifted the bowl of fire, which was now beginning to die down, the fuel being almost exhausted. "I have him gagged, handcuffed and leg-ironed in a cabinet of death in which he had promised to execute me. How's that?"

His voice was almost gay. Now that Rose Kellar was at his side again he felt as if all dangers were removed; the possibility of interference from any one else in the house worrying him very little. He felt equal to conquer a whole regiment of men like Doctor Grim, and every pressure of Rose Kellar's hand on his arm increased the size of the regiment.

As he came to the door again he fancied that he heard a slight noise in the room where he had left Doctor Grim a prisoner, but he was certain it was impossible for Doctor Grim to have escaped. Yet there was some little foreboding expectation of trouble in his breast, as still clasping his assistant tenderly he stepped again into the brilliantly lighted room.

But he was not prepared for the sight that met his gaze. Doctor Grim was not there. But Alphonse, a German-looking individual with a French name, was there. He was standing respectfully in the center of the room, as if waiting for orders. His eyes were on the floor.

In silence LeMar stood in the doorway regarding him. The long quiet soon struck the man as unusual, and he opened his eyes, resting his gaze upon the magician.

"*Gott in himmel!*" he yelled. "Go back! Doctor Greem!"

He whirled about and then ripped from his pockets two weapons. In one hand he clutched a long knife, in the other a revolver.

"Two for two!" he snapped, brandishing the knife threateningly. His evil little face was distorted by an expression of confident power. "Vat a fine business! Vy de h—I don't Doctor Greem come on!"

LeMar saw the plight of Rose Kellar. She was seated, with her hands resting on a sort of stock in front of him.

Swaying, overcome almost at this fresh trial, Rose Kellar leaned heavily on LeMar's arm. But he reassured her in tones in which there was not the slightest tinge of doubt or uncertainty.

"Don't be afraid of this German!" he cried. "Just let go my arm, dear, and stand behind me. He can't hurt you, and he can't hurt me."

Alphonse was dancing back and forth, trying to prevent their escape until his master came, and only too eager to use his weapons if he dared. It was plain LeMar's words had had no effect upon him; he believed the man and woman before him were utterly at his mercy, but he feared the will of his master and would not strike until it became what he considered necessary.

But LeMar was not disposed to wait. What he had done to Doctor Grim he could do to his man-servant. He raised his arms on a level with his shoulder and extended his hands toward the mouthing servant.

But before he could bring to pass what he wished, there was a startling interruption. In the outer hall there was a sound of rending, snapping wood and glass, and then the fall inward of a heavy door.

Immediately afterward a rush of feet resounded through the house as men came rushing down the hall. They pushed open the door and crowded in.

Leading them was a familiar figure. It was Jack Brown, and he had a squad of police with him!

CHAPTER TWENTY
WHAT HAPPENED TO DOCTOR GRIM

"WE'RE HERE!" CRIED JACK EXCITEDLY, glancing all around, as if expecting to find a roomful of men to subdue.

"Well, we can use you, all right," answered LeMar. "Here, officers! Seize that man!"

With a howl Alphonse darted back toward the door which led into the room of the Kultur illusion. He was half-way across when LeMar, bounding after him, caught him in an iron grip, and led him whimpering, mouthing and praying back to the little group of policemen. A lieutenant stepped forward with an air of authority and asked LeMar what had happened.

"Lieutenant, you're going to take back to the station-house the biggest feather you ever secured for your cap," replied LeMar. "I've caught you a rare bird—a raven—and this is his cage."

He walked over to the cabinet, which was now back in its corner, and placed one hand on its knob. The lieutenant cleared his throat, reddened and said impatiently:

"I don't get you, Mr. LeMar, but I want to know what's happened here."

But LeMar did not answer him. Instead he quickly drew back his hand from the cabinet, as if he had suddenly been stung, and when he again faced Jack and his blue-coated friends, his face was very grave.

"It's very singular," he said. "It is extraordinary!"

His obscurities were driving them to exasperation. The irate lieutenant repeated his demand. He wanted to know what had happened here. LeMar finally told him enough to satisfy him for the moment.

"The facts are simple," he said, "but it will require some little while to explain all the details. I do not understand them all myself. But the main facts are these. Dr. Raven Grim is a man for whom the governments of many countries would pay a handsome price, just to get him into their criminal courts, but none of them has as great a cause for securing him as the government of the United States. For reasons of his own, Doctor Grim abducted this young lady, who was an assistant in my magical entertainment, and brought her to this place. I followed him here. He set out to kill me, but, by means which it is not now necessary to describe, I overcame him, and placed him for safe-keeping in this cabinet. The most extraordinary thing is that I just burned my hand."

"You are sure of your facts?" asked the lieutenant, ignoring the last remark.

"I can prove them all!" answered LeMar.

The lieutenant then assumed charge of the situation. He ordered two men to make a search of the house, he ordered another to guard the door, and another to watch the terrified Alphonse. For himself he reserved the task of opening the door of the cabinet. He walked up to it confidently and placed his hand on the little ornamental brass knob.

Then he darted back, with a muffled little exclamation of acute pain.

"What in—? My hand is burned almost to the bone!" he complained, nursing it and staring blankly all around.

"I warned you," reminded LeMar. "It is a most extraordinary phenomenon."

"Did you say there was a man in there?" asked the lieutenant, looking seriously at LeMar.

"I handcuffed, and leg-ironed, and gagged Dr. Raven Grim and I put him in that cabinet," replied the magician. "I closed the door and locked it for safe-keeping."

The lieutenant turned to the man who was guarding Alphonse. They all noticed the chalky whiteness of abject fear on the face of this confidant of Doctor Grim. Now he was ghastly in his terror, and his eyes were fixed with an almost hypnotic stare on the cabinet.

"Make that man lead you to where there is an axe," commanded the lieutenant. "Keep the nippers on him so that he won't turn on you. Bring the axe here and break open this cabinet."

In a silence that was oppressive, the rest of them waited, all of them with eyes fixed on the cabinet. What would they find inside? That was the question that agitated them all. Though they knew the villainies of Doctor Grim, though they were fully aware—at least LeMar and Rose were—that he was capable of unspeakable cruelty, that he was a genuine example of a man possessed of an evil spirit, yet they dreaded the opening of the door. Tragedy, they knew, must be behind it—but a tragedy they feared to look upon.

And then, at last, the policeman reappeared, with one hand guarding the steel bracelets on the wrists of his prisoner, the other holding before him a sturdy axe. He set the axe down with a resounding thud and saluted.

"Open the cabinet door," commanded the lieutenant.

Another policeman came forward and relieved his companion of the care of Alphonse. But the latter really needed no guarding. He was watching that cabinet door as a damned soul might watch for judgment day. He was shivering, though it was not cold, and beads of icy water stood on his forehead. His color was ashen, and his breath was coming in spasmodic little jerks.

"*Gott in himmel!*" they heard him whisper. "Break it open! Break it open!"

The policeman raised the axe and swung it with one fierce, mighty blow. There was a crashing sound of breaking wood and the door pitched drunkenly inward. The bluecoat pounded on it mercilessly, until it cracked asunder, and two big pieces of board rattled to the floor.

The cabinet was gaping wide for them to see. They crowded around, breathless, expectant.

But all they saw was vacancy. There was no trace of Dr. Raven Grim— not even his leg irons, or handcuffs remained. He had utterly, completely, totally vanished.

"A magical death!" cried LeMar. "That is what he had promised me!"

CHAPTER TWENTY-ONE
THE PARTING OF THE MISTS

AFTER ONE HAS CROSSED BROADWAY, not far from Union Square, and has passed by the inviting but altogether artificial entrances of three or four French eating-places, he comes to Brussier's. Every one who has imagination eventually comes there. There are enough artists there on a single night to form a regiment for the Camouflage Department; enough literary men to write the history of the war. They like it because it is not Bohemian. It is just a good place to eat, with an atmosphere altogether its own, altogether unforced, and altogether interesting. Moreover, there are tables so arranged that one may talk without being overheard, and still enjoy the fun of the ensemble. A great place, this Brussier's.

There was a little dinner party of three at Brussier's seven o'clock on the evening of the day on which Dr. Raven Grim finally and totally vanished. It is hardly necessary to add that the three who had thus assembled to break bread together were LeMar, the celebrated magician; his beautiful assistant, and his business manager. But it will be worthy of mention that in spite of the trials and tribulations through which they had passed during the preceding twenty-four hours, they were a very merry, very gay little party. Rose's countenance had lost the worn expression of pain and suffering which LeMar had found upon it when he rescued her, and the magician himself was as happy as a boy off on a picnic. It is needless to depict the mood of Mr. Jack Brown. He never changed.

When all the courses had been served, when Jack had insisted on lighting one of his pet Turkish abominations and LeMar was puffing contentedly on a small cigar, the real object of the little gathering bobbed uppermost in the minds of those seated around the table. It was Jack who broke the silence.

"Come on!" he said. "Let's loosen up and ask each other questions."

"I do not think we shall have to ask so many questions," answered LeMar. "While you two have been refreshing yourselves with well-earned sleep, I have been doing a little more investigating work with very interesting results. Rose, as you know, I have asked you a great many questions, and, Jack, I have asked you quite a few. I think I now have this abominable business quite clear in my head."

"Then you explain it," suggested Rose, and Jack thoroughly agreed.

Accordingly LeMar began:

"We must go back quite a bit, in order to understand the checkered career of Dr. Raven Grim, and the reasons which led up to the sad occurrences of the last few hours. Raven Grim was not his real name—it was a fanciful name which he assumed himself, and which, while fantastic, was curiously suggestive of his character. Doctor Grim's real name was Harris—Brace Harris—and he was born in Australia, of a very fine stock. In his youth, he was sent back to England, where he received a magnificent education, carrying off two or three insignificant honors at Oxford. Then he returned to Australia, and drifted down the stream, until finally he became lost in the wilds of that continent.

"The sensational exploits of Brace Harris, ten years ago, you will recall, if you read the newspaper accounts at that time. He was one of the most daring outlaws the Anzacs ever knew, and he was never caught. But things were getting too hot for him, and he had to get out. Now here is where a curious feature enters into the man's history. Like many another college man, he had taken up a hobby while in England, and in his case the hobby happened to be magic. Probably he had seen Devant or Maskelyne in Egyptian Hall in London. Anyway, he was much interested in the subject, and, as he always did, he made himself a master of it before he was finished.

"This knowledge of the art of mystic entertaining he utilized in order to escape from Australia. There was a magician there, who had come from England, and who was about to return. Harris, or Grim, waylaid the troupe in its wagon, which was their means of transportation inland, and killed the outfit. Then he and two of his men, one of whom was Alphonse, from which I gleaned this information, disguised themselves as best they could, drove to a seaport, and using faked credentials managed to get out of the country.

"That was how it came to pass that Dr. Raven Grim, the celebrated illusionist, suddenly startled the theatrical firmament of the United States. When he reached this country, he realized his salvation from arrest depended for a year or so, at least, on his emerging into the personality of another man. So he, Harris, the bandit, created Dr. Raven Grim, and made a transcontinental tour of the United States.

"But he was not slated so easily to succeed. Somehow, some one in authority in Australia, who was on a visit to this country, or some agent, or in some other way—Alphonse, the German with a French name, is not quite sure—recognized the magician, and started machinery to trap him. It of course would be an international complication, and he had to work slow. But meanwhile Dr. Raven Grim worked fast.

"One night he disappeared, taking Alphonse with him. All his apparatus and paraphernalia were left in Kansas City, where a kindly physician much interested in magic sold them off and gave the money to charity. But Dr. Raven Grim and his man Alphonse had passed utterly off the face of the earth.

"Now what Dr. Raven Grim did at that time is an example of his own superhuman skill and foresight. He had tried the trick of emerging into another personality, and it had failed him. Now he went that trick one better. He emerged into two personalities, and he did it with masterly skill. As Doctor Raven, he opened a sanitarium for nervous wrecks; as old man Neck, he opened a bogus fortune-telling establishment in the suburbs. From one place to the other he passed in an automobile, playing the part of client or patient or dupe in transit. It was—"

"Wait a minute!" pleaded Jack, with widening eyes. "Do you mean to tell me that Dr. Raven Grim and old man Neck were the same?"

"Exactly," smiled LeMar. "I had guessed that long ago."

"Well, who was that infernal old sister of his—the one with the diabolical chuckle?"

"Alphonse!"

Jack sat straight up in his chair, looked from LeMar to Rose for a moment, and then lifted his glass.

"Here's how," he said. "Forgive me, but I need refreshment."

Then LeMar proceeded:

"These two agencies which Doctor Grim now opened were not chosen at random. They had long been planned; indeed, arrangements for both places had been completed; the discovery by the Australian merely hastened matters. They were designed to further certain schemes which Doctor Grim and his man Alphonse were fostering. Alphonse, you see, is really a well-educated German, and he has been in the confidence of the German intelligence office for a long time. Coming to America with Doctor Grim at a time when the United States was verging on war with this country, he saw his opportunity, and suggested to Doctor Grim that they place themselves at the disposal of the Kaiser.

"To this Doctor Grim readily agreed. His plans were elaborate, but they had, too, the virtue of simplicity. From his clients who were taking treatment for nerves, and from superstitious people who came to get their fortune told, they could glean bits of information that would be exceedingly valuable to the Imperial Government—may it be blasted to smithereens! Such a spy system is, in fact, in general operation throughout the United States at the present moment, and the agents of the Department of Justice are busy tracking them now.

"It is here, my friends, that Miss Kellar enters on the scene. She answered an advertisement, and found that old Neck needed an assistant. The work did not strike her as being entirely as honorable as she could wish, for it consisted mostly in rummaging through the coat pockets of old man Neck's clients' coats, which they entrusted to her before they entered the séance chamber. The information she could glean from what she found in their pockets, she wrote on a slip of paper and slipped secretly to the old man, who, a little while later, retailed it as inspired messages to the sitters. But she does not mind admitting that she and her sister, Madeline, were up against it, and the work appealed to her love for the odd, the unusual and the adventurous.

"One day, however, something happened. An army officer came in and did a very indiscreet thing. He had in his pockets a secret formula for a new trench gas which was about to be introduced by the United States government, and he had an engagement with another officer to overlook the situation with him. Finding an hour hanging heavy on his hands, he had wandered around the neighborhood until he came to Neck's place, and being curious after reading the sign, he went in. The formula was in his coat pocket, and he gave that coat to Rose.

"She sent the information to Neck that a gas formula was in the officer's pocket. The medium became tremendously excited, and rushed out into the hall where she was, demanding to know the secret. Being a patriotic girl, and knowing the care with which such matters are guarded by the government, she refused to tell him, for in his eyes she had read there was more than ordinary interest. Of course, the Kaiser and his slaves would have made a man a millionaire to possess such a secret. Neck, or Harris, or Grim, or whatever you choose to call him, rushed at the officer's coat himself, upon which Rose screamed for help, and the officer got out in time to prevent Neck from going through his clothes. Rose, fearing the old man's wrath, for his eyes by this time were murderous, asked the officer's protection, and he led her from the house.

"Being a girl more than ordinarily wise, she did exactly, what Neck, or Grim, would have done under the circumstances. She disappeared. The officer took her to her boarding-house, where she and her sister Madeline lived alone, got her sister, and moved to a distant suburb immediately. Fortunately for them, they were not discovered, though Grim, you may be sure, sought for them diligently.

"Meanwhile, she answered an advertisement in the paper which I had inserted, and so I secured her two weeks before my show opened. She always came veiled to the theater and went away the same, to avoid detection in the street. However, she feared that something might happen, and so she had always taught her sister, day by day, what I had taught her. Several times her sister accompanied her to the theater, sitting in the dark at the back of the house. Rose did this, because she did not want me to lose out—it was an evidence of what a wonderful girl she really is!"

Here LeMar gazed fondly at the beautiful girl, and Jack lit another Turkish cigarette, begging meanwhile that LeMar go ahead.

"Rose had hoped," the magician continued, "that by traveling with my show she would be safe from Doctor Grim, or Neck, as he had been known to her. But she reckoned without the knowledge that Grim himself had been a magician. It was entirely a natural thing for Doctor Grim (in the rôle of old man Neck) to stop in at this theater, when our photographs were put on display in the lobby. And in looking at them, he saw Rose's picture, instantly recognizing it.

"Now Doctor Grim had made up his mind to get the secret of that formula, and he believed that if he could abduct Rose and get her to his mad-house he could force her, by tortures and threats, to divulge it. She had admitted to him that she knew it, but would not give it up. Accordingly, he laid his plans for the kidnapping.

"That was how it came to pass that old man Neck got behind the scenes of the Globe Theater, on our opening night, after heavily bribing the doorman. His purpose was to get the lay of the land. The doorman had been well paid to fix the preliminaries, the most important of which was the placing of a glass of drugged water in the dressing-room of Miss Kellar.

"But here again Doctor Grim had not counted on chance, which in a number of instances had befriended him, but which had also played against him. Rose had seen him when he was buying a ticket at the box office, but he did not recognize her because of her veil. She was certain he would discover her when she appeared on the stage.

"That was the reason she did not want to go on that night. She had gotten in touch with her sister by phone, and the latter was hurrying to the theater, for Rose had determined not to go on this night, when she knew Doctor Grim would be in the audience. She planned to return the next night and say that she had been ill.

"She escaped by passing through the private boxes, into the lobby and then into the street. By a prearranged plan she was to wait in a closed taxicab outside the theater until her sister came out. Her sister Madeline had promised to explain all that could be explained to me, as soon as an opportunity presented itself.

"All this was carried out, as had been scheduled, with this important difference—that Madeline Kellar drank the drugged water which had been placed there for her sister. Its effect was not instantaneous, but gradual. She was able to get through the levitation, but when she was taken into my dressing-room and we questioned her, Jack, as you well remember, she found that her speech and hearing were affected, and presently she was in a complete stupor.

"Then we got an ambulance and took her to the hospital. From her position in the taxicab, Rose had also seen her sister carried out, and so she followed us to the hospital. But when she saw us emerge again, and heard us talking of what had happened, she realized it would be better for her to follow us, rather than show herself at the hospital, where Grim might appear at any moment.

"There her reasoning was false and unfortunate. As a matter of fact, Grim, who was in the theater, and who had had all his plans laid for a speedy and sensational abduction, with the aid of some assistants, had observed the substitution, and he was following Jack and myself. He believed we had made the change deliberately, and that we would lead him to Rose.

"When we got to the house of the Necks, Rose began to get frightened. Knowing, from some experiences, the kind of man Neck was, she wanted to call us off, so that the matter might be dropped, and we might not suffer. She feared if we stirred things up it would only make matters worse. So, when she saw us standing on the porch, she slipped around the back way, an entrance she had used when working in the medium's parlor, and unlocked the door. Knowing her way so wall, she could get around in the rickety old house with her eyes shut, and so she did not mind the darkness. She hastily scribbled the note, and standing on a shed outside the upper stairway, thrust the note into our hands.

"Then a stunning surprise awaited her. Doctor Grim, who had followed us, had seen her as she entered his house, and that was exactly what he had come for. He clapped his hand over her mouth, thrust her into his machine which he had been tracking us in, and then proceeded to make her fast.

"While he was thus engaged, we emerged to the street and walked down to the corner. We were just in time to be there when Grim's machine turned the curb, and Jack, luckily, was whistling our manipulation waltz just at that second. The sound of this gave Rose a superhuman strength and courage, and she managed to free herself and open the door. She had almost escaped, when the machine darted off, under Alphonse's skillful guiding.

"Then, as you know, we raced after the machine, but when we got in, it was empty, except for Doctor Grim. It was this that gave me my first clue as to the man's identity. His face was hauntingly familiar, but I could not place him. But when I found the girl gone, though staggered for the second, I speedily solved that riddle, and it helped me win out finally.

"What Grim had done had been simply to have the interior of his automobile fitted up like the illusion known to magicians as the appearing palanquin. It is an illusion of angles, in which you have space enough to conceal a human body, although you appear not to. Rose was really under the seat, although when I made a hasty examination I thought I was looking at empty space. She was behind a mirror there.

"Then Alphonse put the butt of a revolver through the little window over our heads and knocked us both senseless. Grim, with his really grim sense of humor, took us back to our hotel, and wrote that warning message on the bell. When I came to, I was sure Nagen would help me place him, and I was also sure we would be watched, and so on the double chance, Jack and I set out. We went to Nagen's house and completed our identification of Dr. Raven Grim. Then we went out, turned the trick on Alphonse, who had been trailing us, through Jack's operation. But here Jack turned a trick on me. His orders were to take an L car downtown, go to his hotel and go to bed.

"Instead of doing that, he went up on the L platform, let the next train go by, and then risked his foolish life by crossing those trestles. He got to the other side, where the uptown trains stop, and went down, emerging on the other side of Third avenue. I followed Alphonse, and Jack, all unknown to me, followed both of us. Jack saw me go up and ring Grim's doorbell, and that was how he took matters into his own hands and brought a raiding party to the rescue.

"There is little left to explain, except how I managed to outwit the odious Doctor Grim in our final grapple. He had invented a most diabolical thing. That cabinet was a nest of wires, connected with a special battery, worth thousands of dollars. By closing those doors, the thing was hermetically sealed, and enormous heat created, which practically disintegrated whatever was there. It was his dream to produce a real vanishing illusion, and in this he succeeded, though he really destroyed whatever he vanished. That was how he instantly planned to kill me, as soon as I crossed his threshold.

"But I was armed with a more innocent, yet equally as potent a weapon. And yet it was a very simple one. You remember my balloons from the hat illusion. At the beginning of my second part I borrow a gentleman's hat. I show it empty, and then I produce from it a dozen toy balloons, inflated, and they float over the heads of the spectators with a vary charming effect. Now this is accomplished by having a rubber reservoir of gas at the small of the back, under the coat, connected with a tube running down the right arm. An ingenious small appliance controls this flow of gas. The balloons in a small form, uninflated, are secretly introduced into the hat, and then the mouth of the tube placed against the opening. They are thus inflated, and secured with bands, and produced, one after the other. I had this apparatus in place before we left the hotel.

"Now I have discovered that this gas is very poisonous, if inhaled. It produces unconsciousness almost instantly. And I knew, with such a gas, I could knock Doctor Grim senseless before he knew what I was doing. That is exactly what I managed to do, and then, I am sorry to say, I sent him to the very fate he had prepared for me."

Rose shuddered at the memory, and they quickly turned the conversation toward brighter topics. They had much to talk about, and soon the horrors of Doctor Grim and his mysteries were forgotten in making their plans for the future—plans in which a wedding figured conspicuously.

The Thing That Wept

WHEN JOE BLUNT WAS APPRENTICED TO HIS UNCLE JACOB, who was an undertaker, he had never seen a corpse.

This is not so surprising, when it is considered that Joe was born on a farm and had never been more than ten miles away from it since he was born. There were many other things Joe had never seen besides a corpse. He had never been to a moving-picture show, did not know how to talk through a telephone, and did not believe in air planes. His folks were old-fashioned and did not hold to giving a boy too much rope. So on the farm he remained until he was sixteen years old and too lazy for plowing.

Then his father bundled him on the train, and Jacob Blunt, the uncle and undertaker, met him when he got off at the city station. On his way to the embalming establishment, which was far up in the residential district, Uncle Jacob pointed out a thousand wonders to the pop-eyed Joe.

They arrived at Uncle Jacob's funeral parlors about noon. In the dining room, which immediately adjoined the chapel, they ate a cold meal, and then Uncle Jacob got down to business.

He explained carefully to Joe the nature and scope of the undertaking profession. A point on which he laid particular emphasis was that it was a sure business; everybody had to die at some time or other, and the mortician had a first mortgage on the insurance. He winked an eye as he hinted that the profits were high. He sketched, with some detail, the process of embalming, so that Joe would have an idea of the kind of work he was to do. Then he took Joe into a darkened room at the rear and showed him a body.

When Joe recovered consciousness Uncle Jacob remonstrated with him gravely on his weakness, but seemed reassured when Joe confessed it was his first sight of a dead man. The uncle then continued with his elucidation of first principles. He took Joe into the front office, where he had an elegant coffin near the window, flanked with palms.

He showed Joe the telephone, and carefully impressed on him what he was to do when the telephone rang in Uncle Jacob's absence. He was to take the name of the person calling and the address, and write it on a pad. Through the remainder of the afternoon Joe answered telephone calls, and finally Uncle Jacob said he would do. Then they had supper.

Immediately after the meal Uncle Jacob announced that he was going out and would leave Joe in charge for an hour or so. Joe requested that he lock the door on the dead man before he left, but Uncle Jacob only gave him a reproachful scowl, and, with parting cautions and instructions, went out.

Joe drew his chair as near the front door as he could. In all undertaking parlors the light is burned low as a business principle. Joe wished it were brighter. After a while the ticking of the desk clock grew monotonous. The cracking of the furniture made Joe jump and start. He fidgeted in his chair; he whistled and stopped in the middle of the tune; he got up and walked around the office. Every second or so he glanced at the half-open door in the rear. Finally, with a burst of bravado, he walked to the door and looked in. He got a second glimpse of the body in there, and with a howl sprang back to his post at the door.

Just then the telephone rang. Still shaking, Joe forced himself to answer it, and blundered through the conversation desperately. When it was over he set the receiver on the desk with a gasp. Apprehensively he gazed over his shoulder. He was convinced the dead man there might come out after him at any moment. The silence was startling.

A low sound reached Joe's ear. It was soft, like the purring of a cat. He glanced rapidly around, trying to find from where it came. With a bound he dropped to the floor, looking under the chairs, under the desk, under the coffin, for the cat. The soft, purring sound continued. But he saw no cat. Then, with a sinking of the heart, he remembered a casual remark of Uncle Jacob—that undertakers never kept cats; they wouldn't do around dead people.

Dizzily Joe rose to his feet. The purring noise was growing louder. It rose to a high-pitched whine, and it twisted and worried itself as if it were some lost thing in pain. Joe could stand it no longer. He scrambled awkwardly to the door, flung it open, and rushed out into the street. He almost fell into the arms of a policeman.

"What's a matter?" demanded the offended guardian of the peace.

"Somethin'—*in there!*" cried Joe. "It's ha'nted!"

"Get out of here!" snapped the policeman. "Don't try to kid me!"

He brushed past the panting Joe and strode in the door. For a moment he paused, then walked up to the desk. He rearranged something, and then reappeared, glowering, in the doorway.

"Say, you!" he growled. "Whadidja leave yer receiver off the hook fer? That was central jazzing yer buzzer—ya poor fish!"

MYSTERY MAGAZINE

VOL. II. N°43 AUGUSTUS 1919 PRICE 10 CENTS

FEATURE · DETECTIVE · STORY

The Mystery of the Seven Shadows

by
CHARLES · FULTON · OURSLER ·

The Mystery of the Seven Shadows

CHAPTER ONE
CRIMSON CANDLES

A RAP SOUNDED ON THE BED-ROOM DOOR OF GORDON KEENE.

"A gentleman and a young lady say they must see you at once, sir—a matter of life and death," said the voice of a man-servant.

Gordon Keene sat up in bed and his groping hand found the electric switch.

"Come in, Blake," he called, as the lights were flashed on. A young man, scantily dressed, opened the door and stood, half-awake, on the threshold.

"A young lady and a gentleman at this hour?" asked Keene, amazedly. "Why, look at the clock. It's three in the morning."

"They pounded on the door and rang the bell like to rouse the dead," answered Blake, ruefully. "The gentleman gave his name as Professor Rust. He said—"

Keene bounded from his bed excitedly.

"Show them into the library," he ordered. "Tell him I'll be right down. If Professor Rust comes here like this, he must have something—hurry up, Blake! Serve them some hot coffee and anything you can find in the pantry. Be quick!"

Blake was gone on the instant, and Gordon Keene busied himself with his garments. In less than ten minutes he was in a Tuxedo, as fresh as if about to attend an evening function, and walking down the stairs to meet his guests.

Professor Rust came forward eagerly to meet him.

"My dear Keene," he burst out, "it is beastly to break in on your sleep at such a ghastly hour—but this is a ghastly business, God knows, and if any man can help us, you can. Let me introduce Miss Marian Dale."

Keene bowed before as beautiful a girl as he had ever looked upon. She was a slender, brown-haired creature, with sympathetic eyes. What impressed him most was the death-like pallor of her face—the pinched expression that betokened an acute suffering, a mental anguish that was breaking her heart. The finger of horror had left an unmistakable mark upon a beautiful face.

"Won't you sit down, please?" said Keene, easily. "I do not mind the intrusion—particularly if I can serve you in trouble."

Marian Dale flashed a shy look of gratitude as she sank into a large chair. Professor Rust sat down abruptly, all eager to get at the business that had brought them there, but Keene, ignoring the over-strung tension which both of his guests exhibited, insisted that Blake serve them refreshments before they talked. He offered the professor a cigar, after receiving the permission of Miss Dale, and himself lighted a cigarette as he sank comfortably into an easy-chair.

"Now, Professor," he said, smilingly, "tell me the story."

Professor Rust waved a sandwich tragically.

"It is the most damnable piece of business ever contrived," he cried, shrilly. "Either there is some fiendish occult agency at work to crush the life out of Miss Dale, here, or else there is some human fiend whose object is the same. Whatever the agency, the object is being achieved!"

"Please come to the point," prompted Keene.

Professor Rust paused a moment as if at a loss how to proceed. Gulping down a final bite of the sandwich, he resumed:

"I have been what you might call a guardian of Miss Dale here since her childhood, when she was left an orphan. That is to say, I supervised her education and in other ways looked after her. Consequently, although she has been of age these two years, it was to me she turned when this terrible thing began. I confess that—"

Gordon Keene was getting a trifle irritated at the impossibility of getting Professor Rust to come to the actual relation of the facts in the case.

"Tell me about that afterward," he interposed. "I am all eagerness to know the actual cause of this extraordinary visit."

"That you shall know," exclaimed the professor, dramatically. "The facts in the case are these: About two years ago Miss Dale was engaged to marry a certain young man, with whom she believed she was deeply in love. But you will understand that, as is the case with any young woman of independent means, she had many others who admired her. Finally she met another young man, and discovered that her first affair was a mistake, that her heart really belonged to another. She told her fiancé of that fact and asked to be released. He made no trouble, but"—and here the professor rose dramatically, while Marian dropped her head—"from that moment her trouble began.

"One evening, not long afterward, she had just said good-night to her future husband—Jack Eastwood—and was reading in her bed-room. Her maid had retired and she was quite alone. Marian, tell him what happened."

The girl lifted a haggard face, and shivering a little at the recollection, took up the thread of the narrative.

"All at once," she said, "I dropped my book, with the uncanny feeling that some one—or something—else was in the room with me. You know how one can feel things like that, Mr. Keene. I glanced hurriedly behind me, but there was no one there. I got up and tried the door, but it was locked, as I had left it. Then I turned, and what I saw above my mirror nearly made me faint. There was a round circle of light in the very center of the wall—a circle of white, brilliant light. I could not imagine where it was coming from, and it looked so fearful and so strange that I felt sure it was something ghostlike. I watched it, very frightened, and then across it there suddenly appeared a shadow.

"Mr. Keene, that shadow was uncanny. I did not stir. It was the figure of a little dog, and it stood on its hind legs, and held out its paws and begged. All at once the light went out—the light and the shadow were gone."

A hush fell on the three of them there, and Gordon Keene smoked in earnest silence, waiting for the girl to resume.

"I had a little dog as a household pet, Mr. Keene," she continued. "He used to beg just like that shadow did. The very next day it died!"

Professor Rust again leaped to his feet.

"A little thing, Mr. Keene, but an evil omen just the same, and in the light of what has followed, a damnable evil thing. That is why we are here to-night. You have a reputation as an unraveler of mysteries. You are more than a detective—you are a master scientist. And if this thing can be explained, then you—"

Gordon Keene interrupted him with a gesture.

"Go on, Miss Dale," he urged. "I am tremendously interested."

"I told my friends of this experience," she said, "and they laughed at me. They all insisted I had dozed over my book and had dreamed this thing. But I was sure I had not, until their repeated arguments convinced me, and I believed at last they were right. Then—" Her voice broke, and it was several moments before she could go on. "Then I saw a second shadow, and under the most extraordinary circumstances. It was in the same room and about the same hour. I was in bed, almost asleep, and the room was dark. Suddenly the room was lighted, not by the electric lights, but by three small jets of flame. They were from three blood-red candles on my dresser and they seemed to have been lighted by an invisible hand. The candles had not been there when I went to sleep.

"I was too horror-stricken to cry out. All that I could do was to lie there, petrified, frozen with fear, and watch. The three crimson candles cast a glow over the wall, and almost instantly a shadow appeared there. This time it was not the harmless form of a terrier. It was now a miniature silhouette of a highwayman, with a revolver held out. The apparition—if you could call a shadow two feet high such a thing—was fixed and still. It remained there for a few moments and then something snuffed those candles. They went out all at once. In the darkness I found my voice and screamed so that I aroused the neighborhood. My maid rushed from her bed, and others in the apartment hurried in. When they got to me, I was in hysterics, and babbled incoherently about the shadow. When they had finally quieted me, however, I would not speak. I dared not tell them what I had seen; I feared they would call me mad. So I hugged the dreadful secret to my breast; told them I had simply had a bad dream, and asked only that Annette, the maid, remain with me for the rest of the night.

"The next day, as I was coming through Central Park, just about dusk, a man leaped out of the bushes, and sprang upon me. He attacked me like a raging maniac. His one purpose seemed to be to beat me; his fists struck repeated blows on my face, my breast, all over my body. I lost consciousness before he had left me."

Sobbing at the memory, Marian could not go on. Professor Rust was about to orate again, but Gordon Keene hastily prevented him. The detective's eyes were glittering with intense interest at Marian Dale's story. Gently he soothed her, and asked her to continue.

"I lay in the hospital two months following that," she went on. "My body was a mass of bruises and cuts as a result of that brutal assault. Two days ago I came out of the hospital and returned to my apartment. While in the hospital, I had told one of the physicians my story, and he had promptly summoned a psychiatrist to examine my mental condition. He thought I was mad. I resolved then and there never to tell it again to any one, not even to so kind and generous a friend as Professor Rust. But what I saw to-night banished that resolution. I am afraid.

"My maid had just left the room, about eleven o'clock this evening, when I saw the third shadow. This time there were no red candles, no white circle of light on the mirror. There was simply a shape crawling across my wall—a shadow shape, a black, coiling shadow—the apparition of a giant snake!"

Shuddering and sobbing, the girl rushed over to the side of Professor Rust, who soothed her with an awkward tenderness that was pathetic.

Gordon Keene paced the floor excitedly. No man loved mystery better than he; certainly none had ever encountered and solved deeper enigmas in his day and generation. Here was a challenge to all his theories and all his resources—a problem the like of which he had never heard before.

"To-night you saw the shadow of a snake!" he commented. "And nothing has happened?"

"Nothing has happened—yet!" said Professor Rust, significantly.

Keene was silent for a moment, his brows knitted, his fingers working nervously up and down his cheeks—a favorite attitude when he was puzzled.

"It is too grotesque, too utterly unheard of," he argued, more to himself than to his guests. "I gather that when Miss Dale saw this third shadow—the form of a snake writhing across her bed-room wall—she decided to go to you at once and tell her story?"

"Exactly," answered the old scholar. "She came to me almost at midnight and laid the facts before me. More sophisticated men, Mr. Keene, might have laughed at her, but not I. You may regard me as an old fossil, studying my Greek and my logic, but I believe what she tells me is true. And not being anything more than an old fossil, I brought her to the one man I knew could help her, the man who—"

"Miss Dale," interrupted Keene, hopefully, "you have told us a baffling story, it is true, but not necessarily one impossible to solve. There is nothing psychic or ghostlike in what you have seen, of that I would swear. But what it really is, that is what we must find out. This snake thing, now—perhaps we can catch it in time. You did well to act so promptly. Perhaps we may—"

A piercing scream from Marian startled the two men. She rose, rigid with horror, and pointed at a corner of the room.

Coiled in undulating, shivering circles, was a huge green snake, spitting with rage and ready to spring. And no one knew how it got there.

CHAPTER TWO
THE FOURTH SHADOW

"DON'T MOVE!" SAID KEENE.

His voice was low and tense, but there was a ring of confidence, of authority, of stern command which had its effect. The panic-stricken Professor Rust sat, pale and staring, like a frozen image of fear, on the edge of his chair. Marian, her finger still pointed in loathing terror at the reptile, remained half crouched, her breath coming in gasps. Keene remained transfixed in the center of the room, his eyes on the snake, completing the tableau.

It was a monster reptile, a cobra, with sleepy, wicked eyes, and its sickening odor filled the room. Its body, in its thick coils, trembled; its forked tongue moved in lightning darts; its flat head was drawn back. The yellow spots that marked its greenish black coat gave it a sinister, devilish appearance—an evil thing of power. It was poised for a spring, and its ugly eyes were on Marian Dale.

"Don't move!" crooned Gordon Keene.

A flash of hope came to Professor Rust. Keene had been in India; Keene knew about everything; perhaps he could charm the reptile. He waited to see if the detective would make any move to fascinate the creature and render it harmless by some occult means. But such was not the intention of the detective. Second after second ticked away, and not one of the three moved a muscle. The reptile made a sudden, hissing noise and a long, lithe movement of its neck.

"Now!" said Keene.

Out of the shadows of the book-case draperies darted a long riding whip, looped at the end. With a swish it came down over the squirming neck of the hissing snake; the arm that held the whip twisted the loop with sudden ferocity, and pushed it downward.

With a bound Gordon Keene leaped across the room, snatching an ancient sword that hung on the wall, and bringing it down with a merciless blow on the head of the snake. Again and again he struck, and then stepped back with a smile and a chuckle that were his only outward signs when danger and crisis were over.

"Who—who did that?" croaked Professor Rust.

"Yes—who?" breathed Marian earnestly.

Keene smiled, a little whimsically.

"A man who monkeys with crime and criminals," he replied, "must be forever on the alert against his enemies and the enemies of his clients. If not"—he made a significant movement across his throat—"he will soon cease to figure as a detective. Consequently a detective must not depend entirely upon his own resources in matching wits against evil-doers." He turned and faced the draped book-case at the end of the library. "You may come out now," he called.

And out of the draperies, erect and unmoved, stepped Blake. The young man's face was as calm and inscrutable as if nothing whatever had occurred.

"Blake," explained Keene smilingly, "is more than an attendant. For two years he has been my companion, more my comrade, in a hundred devilish adventures, and more than once he has saved my life. He is brave, faithful and sometimes infernally stupid. You can never tell where he is—he is likely to turn up most any place, for he is always on the job. To-night, one of us at least owes him life itself."

Marian went up to the blushing Blake and put her hands on his shoulders in unaffected gratitude. She began to tell him, almost incoherently, how much she owed to his presence of mind, but he grew so confused that Keene kindly interfered, and sent him away. As the door closed behind him the detective confronted his two clients soberly.

"The situation," he said, "is not materially altered by this thing," and he kicked the carcass of the snake angrily. "It does confirm my opinion, however, that we are dealing with a human and not a supernatural agency. Perhaps this dead monster will provide us the clue that we shall need. In any event, it will not do to discuss the matter any further here at this time. I feel quite certain, Miss Dale, that you will not suffer any more annoyances tonight, and I shall see that you are protected to the limit. If you will not object, I shall arouse my housekeeper, Mrs. Stone, who lives here with me—oh, she will be delighted, I assure you—and you shall pass the night with her. I think it would be a grave mistake for you to go out from here at such an hour. Professor Rust can call for you in the morning, and in the meantime I shall spend the two hours that intervene between now and dawn to working on this problem, and I hope to be able to tell you something definite at breakfast. Is that agreeable?"

Professor Rust thought it an excellent idea, and Marian was delighted to know that she should end the night in such protected surroundings.

Accordingly, Keene left them in the library and soon had summoned Mrs. Stone, a sweet, peaceful-faced elderly woman, who came down at once, and immediately went up to Marian, put her arms around her, and led her away.

Left alone, with the carcass of the snake between them, Keene and Professor Rust faced each other with blank faces. The old professor was plainly out of his element; hopelessly confused and very much over-wrought. Keene was obsessed with the baffling mystery with which he had been so suddenly confronted, and rather anxious for the professor to say good-night and get out. He liked to work in silence, with no one near but the faithful Blake.

"What do you make of it?" barked the professor.

"Nothing!" snapped Keene. "Professor, I want you to say 'good-night' and go, so that I can work this thing out without delay. You won't mind?"

"Not at all! Not at all!"

The professor picked up his hat and a traveling bag, and reluctantly started for the door.

"Just a moment!" called Keene. "A question about your ward. She is wealthy?"

"Worth about half a million! Manages it herself, too. I turned the whole thing over to her when she came of age."

"Who does the money go to afterward?"

The professor looked meaningly at the detective for a moment, sat down his bag, and came closer.

"She has just made a new will," he whispered, hoarsely. "Left it all to Jack Eastwood!"

"What! To her fiancé?"

"Exactly. I was one of the witnesses."

"But she hasn't married him yet!"

"Exactly!"

"What became of that man she turned down for Eastwood?"

"I don't know. He disappeared. But I have always believed—"

"You knew her mother?"

The question evidently struck home to the old professor. He dropped his eyes, and then answered slowly:

"I was once a suitor of her mother, but she married another man. She lived to repent of it, Keene. She died almost the day Marian was born, and with her dying breath she asked that I be her guardian."

"What do you think of this Jack Eastwood?"

"Bah!" cried the professor.

"Good-night, Professor."

"Good-night, Keene. Take good care of Marian."

The door shut softly behind the old man, and Keene heard his footsteps down the hallway; heard the front door slam, and the sound of the automobile outside as it carried him away. As the last faint chugging of the motor came to his ears, the curtains of the book-case were parted again, and Blake came forth. He was as inscrutable as ever, and stood like a soldier at attention, waiting for his orders.

"Go upstairs," ordered Keene, "and tell Mrs. Stone I want Miss Dale's outer garments sent to me at once."

Blake disappeared through the doorway. Keene paused uncertainly in the center of the room for a moment, then stalked to the corner where the snake had first made its appearance. He examined the floor minutely, getting down on his knees, and peering at the boarding in the floor, lifting the thick Persian rug every now and then, and examining the most insignificant details of the woodwork.

"How in the devil!" he muttered to himself.

Still on his knees, he crawled back and forth across the floor, until at last he knelt beside the vile-smelling length of the reptile. Starting at its head, he examined the carcass with the most circumstantial care, every once in a while rubbing a tentative finger against its oily green coat and yellow spots. His brows were drawn close together, his forehead was furrowed, and every now and then he grunted in a way that Blake would have interpreted as extreme annoyance at finding no clues.

"There is no such thing as the fourth dimension of space," he said as he stood upright. "There was a physical way in which that snake crawled into this room, and by thunder I've got to find it!"

The door opened and Blake came in, bearing in his arms the brown skirt and coat, the white silk waist which Marian Dale had worn. With an air of profound gravity he deposited these in the chair so lately occupied by Professor Rust, and then stood back to await further orders.

"Did you notice anything peculiar about those garments?" asked Keene, casually, as he lifted the coat and held it to the light.

"They have a peculiar perfume that I don't quite understand," answered Blake.

"You noticed that?"

"Yes, sir!"

"Go into the laboratory, Blake, and bring me one of those small garden snakes that I have been using for the back-pressure experiments. Try to get a young one."

Again Blake vanished through the doorway.

Keene took the coat and placed it behind the draperies of the book-case, and on top of them he laid the skirt and waist. This done, he drew the curtains tight, and walked to the other side of the room, just as Blake opened the door, with a small green serpent dangling by the tail from his fingers.

"Put it on the floor," commanded Keene.

Blake obeyed, and the thin little snake lay quite still for a moment, except for the nervous wriggling of its tail. Suddenly it lifted its head a trifle and then began worming its way rapidly across the carpet. It was making straight for the book-case curtains. In an incredibly short time it had reached its goal and passed beneath the hangings.

Keene, followed by Blake, hurried across the room and drew back the curtains. The snake had coiled itself contentedly against the brown coat of Marian Dale.

"I was positive of it," said Keene. "That coat has been perfumed with thorn root, an East Indian herb, and a sure attraction for any kind of snake. A cruel coward, this devil we've got to find, Blake. He wanted to make sure of his victim this time, so he daubed thorn root over her clothing to attract that monster. Well—carry out that carcass now, and take the little snake with you. We've learned that much, anyhow. The snake placed in waiting outside, followed her in here, attracted by that odor."

Lighting another cigarette, Keene threw himself into the depths of an easy-chair, while Blake, without a grunt of protest, proceeded to drag away the corpse of the cobra. The detective quickly forgot his surroundings as he began to marshal the facts of the case before him in orderly array, seeking to find a common denominator for them all. In this, Keene adopted a method not practiced by any other detective he had ever known. Instead of piecing fact upon fact together, he visualized pictures of different objects associated with a crime. He would close his eyes and his imagination would bring up before his mental vision such pictures as would enable him intuitively to reach out and snatch an explanation, where logic would not have helped. Keene was not a logician. He was a scientist with imagination, who, once he knew what course to pursue, could bring surprising results forth by using unsuspected secrets of his laboratory. But he arrived at that proper course more by inspiration from his mental pictures than by theorems, hypotheses and logical thinking.

As he closed his eyes now, a strange array of objects were presented to his mind. He saw a beveled mirror, above which a white light glowed, and in the center of that white light he saw the shadow of a dog. Next he saw a set of three red candles, lighted by an unseen hand. Then he pictured the second shadow—the grotesque silhouette of a highwayman. What an odd business, anyhow! And then the third shadow—the writhing image of a serpent across the quiet bed-room wall of a girl's boudoir—and then the green, loathsome, yellow-spotted thing which had come, as if from nowhere, in the privacy of his own library.

"What devilish brain is behind these things?" he asked himself, and with an uncomfortable feeling that he had not enough clues to work on, he got up and paced excitedly up and down the room. Already he was mapping out what he would do when daylight came. He would visit Miss Dale's rooms; he would interview Annette, the maid; he would find out by what fiendish contrivance those shadows were produced.

That was it! If he could find out how those ghastly shadows were thrown, and actually trace out their origin, he felt the rest would be simple. He was certain the simple knowledge of that fact would lead him inevitably to the guilty man. And if he could only see the actual shadow itself! Give him that opportunity and he would guarantee to put the man responsible for the business behind the bars or in a mad-house.

As if fate had heard and taken up his challenge, the buzzer of the interior telephone sounded harshly, hurriedly, excitedly. Keene lifted the receiver and asked what was wanted.

"Mr. Keene, come up here quick—quick, for God's sake!" came the voice of Mrs. Stone, his housekeeper.

Keene rushed out in the corridor and went up the steps like lightning. In time almost less than it takes to describe, he was at the door. It was opened, and the two women, pale and trembling, were waiting for him on the threshold.

"Mr. Keene, go in there, but be careful," begged the trembling Mrs. Stone. "Look at the wall, just over the mantel!"

His jaws set, his eyes burning with excitement, Keene strode into the room. Instantly he saw what had terrified them.

There was a round circle of brilliant white light on the wall, and in the center of it the shadow of a human hand. The hand was clasping a dagger, and there were drops falling from its point. The hand seemed as if about to lunge at something, and then the light and the shadow went out like the snuffing of a candle—the wall was bare and empty.

CHAPTER THREE
WHAT THE SHADOW FORETOLD

GORDON KEENE SLOWLY STUDIED THE ROOM.

"Stay where you are," he told the two women, and, without stirring from his position, he looked about him. Certainly there was no one else in the room; certainly, in its simple elegance of appointments, it offered no place for concealment. And in his own heart Keene was sure there was no hidden apparatus there to produce the shadow he had witnessed; there was some deeper meaning to it all. Yet he had seen the thing; watched it with his own trained eyes, had beheld it melt away and vanish into nothingness. It was ghostly.

He went up to the spot on the wall where the shadow had been and ran his hand over the wainscoting. All was solid and intact; he put his nose close to it and sniffed—there was no faint trace of chemical there to show that the wall had been daubed with any secret preparation. Keene had thought of that theory when the story had first been told him; of some possible chemical combination which, itself invisible, might produce some such effect under the rays of artificial light. But the shadow had not flickered! He had seen that lunging hand, with its dripping dagger clutched, across the mysterious circle of light.

He faced the two women again.

"There is no use in deceiving ourselves," he said, calmly. "Whoever or whatever it is that is following you, Miss Dale, has succeeded in penetrating my own house, and it seems you are not altogether safe, even here. But I shall see to it that you are safe. Blake!"

A figure separated itself from the shadows at the rear of the hallway, just outside the bed-room door. It was Blake, the ever-watchful, ever-silent assistant, ready at once for his orders.

"Take these ladies to my laboratory," ordered Keene, crisply. "Make them as comfortable as you can there, but under no circumstances leave them alone for an instant. Be ready for whatever may happen—and shout if anything does happen!"

"Why can't we stay here with you and pass the night awake?" pleaded Mrs. Stone, anxiously. Her entreaty was seconded by an eager look from Marian Dale, who was too downcast to speak.

"Impossible!" declared Keene. "This fiend has carried his work inside my own dwelling. There is something sinister abroad in the black hours of this morning, and delay would be dangerous. I have lost too much time already. Good-night!"

Without further words, the two women followed Blake down the broad staircase, and Keene was left alone in the boudoir. In the last ten minutes his manner had changed completely. The sudden appearance of the snake in his library was still to be explained, but there were a dozen different normal means by which its entrance might be accounted for. The shadow which he had seen was different. It transcended anything in his experience. It was so far utterly inexplicable.

With folded arms, the puzzled detective stood long and silently, his thoughts busy upon the problem. That the danger was not past he felt certain. The ugly threat of the dripping dagger assumed a terrible significance in the light of those former omens—first the shadow of a dead dog, then a dog actually dead; the shadow of a highwayman, then a brutal attack; the shadow of a snake, and then a hissing cobra, ready to strike. What new blow was portended now? Where would it strike? Keene raged within, as the problem still eluded him; quick action was what was wanted, and he could not act.

"More facts!" he whispered to himself. "I must get more facts. And before I get them there may be—"

He bit his lips in vexation. It seemed as if his mind would not function. He closed his eyes, and the shadow of the hand clutching the dagger leaped before his imagination. Even the vision of it startled him. It persisted; it would not be gone. And then the idea he had longed for came.

At first he rejected it as being absurd and beneath his notice. Then he argued with himself about it, and at last admitted inwardly that it was worth the trial. Inasmuch as at this stage of the game he was so hopelessly baffled that he knew not which way to turn, and this was the only course presented to his mind, his decision to follow it up was only a bit of common sense.

Switching off the lights, he went downstairs and rapped on the laboratory door. Immediately it was opened by the housekeeper. Miss Dale was resting comfortably in a wicker chair, requisitioned from the reception hall, and Mrs. Stone had taken possession of the chair in front of the table where Dale conducted his chemical experiments.

"Where do you keep your lights on when you are preparing to retire?" he asked Mrs. Stone. "Do you always have them as they were to-night, or sometimes do you have some of them off?"

"I always have all the lights on until I am ready to get into bed," she replied.

"Thanks. I hope you are feeling more comfortable—anyway, don't worry! I think I begin to see a way out of this!"

With that the detective turned and was about to retrace his steps across the hallway to the library when he was halted by the sudden feeling—a quick impression—that some one was near him. It was a subtle warning to his soul that hidden somewhere out of sight in that corridor was another human being—an enemy. He stopped dead-short.

The house was as silent as a graveyard. Behind the laboratory door the two women were too weary, too frightened to speak, except in occasional undertones. Blake, who kept them company, never spoke except when spoken to. Death-like the stillness seemed, and pregnant with hidden danger.

Was the thing getting on his nerves? Through Keene's mind the question flashed, but something within him answered no! There was unmistakable prompting in his heart; he was in deadly peril at that moment.

And then the peril was revealed. Around the corner of the corridor came a hand—a human hand, wearing a black glove, and its fingers clutched a dagger from which red drops were falling. Only the hand and the forearm were revealed—the rest of the body was hidden behind the curve of the wall.

The hand moved upward with a slow, deliberate motion. It reached a proper angle and then lunged forward with frightful force and swiftness. The dagger came circling in a sudden rush and buried itself into the splintering wood of the balustrade—barely more than an inch from Gordon Keene.

With an oath, Keene leaped forward, just as the hand was drawn back. Whoever the intruder was, he could not escape him now, for he was standing in a niche in the wall, where every possible means of escape, except precipitate flight in full view, was cut off.

Keene had no weapons but his bare hands, but he could have grappled with a troupe of demons, in the rage that now flamed in his heart. With all his strength he hurled himself around the bend of the wall and into that corner; caution and watchfulness he threw aside, to be at the creature who was now so near.

His head knocked against the plastering; his arms blundered wildly against the wall; his hands groped the air in vain. Like the prophetic shadows that haunted Marian Dale, the man whose hand Gordon Keene had just seen, whose dagger still quivered in the woodwork of the corridor stairs, had disappeared.

Keene rushed into the library. He threw aside the furniture in a mad rush up and down the room; he overturned a couch, tore down the hangings of the book-case, and then dashed to the front door, only to discover that the bolts were firm, and that the lock was unyielding.

Keene almost staggered back down the corridor. His brain was reeling at the demoniacal power which seemed to be pitted against him. Give him the carefully plotted bedevilments of human criminals and he would stake his reputation that he could untangle the clues. But what could he, or any man, do against the resources of shadows that came and went; of men who themselves could disappear at will?

Without an effort he managed to dislodge the knife from its position. Evidently the man who had thrown it was not possessed of considerable muscular force, for the point of the blade was not deeply imbedded in the wood. Holding the weapon gingerly by the handle, Keene carried it into the library and placed it on the table.

It was a surpassingly handsome thing, that dagger. Its blade was cut into a dozen sharpened facets, and glittered brilliantly. The handle was of yellowed ivory, carved so that a man's fingers could clasp it most conveniently, and there was a single red stone, a ruby of the genuine pigeon-blood hue, set in the center. The workmanship showed it to be the work of some master craftsman—probably a Dutchman of the fourteenth century. These details Keene observed, but without particular interest. What he did notice, with absorbed attention, was the corroded appearance of the very tip of the blade. It seemed to have recently been dipped in some acid which had eaten much of it away.

"I wonder—" he said, slowly, and then paused. He remembered the scarlet drops he had seen dripping from its point. His hesitation was only momentary; he hurried down the hallway and opened the laboratory door.

"I am sorry to disturb you ladies again," he apologized, and neither his face nor his manner gave them any hint of the extraordinary incident he had just passed through in the corridor, "but I find I need something else if I am to find out the truth of this affair."

He passed over to a box-like cage in the rear of the room and presently emerged with a squirming white rabbit in his hand.

"Mr. Keene, what are you going to do with that poor little thing?" asked Marian.

But Keene put his finger mysteriously to his lips, and passed out of the laboratory. He watched cautiously as he moved down the corridor, for he felt certain the hidden enemy had other weapons besides his dagger. But the detective reached the library safely, and having closed the door, he placed the rabbit on the table, where he held him firmly.

"Bunny," he said, "I'm sorry to sacrifice you like this, but it's on the altar of a sacred cause, and your reaction now to this experiment may save the lives of your superiors."

Seizing the dagger, he pricked the tender skin of the rabbit on one side, as gently as he could, so gently in fact that the little fellow barely winced at the miniature operation. But a moment later it seemed suddenly galvanized; its body grew rigid, and then relaxed into a pitiful little heap. It was dead.

"A poison dagger!" muttered Keene beneath his breath. "And this time it was meant for me. Lord, what an—"

He stopped, listening intently. The floors of his house were carpeted with the handwork of Asia, yet he had heard a footstep; the sound of some one moving cautiously, so very slowly, just outside the library door.

Keene's hand noiselessly felt for the drawer of the library table, while his eyes never left the door. Soon his hands closed over the butt of a revolver, and with this leveled before him, he began stealthily moving toward the door. The footsteps had ceased, all sound had seemed to come to an end in the frightful tension of these minutes. Keene knew the man was there, and he knew—he was certain—that a real clash was at hand.

Still no sound came from the doorway. Keene, creeping noiselessly forward, wondered if it were a trap—if the hidden foe might not be decoying him into the death which he had so narrowly escaped from the dagger. It made him cautious, but it did not deter him.

His hands reached forward and seized the knob. With a terrific pull he hurled the door backward and leveled his revolver through the doorway.

"Hands up!" he cried.

He had covered a stalwart man, whose rather youthful face was gone suddenly white, and whose eyes were blinking in fear and amazement.

"Put down that gun," cried the stranger.

"You are under arrest," snapped Keene, cool and serene. "The charges are burglary, attempted murder and several other things. I shall hand you over to the police in a moment."

The stranger smiled a little weakly.

"There's a mistake somewhere," he protested. "This is—er—an important call."

"A call?" mocked Keene. "A friendly call at five o'clock in the morning, when a man's house is locked up?"

"Not to see you," insisted the man, with a dazed and bewildered air. "I came to see Mar—Miss Marian Dale!"

"So I understand," retorted Keene, sarcastically. "Do you mind giving me your name?"

"Certainly not," the man replied. "My name is Jack Eastwood."

Chapter Four
who's guilty now?

That was the last name Keene ever had dreamed would come from the intruder's lips. And the man said it with the utmost frankness and sincerity, as if that very remark should explain matters without much additional comment.

"Eastwood!" exclaimed Keene. "I understand that you are a very good friend of Miss Marian Dale?"

"That's why I am here."

"Indeed?"

Keene's voice was cutting. Eastwood's assurance had returned to him, and there was something akin to insolence, almost a threat, in fact, in his manner.

"Yes. That is why I am here. And if I am not conducted to Miss Dale at once, there is quite likely to be a little trouble. You see, my dear Mr. Whoever you are, I am not much concerned at that loaded gun in your hand—I've met them before."

It occurred to Keene that he was having quite a remarkable time of it. Far from evincing any fear at being detected prowling around the house under suspicious circumstances at such an hour, Eastwood was making himself the aggressor, actually threatening to make trouble.

"You seem to forget," snapped the detective. "You are a burglar in my house, and my prisoner. I think you know what you are guilty of. And if you start any monkey business, I'll shoot—straight."

Eastwood looked frankly puzzled. He stared hard at Keene for a moment, and then smiled in a manner intended to be friendly and capitulating.

"Perhaps we are talking at cross purposes," he hazarded. "I'm not a burglar, and I don't know what all your mysterious accusations mean. I was in bed, asleep, in my apartment, an hour ago. My telephone rang. Some one—it was a harsh, low voice, more like a boy's than a man's—told me to come here at once—that Miss Dale had been kidnapped here in an automobile, and that she was in terrible danger. Whoever it was told me your basement door would be left open by a friend. Now you will understand I didn't know what to believe; whether it was some impossible practical joke or not. But no man would take a chance on a message like that. I jumped into my clothes and came here in a taxicab. The door was open downstairs when I got here, but no one was waiting for me. I came right in, and all at once you jumped at me with that revolver. That's what I am doing here!"

Keene smiled skeptically.

"It doesn't sound good, Eastwood," he replied. "Not in the light of what has been going on here in the last few hours. Suppose you come in and sit down. I'll have to figure what to do with you."

"Not on your life," snarled Eastwood. "I'm going to find out if there's anything in that message now. I'm going to look for Marian Dale."

He clenched his fists and was about to rush upon Keene. But the latter's face was grimly set, and the weapon leveled directly at Eastwood's head.

"Miss Dale is here," the detective assured him. "She came here, voluntarily, to be under my protection. If I think it wise I may even allow you to see her. Meanwhile, sit down."

His face flushed, his manner nervous, Eastwood sat down unwillingly, while Keene still covered him with the revolver. Without relaxing this precaution, the detective backed to the house telephone, plugged the proper connection and pushed the button for the laboratory. Then, with his free hand he lifted the receiver to his ear.

"That you, Blake?" he asked. "Did you lock up the house to-night? You did. At what time? Nine o'clock? Do you remember locking the basement door? You do? Thanks."

As he dropped the receiver, the detective once more addressed Eastwood.

"Where is your apartment, Mr. Eastwood?"

"96 West Kenwood Avenue."

"Your telephone number?"

"Claxton 1077."

Keene picked up the receiver of the exterior phone and gave the number Eastwood had just told him. In a few moments he had the apartment-house operator on the line.

"Is Mr. Eastwood in his apartment?" he asked, smiling grimly at the indignant glance of his prisoner.

"No, sir," came the telephone girl's reply. "He left here in a taxicab about an hour ago."

"Do you know where he went?"

"No, sir. He got a telephone call, and the party told me at the time to get him quick—it was a rush message. Five minutes afterward Mr. Eastwood came rushing downstairs and called a taxi. There's an all-night stand near here, you see, because of the—"

Keene dropped the receiver. That much of Eastwood's story at least was verified, the situation was far from reassuring. Certainly Eastwood's story was most improbable, and yet— Another idea came to the detective. Picking up the telephone again, he asked for the chief operator.

"I am investigating a burglary in my house," he told her. "This is Green 7666. I wish you would let me know if any telephone call has been made from my house within the last hour and a half—with the single exception of one I have just made, two minutes ago."

"Just a moment," was the response. There was an interval of waiting, and then the chief operator's voice came droningly to the detective's ear:

"Some one called Claxton 1077 a little over an hour ago. They told the operator it was a rush message—to hurry. Can I help you any further?"

"No. Thanks."

Keene dropped the receiver and faced Jack Eastwood, replacing his revolver on the library table as he did so.

"Eastwood," he said, "whether you're a criminal or an honest man I'm not prepared to say, but you've told me the truth so far. Your presence here is damned suspicious—if you are innocent you don't know how prejudiced your position is. But I'm going to give you the chance to prove your innocence, principally for the sake of the girl in there, who loves you. Right from the start you may as well understand that she has been in deadly danger, and I believe she still is. If you are sincere you will do everything in your power to save her. And I can tell you what to do."

All the traces of resentment were gone from Eastwood's face. His eyes were anxious as he thrust out his hand and Keene clasped hands with him.

"I'll do anything at all," said Eastwood, huskily. "What shall I do first?"

Keene did not immediately reply. He was studying Eastwood's hand—a most unusual hand it was for a man. It was long and well groomed, the fingers were supple, and the flesh soft. An artist might have had such a hand, or a psychic, or a poet, or even—

"What do you do for a living?" asked Keene, abruptly.

"I'm a salesman," answered Eastwood. And then, with a flush of understanding, he glanced down. "You're looking at my hands. I play the violin, and that naturally has made me be careful with them. To get the *vibrato*, you know, one must have the proper sensitiveness as well as strength. I have developed them for years, and the best practice I have found to be shadowgraphy."

"What do you mean?"

Keene's voice was casual—there was a silken nonchalance in his words that cloaked a sudden and tremendous shock.

"Shadow pictures. You know how. By manipulating the hands—particularly the fingers—one can make shadow pictures on the wall. I am quite an expert at it."

Was the man a babbling lunatic? Didn't he know—hadn't Marian Dale told him of those early shadows—those sinister forerunners of what she was suffering now? Keene studied the man before him incredulously. Yet Eastwood met his gaze frankly, as if he had nothing whatever to conceal.

"So you make shadow pictures," remarked Keene. "You can double and twist your fingers to produce small silhouettes on the wall?"

"Surely. But I don't quite see—haven't we more important things to talk about?"

"You can imitate the shadow of a dog?" Keene's voice was edged now.

"Why, yes, I can."

"Could you make the silhouette of a highwayman?"

Eastwood regarded the detective coldly.

"Just what is your drift?" he inquired.

"Could you do what I asked?" repeated Keene.

A shot rang out, and something whizzed between them. A flood of smoke came through the doorway, the glass of a picture crashed into a rain of fragments, and they heard the sound of rending wood as a bullet tore its way through the wainscoting.

Both sprang to their feet. The shot had come from the hallway. With one accord both rushed out, but as Keene knew in his heart before he got there, the hallway was empty. At the same moment the laboratory door was flung open and Mrs. Stone, followed by Marian Dale, came impetuously down the corridor.

"What is it? What has happened?" they cried.

Then Marian Dale screamed: "Jack! Are you hurt? What are you doing here?" She rushed into Eastwood's arms and laid her sobbing head against his breast. Mrs. Stone, white-faced and unnerved, looked questioningly at the detective. Blake stood alert and expectant in the background.

"It is nothing," Keene assured them, his voice pitched high and confident. "Our man got away again—that's all. Next time we'll get him. I called Mr. Eastwood here because I thought he might be of some help. I am sure you don't mind, Miss Dale?"

Marian's answer was to wrap her arms tighter around Eastwood's neck and cry out her troubles. It was up to Keene to break the tableau.

"I think it will be best for you ladies to remain in the laboratory, as I instructed you," he said, sharply. "You should not have raced out here as soon as you heard that shot—no one knows what's going to happen around here. It will be better all around if you will return there now."

Eastwood released Marian, and she stood aside, wiping her eyes and still shaking with weeping. Mrs. Stone went up to her gently and was about to lead her back down the corridor when the girl gave a gasp of astonishment.

"Look!" she cried. "Where did that come from?"

She pointed at her feet, where a sealed envelope lay, the address-side turned upward, and the superscription written so boldly that even from where they stood they could read it. The address was:

TO YOU POOR GROUP OF IDIOTS!

Keene stooped and picked it up, and ripping open the flap, took out a sheet of notepaper. Both the address and the message itself were in the form of printed characters—there was no possible hope of identifying the writing.

"I failed twice to-night," it read, "but I shall not always fail. Perhaps it was better that I should. You may be sure that my purpose will be achieved. The Dale girl will see her lover die before her eyes—a torturing, terrible death. She herself will shortly follow, but not until she has suffered first as is proper and just under the circumstances. And, finally, this mystery will be explained to the full satisfaction of your impossible scientific detective—but he shall not know before. When the seventh shadow creeps on the wall, two shall die, and Keene will understand.

"Why not go to sleep now, like sensible people? Dawn is on the hilltops; pink, beautiful dawn. I am weary with the night's revel, and shall not trouble you—for a few hours at least.

"Pleasant dreams!"

CHAPTER FIVE
THE DAGGER STRIKES

"DAWN IS ON THE HILLTOPS!"

The mysterious sender of that extraordinary message had spoken truly. Already, as he looked down the corridor through the open door of his laboratory, Keene could see through the windows the first streakings of pink and gray that foretold the coming of the morning. As he confronted the silent figures before him; as he looked into the puzzled, sympathetic face of Mrs. Stone, the care-worn, harassed face of Marian Dale, the anxious face of Jack Eastwood, the detective was himself a striking contrast to them all. For him the battle was just beginning; the zest and enthusiasm for the chase was now warming his soul; far from showing fatigue or discouragement, his face was bright with a fresh glow. He had asked for more facts; now he was getting them.

He tapped the note tentatively against the open palm of his left hand.

"Our foes confess their weariness," he said. "Whether we can trust them is quite another question. But we need not trust them. When the sun comes the shadows flee away. I believe the danger is over—for the present. Mrs. Stone, I wish you would take Miss Dale to your room now, and she must sleep for the rest of the morning. You must remain awake and guard her until I secure some one to relieve you. Mr. Eastwood, I am going to ask that you remain in the library until I have time to talk to you. You and Blake had better come in now."

The two women went up the stairway as Keene and Eastwood crossed to the library, followed by the silent Blake. Eastwood protested against Keene's course; he said that the danger was undoubtedly still present, and that they should organize a search through the house at once. But Keene, after hearing him through patiently, merely shook his head in cryptic silence and passed thoughtfully into the library. Abstractedly he motioned Eastwood to a chair, and he threw himself into an easy position on a sofa.

"For the next ten minutes," he said, "I wish that neither of you would disturb me. I have got enough to keep my mind busy for that long—and I can't think if I am interrupted."

Blake cast a reproachful glance at the detective. He seemed to take the remark as a personal aspersion. If so, it was certainly unjustified, for Blake never spoke except when spoken to.

Keene's mind was ready now to grapple with the problem. In orderly array, the problems of the case shaped themselves before his mind. He must find out how the shadows were produced, the mechanical means by which they were effected. The crimson candles, too. He must learn how they had been smuggled into Marian's room and placed on her bureau, without discovery. And how had they been lighted? He must see those candles—Marian had not told him whether they disappeared with the shadows or had remained on the bureau. Candles that lighted themselves should be worth seeing. He must make a careful examination of Marian's apartment; the arrangement of the place undoubtedly would suggest something. The letter which he held, the mysterious communication which had suddenly appeared in their midst, that was a physical clue, which, under certain chemical treatments in his laboratory, might disclose secrets regarding the writer that might lead to the discovery of his identity.

The fact that the mysterious enemy had gained entrance to his own home, and was there working about his scheme of terror and death, goaded every instinct within Keene to do his utmost. In swift retrospect he went over every detail that had been told him by Marian Dale and by Professor Rust; he recalled every dramatic detail of the exciting incidents within his own walls during the last few hours, and tried to reconcile some basic fact to harmonize them. It was a difficult, indeed, it seemed a hopeless, task.

Ten minutes and five more had flitted by, and the detective had not yet opened his eyes. He was considering the various possibilities of guilt, and seeking a possible motive. Jack Eastwood? Yes, he had a motive, at least a possible one. Marian had willed him all her money. That was a preposterous thing to do; possibly he had urged her to do that very thing. Suppose that he was married already and was playing a crooked game? He might conspire to murder her, and then claim her fortune. But—and here was the question Keene could not begin to answer—why should he adopt such bizarre and unheard-of tactics to accomplish that end?

The fact did remain, however, that Eastwood had been discovered under strange circumstances in the corridor. And it was a fact which he himself admitted that he made a hobby of shadow pictures. He had a well-substantiated yarn about his presence in the house. That was the case, for and against Eastwood.

Annette, the maid of Marian Dale? Perhaps. She might have a motive, though Keene, of course, knew of none. He would interview Annette that morning.

The discarded suitor? There was a possibility. Keene would interview Miss Dale, find out more about this individual, and put one of his operatives on his trail.

Who else?

Now, Keene was the kind of detective who never rejected a theory because it sounded absurd. He followed every little lead, until convinced that the vein was exhausted and there was nothing more to be gained. Consequently he also considered Professor Rust as a possible factor.

Rust had made a remark that stuck in Keene's mind. It was the remark that Marian's mother had once been his sweetheart; that she had thrown him down for another, "and lived to repent it," as the professor had added bitterly. Was he wreaking the accumulated venom of years in a bizarre revenge upon Marian? Such things were not unheard of.

Suddenly two memories, exactly opposite, came together in the investigator's mind, and he sat bolt upright, his eyes blinking in sudden anticipation.

"Blake," he said. "I have been wanting to ask you a few questions about that cobra. You got into position behind the book-case curtains, through the secret panel, just after serving those sandwiches, didn't you? Well, how did you discover the snake?"

"I knew it was there all along, sir," returned Blake, solemnly.

Keene started in amazement.

"What do you mean by that?" he demanded, wondering if Blake actually knew to be true what he himself had only suspected.

"I smelled it when I brought in the tray," replied Blake. "I knew I could not be mistaken. I acted as I believed you would have me act, by getting the best weapon I could find and taking a position of vantage."

There was a tense silence for a moment, and then Keene asked:

"Where do you suppose the snake came from, Blake?"

In reply, the man pointed at an object left near the leg of the library table. It was a traveling bag, and the initials "P.R." were printed in angular black letters on one end. It was Philemon Rust's bag.

"He left it!" exclaimed Keene delightedly. "That is the very thing I had in mind. Do you suppose he could have carried the cobra in here in that?"

He lifted the suitcase, and then stopped aghast. One end of it was loose; in fact, was nothing more than a dangling flap of curtain, shielding an opening at one end of the case. Two spring catches, operated from the handle of the bag, controlled the flap, which was freely perforated to admit the air.

"There's nothing unusual about that bag," interposed Eastwood, who had been watching and listening intently. "People carry pet dogs on trains in bags like that, and deceive the conductors. You can get them in many leather shops."

"Exactly!" returned Keene. "They are splendidly convenient for carrying around live-stock. Just put that bag aside, in a safe place, for the present, Blake."

When Blake returned, Keene had resumed his position on the sofa, and his eyes were closed. The attendant knew that the scientist was groping with the problem again in the silence of his own heart and mind, and the grim lines around Keene's mouth told him that he was drawing nearer to a solution of the problem.

"Get me an almanac, Blake," ordered Keene, suddenly.

In less than two minutes Blake was back, with an almanac, opened at a certain page. He offered it with a certain pride to Keene, and the latter rewarded him with a bright smile.

"I see your mind is running in the same channel," he remarked, as he saw that the almanac had been opened at the very page he wished. "Now we're getting somewhere."

Eastwood scratched his head meditatively.

"You'll excuse me," he said, "but I am a little puzzled. I don't know yet why Marian is here with you. I don't know who you are, or what your game is. I don't even know your name. And I'll be damned if I know why, in all this mix-up, you have to consult an almanac!"

Keene smiled whimsically.

"You may be the guilty man," he said reflectively, "and yet you haven't got the look of a criminal about you in any way. At all events, I think you are entitled to some sort of explanation—you may help out in an emergency at that. But I shall have to defer a translation of the almanac until a later date!"

Upon which he sketched briefly the extraordinary circumstances in which Marian Dale had found herself involved in the last few hours. Time and time again the big handsome fellow clenched his fists as he learned to what the girl he loved had been subjected. He begged Keene to allow him to explore the house.

"There are to be seven shadows, you remember," Keene reminded him, "and so far there have only been four—the dog, the highwayman, the snake and the dagger. 'When the seventh shadow creeps on the wall' says this charming little message, so you see we have three to go. And from the looks of this case I believe we shall actually see all three of those shadows."

"You have formed a theory, then, Mr. Keene?"

"Not a bit of it. I have seen several floating nebulously in the ether. Any of them may be right; all may be right, in fact, and yet, very probably, all may be wrong. But one thing I'll swear to, that after I have a look over the ground, with Blake at my side, this morning, the theory of this thing will leap into my mind almost unbidden. I am working toward the light now!"

"Great!" breathed Jack Eastwood. And then, with a deep frown he leaned forward.

"Why, do you suppose, they shot at me a little while ago?" he asked, pointing at the bullet-hole above the library mantel.

"The note explains that," answered the detective. "You are to die so that Marian Dale will suffer. That, in itself, suggests the real motive, and yet it may be only a clever blind. Don't forget that we're dealing with an infernally clever man."

Keene relapsed into brooding silence again, a silence that was broken at last by the tingling of the telephone bell. Blake answered it, and then, with a solemn nod, passed the instrument into the detective's hand.

"Mr. Keene speaking," he said, briskly. Then, with a face as expressionless as a dead man, he listened to the message that was spoken sharply, hurriedly, excitedly, into his ear. A short "All right!" ended the conversation, and he hung up the receiver.

"Professor Philemon Rust is dead," he said, sternly. "He was discovered murdered not an hour ago—stabbed to death! And his body was in the apartment of Miss Marian Dale!"

Chapter Six
KEENE IS WARNED

So it was murder at last! The fiend who had painted his devilish moving shadows, omens and portents of evil, upon the walls, had struck the killing blow. Where the flying knife aimed at Keene, the poised cobra and the shot had failed, the dagger had won. And its victim was an innocent, scholarly old gentleman!

Yet, was he that?

As Keene sat forward, his head in his hands, trying to absorb this latest development in the problem, that question was uppermost in his mind. Rust had not been above suspicion in his own mind not half an hour before. And what had Rust been doing in Marian's rooms? Had he means of access there? If so, might not that very fact throw a great deal of light on the problem?

And yet, if he were guilty, who would have killed him? Where had Annette, the French maid, been when he was slain? Where was she now?

There was no time to be lost. Torn between his anxiety to be at the actual investigation of the facts and his desire to protect the girl who had been brought under his own care by the very man who had just been murdered, Keene felt at a loss how to proceed. Fiercely he swore to himself that nothing should harm Marian; that the vile plot against her should not succeed; that, cost what it might, she should be protected.

"Eastwood," he said, suddenly, "I believe you are innocent in this business, and I've thought so all along. Somebody has got to protect your fiancé and I cannot remain here to do it. Are you willing to take that as your job? To stay here and guard her door with very life until I return? For I tell you, man, against this fiend we are fighting now, we've got to put our very best. Are you—"

"Am I?"

Jack Eastwood stood up his full six feet and his chest swelled with pride.

"I'd just like to get within arm's reach of one of them," he grated out, savagely. "By thunder, I'd—"

But Keene didn't let him finish. He was too busy giving him instructions what he should do and how he should do it in his absence.

He suggested that he remain where he was, in the library, and promised that breakfast would be served him in a little while, when Mrs. Stone would assume direction of the servants who had not been aroused through all the weird happenings during the small hours of the morning. To this Eastwood acquiesced, with the stipulation that he would prowl around occasionally and follow up any unusual sound he might hear. To which Keene agreed, remarking that about the only unusual sound he might over-hear would be the bacon sizzling in the kitchen downstairs.

Keene then went upstairs and rapped softly on the door of Mrs. Stone. That faithful guardian of the persecuted Marion answered the rap, and told the detective her charge had fallen asleep only a little while before. Already Keene had determined not to break the news of Rust's murder to the girl until he had to. As a scientist, with considerable medical training, he realized that this additional shock might have the most dangerous consequences.

With some parting instructions to Mrs. Stone, Keene came downstairs again and bade Eastwood good-by. Blake, who was always everywhere and nowhere at once, who never asked questions and always knew what to do, was ready with his overcoat and small satchel in which Keene carried mysterious appliances of service to him on criminal cases. During Keene's absence, Blake had telephoned for Keene's automobile, which was now panting at the curb outside, and the detective and his assistant went speeding down the long avenue within three minutes from Keene's parting from Mrs. Stone.

Glancing out of the window, Keene noted that the sun was already glowing warmly across the east, and that the day would be a sweet one. Unconsciously he contrasted the calm, serene loveliness of the morning with the deadly terrors of the night, horrors which had come to a climax in the murder of Philemon Rust.

"What do you make of it, Blake?" he asked.

Blake glanced at him shrewdly.

"Had you thought of the motive, sir?" he asked.

"Several."

"Don't you believe there is one underlying characteristic of the whole job?"

Keene smiled appreciatively.

"You'll be a detective before you're through," he said, joyously. "Your thoughts often echo mine, sometimes I fancy they are ahead of me. You are right. That underlying characteristic is the big thing—the tell-tale clue—after all. They may cover up their tracks—and they've been damned clever about it—but that one tell-tale characteristic leaves them wide open to any one possessing ordinary horse sense."

Blake nodded his head sagely and agreed.

The car drew up close to the curbing, and stopped. Blake was out in a trice, and Keene followed him, to find himself before a handsome twelve-story apartment house, recently erected, on the lordliest portion of what Albert Noyes called the "lordliest street in the world." A policeman came up to them.

"Mr. Keene?" he inquired, touching his hat respectfully.

"I am Mr. Keene."

"The chief's upstairs, sir, and told me to watch out for you. It's a terrible business, Mr. Keene—not another murder like it in the history of the department. Better hurry right upstairs, sir; it's on the ninth floor, Apartment B."

With a friendly nod, Keene passed into the austere lobby of the apartment house and made his way to the elevator. One question was agitating his mind considerably at this juncture. In many celebrated criminal cases his profound knowledge of science had frequently been of great service to the city detective department. This much the detectives themselves were quite ready to admit. What they would not confess so readily, however, was the fact that Keene's shrewd deductions, sometimes amounting to an almost uncanny insight into the secrets of a problem, had put them on the right track at times when the whole force was hopelessly puzzled. Some newspapers had given Keene considerable hysterical publicity over one or two recent cases, and this, he had realized, had stirred up antagonism among some of the regular operatives. He had been quick to sense and identify this feeling of professional jealousy.

Consequently the sudden telephone message, apprising him of the murder of Philemon Rust, was a surprise to him. The chief, Burkehart, himself, had called him. Why should they call upon him so quickly, so frantically, within an hour of the discovery of the crime? This was the question that was bothering Keene as the elevator bore him swiftly upward to the ninth floor.

Followed by Blake, he emerged into the corridor and the shrill sobbing of a high-pitched feminine voice told him that a woman, most probably Annette, the maid, was making the situation worse.

As Keene stepped to the door, Chief Burkehart, a big, bluff man, with bristling grizzled mustache, came up to him with an air of brusque politeness and greeted him.

"Sorry to get you down here," he barked, "but this is a case where nothing else could be done. Come in and see for yourself."

Keene followed him down a narrow hallway, through an elegantly fitted reception room, then through a library, and passing through a second doorway toward the left, found himself in the boudoir of Marian Dale. By its daintiness, its girlish charm and simplicity, Keene identified it at once. But his attention was chained to what lay before him on the floor.

Philemon Rust, the man who had left his door so short a while before, lay stark in sudden death. Flat on his back he lay prone, with his arms flung wide, and his stiff fingers distended as if about to close upon some ghastly antagonist. The face was like a mask of despair; such an expression was on it as Doré gave the condemned souls in his pictures of the Inferno. It was as if the old scholar, detected suddenly in his ward's apartment, had seen instead of some human person a phantom or a fiend. His wide-staring eyes, his sunken jaw and wide-open mouth, the furrows of the forehead, all spoke of a mortal fear. A dagger had been thrust in his throat, the floor was stained scarlet. And there was something white pinned to his shirt front.

"That," said Burkehart, grimly pointing, "was what made us send for you. That's a little love-note, addressed to you."

Keene bent low beside the fallen form and examined what he saw to be a sheet of white paper, on which a message had been written. The words, with their oddly printed characters, seemed to leap up at him, and he could not restrain a gasp of astonishment. For the characters were too familiar to be mistaken; the same hand which had traced that note which had fallen at their feet in his own home had written this second communication.

"Let this be a warning to Mr. Gordon Keene," read the note. "Let him look long upon the corpse of the man who brought Marian Dale to him. Professor Rust has learned too much. Mr. Gordon Keene had best look to it that he himself does not make a similar mistake."

Keene looked up quizzically at the stern-faced detective chief.

"You're not putting any skids in my way, are you?" he remarked. "I am not usually disturbed by threats, but this fellow means business. And," he added, raising his voice, "if he is within sound of my voice now, he may as well understand that I know far more about it now than he suspects, and that I am going to get him within twenty-four hours."

Without pausing, the investigator stood up and walked nearer to the chief.

"Tell me what led up to this," he asked.

In a few, terse sentences, Burkehart explained. At midnight Miss Dale, the lessee of the apartment, had suddenly left the building. That, reflected Keene, was when she went to see Rust and tell him her story. Annette Desiré, the maid, being left alone in the apartment, locked it up and went out, informing the telephone operator that she was going home to spend the remainder of the evening with her mother. That left the apartment deserted. Several hours later, Professor Rust appeared in the corridor. He was a familiar visitor and was immediately recognized by the attendants. He informed them that Miss Dale would not return home that evening, but that she had asked him to get some articles for her. The clerk lent him a pass-key and he was taken upstairs in the elevator.

"That," Keene decided, "may be explained on several premises. But the most probable explanation is that the poor old fellow meant to go up there and do some detective work on his own account."

No one, continued Burkehart, had seen him come down, and his presence upstairs was forgotten. About six o'clock in the morning, Annette Desiré had returned, complaining that she had lost her key, and asked the clerk to let her in. He told her that he believed Professor Rust was still up there, but she laughed at such an idea as preposterous, and insisted that he unlock the door for her. Accordingly, the clerk lent her a second pass-key—the one Rust had taken had not been returned—and, remarking jokingly that he would not lose a second one, went up in the car with her. It was the clerk himself who opened the door, and who was surprised at seeing all the lights in the apartment on, and some evidences of confusion; an overturned chair, and a smashed reading lamp. Followed by the French girl, he had hurried through the various rooms and come finally upon the corpse of Professor Rust.

The detective stared moodily over the officer's head. In many ways he had a great respect for the force, but he did not credit it with too much initiative, or imagination. And he did not believe that the officer would get much further in his investigation, if he were to see what Keene was seeing at that particular moment.

Keene was looking at a shadow. It was the fifth of that mysterious series, and it had suddenly appeared in a circle of morning sunlight on the bed-room wall. It was the shadow of two hands—long, thin, tapering hands. One held a tiny tumbler, the other a vial. And from the vial, drops were falling into the tumbler.

CHAPTER SEVEN
A DOUBLE MYSTERY

POISON! AND DEFIANCE!

Those were the words that flashed across the mind of the detective as he beheld that sinister shadow on the wall. It was a clear and definite prophecy of the form the next attack from the enemy would assume. And, defiant of his powers of penetration, scornful of the possibility of detection, the singular shadow came upon the wall almost immediately after he entered the room.

It was as fleeting as all the others had been. Scarcely had the detective time to understand its meaning before it disappeared. There was no blurring of its lines; no gradual melting away—it simply vanished while he was looking at it.

"What are you staring at so hard?" asked Burkehart, suspiciously.

"Nothing at all—just thinking over matters," replied Keene abstractedly. He turned to the doorway and saw Blake there, with an expression in his eyes the detective had seen there many times before. It was a signal light, and it meant that Blake, acting under instructions given him by Keene during the ride in the automobile, had found something.

"Do you mind if I look around a bit on my own account?" asked Keene, casually. "You know my methods and you will understand that I did have a little hand in this game before it became murder. Now, don't ask me to open up just this minute. Give me an hour in this apartment, and then I'll tell you all that I know."

Burkehart looked undecided. He felt he should get everything out of Keene then and there. But he also remembered that Keene had saved many a case in the past, and he was unwilling to risk antagonizing him.

"Very well," he assented grudgingly. "Look around as you please. But I don't think you'll find very much—I've been busy myself, you know."

Keene's reply to that was a little laugh which Burkehart did not understand.

He passed out of the room of death, with a last glance at the body of Philemon Rust, and stopped in the hallway, where Blake had retired to wait for him.

"What?" he whispered questioningly.

"Look on the sill of the bed-room window," advised Blake, eagerly.

There was no time for anything but the most hurried consultation, for at any moment they might be interrupted, and Keene did not want the police to know the inside facts—or rather mysteries—of the affair, until he had it further in hand.

"Your orders are these," he snapped, crisply. "Get an absolute lay of the land around here. Get it so clear in your mind that you can draw a perfect map of it. Then make a careful examination of the fire escapes. You know the methods I have shown you. After that, get out on your second job. I want a complete life history of Marian Dale's parents, individually, before they were married. Also find out every detail you can about the private life of Annette Desiré. Get me a picture of Miss Dale's father and mother, if you can. But particularly find out about the maid. She is very important!"

Blake touched his hat respectfully.

"Floor plans. Fire escape. Miss Dale's parents. Annette Desiré."

He repeated the words like a parrot. And then he slouched off down the hallway to mingle with the many policemen and men from headquarters who crowded the apartment. As Keene turned to go back to the bed-room, he could hear the agonized voice of the maid, as she answered the searching queries of the detectives, who were already applying a premature "third degree."

Blake had said: "Look on the sill of the bed-room window." So that was Keene's next step. In Blake he had found an assistant at once wily and wise, and he knew that he could depend on him to ferret out something. Without an original cell in his brain, he could adopt the methods shown him and apply them with marvelous facility. And so, while Keene had been talking to Burkehart and examining the body of Rust, Blake had not been idle, and had come upon something on the window sill. It was with a suppressed curiosity, therefore, that the detective strolled across the room, stopped to examine the pearl-handled, antique dagger with which Rust had been slain, and finally stopped moodily, as if reflecting, before the window at the far end of the room.

There was nothing on the window sill. Keene waited for a moment, and then passed on until he stood before the center one. Instantly he saw what had stirred Blake so. Tucked away in one corner, against a bit of carved moulding, which prevented them from falling to the street below, were three red wax candles.

Keene glanced behind him. The room was empty, save for himself and the dead body on the floor. Burkehart had been called to listen to what Annette Desiré had to say. Quickly he lifted the window, his hand seized the three candles and hid them away in his pocket. Gently lowering the window, he turned away. One clue that was worth while at last was in his possession.

Burkehart bounced in the room at the next moment.

"Well, Keene," he said, "how much more time are you going to spend mooning around this household? Seems to me you ought to be helping justice by telling us more about this man and what you know about this case. What?"

Blake entered just at this juncture and Keene did not reply. The assistant gave Keene an envelope, which was sealed.

"Those are the plans you asked for, Mr. Keene," he said, deferentially. Keene nodded as if the matter were of no consequence and thrust the envelope into his pocket. Blake bowed again and left—to finish the assignments which Keene had given him.

"Well, Burkehart," replied the detective heartily, "I think you are right. I am going to 'spill the whole works,' as the slang dictionaries phrase it, and then, if you are not willing to follow my lead, we'll split, and see who gets there first. For I tell you frankly, I am determined to get there."

"Go ahead and spill," said Burkehart, magnificently.

In rapid fashion Keene related the facts as he knew them, circumstantially, and without embellishment. As various expressions chased themselves across the hardened visage of the unimaginative Burkehart, his countenance was a study for a cartoonist. Interest, swiftly changing to incredulity, then to amazement, to thrilled horror, and then to absolute dismay, were written there as faithfully as the human physiognomy can betray feelings and emotions.

"Great thunder!" he said, in a low, awe-filled tone, as Keene wound up with the story of the fifth shadow on the wall. "It sounds like a story in a book. Have you formed any theory, Mr. Keene?"

"I have!" answered Keene, emphatically. "I believe I know now. But I am not sure. So I ask of you, earnestly, not to interfere during the next few hours. If you will only be guided by me—"

Burkehart growled impatiently.

"Have you any idea how those shadows were produced?" he asked.

"Yes. I know how they were produced. It was the last shadow which absolutely confirmed my opinion."

"What is it then, for the love of Mike? Some sort of pocket projection apparatus?"

Keene nodded his head in a vigorous negative.

"Well, what in—"

Keene got up from his chair.

"You will excuse me," he said, bluntly. "That is only a romantic detail—the product of a particularly vivid and malicious imagination. The essential thing is that murder has been done and that two other lives are in danger—Jack Eastwood and Marian Dale. We can't afford to lose time—that last threatening shadow was not a joke. It meant that one or the other of them was to be—"

"Poisoned!" cried Burkehart.

"You have it. Poisoned! We don't know where or how the blow will fall next. I, myself, am in danger if I press this thing. But I am going to press it to the limit. Now, this much I will tell you—Annette Desiré, your French maid in the room yonder, is an important figure in this case. Hold on to her as tightly as you can. She is not the guiding intelligence, but there is no question in my mind that she has been a facile tool, and more than that, a willing tool, in the hands of some superior, some more cunning, infinitely malicious mentality. When my man Blake returns I expect to find the motive behind this thing. And when I get that motive I will get my man!"

Burkehart considered only a second or so.

"Keene, I'll go you," he said, "and there's my hand on it. If there's any man who can solve this thing, I believe you are the man. There are many scientific features in it which would baffle an ordinary detective in any case. Such as those shadows, for instance. And those candles that lighted themselves. We couldn't make heads or tails of monkey business like that."

"Scientific child's play," retorted Keene. "Better put that woman under arrest and lock her up in solitary confinement. Don't let any one see her."

A commotion behind them caused both men to run. In the doorway, wringing her hands, the tears streaming down her pallid face, stood Mrs. Stone, the light of fright and terror in her face, swaying as if about to fall.

"What's the matter?" cried Keene, springing toward her and catching her in his arms. "Why did you come here? Why didn't you phone? What has happened?"

Dumbly the woman tried to speak. Vainly she sought for words, and at last, croakingly, feebly, she found the power to speak.

"Marian—is—gone!" she gasped. "I left the room just for a moment, when I heard Mr. Eastwood calling and shouting. When I came back—she—had—disappeared!"

Keene was seeing red that moment. His fists were clenched, his eyes blazing.

"What was that fellow Eastwood doing?" he cried, his forehead seared with an ominous frown.

"He was shouting for assistance," gasped Mrs. Stone. "One of the maids had given him—his breakfast—and the—coffee—must—have—been—poisoned!"

With that last, fatal word Mrs. Stone swooned into unconsciousness.

CHAPTER EIGHT
IN THE DARKNESS

A SHUDDER OF HORROR AT THE GHASTLINESS of the series of misfortunes ran through Keene's body as he lifted the weak form of his housekeeper and carried her to a couch. Burkehart, chewing his mustache savagely and too startled to know what to say, followed him like a man in a dream.

Keene turned and confronted him.

"Please watch out for her," he said, pointing to the silent form of the white-haired woman on the couch. "The night has been too much for her. She has been with me two years, apparently as my housekeeper. In reality she is one of the keenest-witted women in the business, a wonder at deduction, and one of my most valued assistants. Perhaps the next blow may be at her."

A grin of admiration broke on Burkehart's face, in spite of his confusion of mind.

"You're a wonder," he admitted. "Who would ever suspect that simple-faced old lady was a detective. No wonder you can get results. Well, what are you going to do now?"

"Back to my own house," answered Keene, hurriedly. "Send Blake there if he should return here. Tell him to hurry. I'll let you know what happens as soon as I get there. And you be guided by me, will you?"

"Sure! We'll work this thing out together," answered Burkehart, grandly. And Keene hurried out to the elevator. As he leaped into his waiting automobile and told the chauffeur to take him home at his best speed, Keene was feverish and impatient. His coolness and abstraction had deserted him the moment Mrs. Stone had brought him this last fearful intelligence. He had forgotten to ask if a doctor had been got for Eastwood. But he felt sure that had been done. He must interrogate the servants who had prepared the breakfast. But, most important of all, he must examine that bed chamber, and try to get on the trail of the missing Marian. What might not be happening to her now!

Some premonition of the terrible truth behind the strange events which he had witnessed, Keene already had sensed. The "underlying characteristic," which he had so cryptically discussed with Blake, had pointed the way. Stirring at the bottom of his mind, the kernel of the real truth of the matter was beginning to sprout, but in his present state Keene was not ready to receive it.

As he reached his own doorway, and sprang to the curb, he was surprised to find Blake waiting for him on the step. Blake's face was solemn. He greeted his master with a manner that showed he knew much.

"The servants have told me," he said, briefly. "Mr. Eastwood is very ill. It is arsenic."

Keene winced. So the fifth shadow had not lied. It had been poison, and its victim had not escaped. If he died the infamous prophecy of the note would be fulfilled, and even if Marian Dale's life were to be saved, her heart would be broken. In a rush of feeling Keene vowed again to himself that it should not be so; that the dastardly plot should not succeed.

They had carried Eastwood to Keene's bed-room, and two neighborhood physicians had been called. They were working anxiously over the tossing figure on the bed. At a glance Keene saw that he was in a bad way; that his life, indeed, was suspended by a thread.

"Hadn't you better take him to a hospital?" he asked.

But the physicians said that all that could be done was being done. They were not willing to offer much hope.

Keene next hurried to the boudoir where Marian Dale had been so peacefully sleeping when last he had been outside its door. The door was wide open now. He strode in impetuously. There was no sign of struggle. Everything was in its place; even the bed clothes were laid back neatly. There was not a single indication to show that anything mysterious had occurred here; the disappearance of the girl had apparently been consummated without making a wrinkle.

"Kidnapped without a clue," muttered Keene, angrily. He went to the windows, he got down on his knees and crawled back and forth across the floor; he peered into odd corners; he went to a thousand pains to be thorough, and spent more than an hour prowling around that single apartment. When he got up, flushed, dusty, and disheartened, he had not learned a single thing.

Blake was standing impassively in the doorway. In his quiet, unostentatious fashion, he had helped Keene a score of times during that wearisome and fruitless search. Now that he saw the detective's work along that particular line was completed, he came forward to ask if he could do anything more.

"Did you learn what I asked?" asked Keene.

"I did. The telephone girl in the apartment house knew their life history."

Blake fumbled in his pockets and produced two portraits, one of a man, the other a woman. These he offered Keene, with that peculiar elation which comes to one who knows that he has served a good cause and served it well.

"Splendid!" cried Keene, heartened a little, as he snatched the pictures. He studied first the face of the woman.

"Look!" he cried. "This is Marian Dale's mother. Lord, how alike they look. Marian must be to-day the very image of her mother at that age."

And then, as his eyes fell on the other picture, he started up, with a look of triumphant conviction in his eyes.

"There!" he cried. "It is just as I could have sworn it to be. Give us one more link, Blake!"

The assistant bowed low.

"Exactly!" he murmured. "That is precisely what I have been thinking, sir. It is up to us to find the missing link."

Keene was still busy comparing the pictures. Evidently he found them fascinating, for he studied them with rapt attention. Reluctantly he laid them on the bureau beside him and turned again to Blake.

"What is the family story?" he asked.

"It is a family scandal," replied Blake, solemnly. "But I can tell you about it in a nutshell."

"Well, do that," insisted Keene. "We haven't a moment to waste!"

Blake made another of his inevitable bows.

"Marian Dale's father had a love affair before he was married," he said, speaking very quickly. "He threw that woman down to marry Marian's mother. The woman he jilted never forgave him. He was a rascal anyway; he broke his wife's heart, and she died when Marian was born. He died under very suspicious circumstances right after that; there was some talk that he was poisoned."

The detective and his assistant looked into each other's eyes and there was a world of understanding in their gaze.

"And then?"

"The woman who was jilted was known to be of a terrible passion when aroused. She was originally an actress, and Dale jilted her, I understand, because she was beneath him socially. She had a daughter by him, which he never recognized. From the day that child was born, the pair disappeared off the face of the earth. But people said that when Dale died so mysteriously—"

Keene interrupted him.

"Light!" he cried. "In darkness there will be light. It has never failed me yet. Here, Blake, take these candles. Search the neighborhood in the vicinity of the apartment house where Marian Dale lived and find out where they were purchased, and if possible, who bought them. Find out where that cobra was secured. Then go to the nearest drugstore and find out who, within the last few weeks, bought a quantity of metallic potassium—flakes of potassium."

Blake stared blankly.

"What did they want them for?" he asked.

But Keene slapped his hands smartly together in his impatience, and Blake vanished from the doorway like a flash.

There was a new light on the detective's face as he got up and stole from the room. Down the steps he went noiselessly until he reached the library, where, only a few hours before, he had first heard the weird story from the trembling lips of Marian. How much had happened since that time!"

He entered the library and closed the door softly behind him. The curtains were still drawn; he flashed off the lights, and the place was flooded with a blackness in which he could not see his own hand before him.

And it was in that utter darkness that Gordon Keene seated himself in an arm-chair and began his final solution of the mystery of the Seven Shadows. Five shadows he had already known. He had the facts now that he needed, and in this blackness he could concentrate all his powers to get at the truth quickly.

For he was determined the remaining two shadows should never appear.

CHAPTER NINE
WHOSE HANDS?

THERE IS AN ANCIENT SCREED WHICH SAYS: "There are more ways than one of killing a dog." It might have been spoken specifically of the detective profession. For there are more ways than one of detecting a criminal. One may be possessed of even less than the average intelligence, yet having the single virtue of tenacity, of bulldog persistency, the spirit that never lets go, may win distinction in the tracking of criminals. That is the way of the average headquarters "shadow." Another sleuth will have a passion for detail; he will insist on making the most minute examination of everything connected with the case. Some pin their success on the adoption of new and unusual principles, such as Burns did with the dictagraph.

And there are a very few who view a crime as an intellectual problem, akin to a problem in algebra. Such investigators require certain salient facts, many of which they secure for themselves, others are brought to them by clever assistants. With these facts as a basis, they retire to themselves and arrange those facts in an algebraic progression, with X as the unknown quantity. And the selfsame "X"—the criminal—is thus discovered by the pure light of reasoning.

That was the way of Gordon Keene.

Utter concentration was what he needed now—a concentration where every extraneous influence was removed. In his darkened library, where not a ray of light now penetrated, he sat smoking and dreaming. No need in the dark to close his eyes. The mental pictures which he visioned rose before him like dimly-lighted, ghostly things; they were the factors in the algebra of crime, and masked among them was the figure of the arch criminal he was determined to detect.

The group of facts with which he had to deal was almost complete. He knew the phenomena with which he had to deal—the singular incidents which began with the shadow of a spaniel, and had come to a climax in the poisoning of Jack Eastwood and the disappearance of Marian Dale. A motive was already clearly established in his mind. The thing to do was to correlate those facts—to put his finger on the vital spots.

An hour passed, and Keene was still puzzling over that array of mysteries. A knock came to the door; it was Blake, back in an incredibly short time with all the information Keene desired. A woman had purchased the candles; a woman had bought the cobra from a dealer in snakes for circus performers; a woman had secured a small quantity of metallic potassium in a drugstore not far from the apartment house. In every instance a woman.

"Did the same description apply in all cases?" asked Keene.

Blake leaned forward and whispered something rapidly into the detective's ear. The detective nodded quickly. Matters were shaping themselves quickly; he saw the crisis that was rapidly approaching.

"Just a moment, Blake," he said anxiously. "On my way back here from the apartment house I studied that map you drew of Miss Dale's apartment. You are certain everything is accurate?"

"Certain!"

"Then, Blake, these are your final instructions."

Rapidly he sketched out a course of plain action for the attentive assistant. He repeated them so that there could be no possibility of a single direction being misunderstood.

"Now," he concluded, "when you have done all that I ask, which should not take more than an hour or two at the most, rap three times on that door. I shall know by that sign that you have succeeded. And by that time, you may rest assured, I shall have completed my case and we will be ready to spring the trap."

Blake gave a last and sweeping bow and departed. Keene shut the door carefully behind him, and retired back through the gloom of the library, finding his chair again with some difficulty. The silence was grateful.

"In every case a woman!"

The phrase was like a song of triumph in Keene's mind. Those words Blake had whispered to him; they told him an infinite story in themselves. Motive? Why, it was clear as—

Light itself, he had been about to say. And it came as a shock that as the word "light" was in his mind, light itself should appear within that room of complete blackness.

It was a very tiny circle, but it was a circle of brilliant light, and it glowed brightly at the other end of the room. Barely had it caught the detective's eye when it began to grow—widening in an increasing circle until it was as big as a dinner plate, larger still, until it was like the miniature glow of a magic lantern.

"The sixth shadow!" he muttered to himself. "What will it be?"

He was not left long in doubt. Two hands appeared again, thin and shapely hands, the same, he could have sworn, that he had seen on the wall of the apartment house a few hours before. But they held no vial of poison now. They held something else, the shape of which was so awkward, so unnatural, so utterly unlike anything that occurred to his memory, that he could not conceive what it might be.

The shadow those shadowy hands clasped was of something round, like a ball cut in half—like a small bowl, though it had edges and bulges that made it unlike either of these things. Apparently it was being handled with great care, as if it must be very carefully adjusted. It was placed prone on one of the hands; then the other disappeared.

Presently the hand came again, and now it held a vial of the same size Keene had seen before. And again drops fell from it but now, instead of falling into a tumbler, they fell upon the oddly shaped thing in the other hand. At the same moment Keene was sensible of a pungent, familiar smell.

"An ether basket," he gasped, but before he could make a move, something moved behind him in the dark; the basket was fastened over his nose, and its overwhelming odor clouded all his senses. But he did not give up. Desperately he held in his breath; he made a mighty struggle to free himself from its influence, but the effort came too late. Taken unaware, he had breathed in, and the influence already was upon him.

Weakly he dropped back into the chair. The light on the wall dwindled away into blackness; all the world seemed floating away with him.

CHAPTER TEN

GONE!

IT IS NOW PROPER TO RECORD WHAT BEFELL BLAKE as he set out with the final instructions of his master still fresh in his ears.

Blake had been told to do certain things that the average man might regard as impossible, but Blake, being by nature obedient, accustomed to delivering the goods when ordered to do so, had no question in his mind that he would succeed in his hazardous undertaking. But even men as careful as Blake sometimes encounter unexpected difficulties. When he left Keene's home, Blake boarded a street-car and within ten minutes was again near the apartment house where Marian Dale made her home. It was not Blake's intention on this particular occasion, however, to return to the apartment upstairs, unless he found it necessary. Instead, he passed around to the rear of the building, waited for a favorable opportunity, and then suddenly disappeared down an opening in the cellar of the great building.

Landing without any appreciable damage to his bones, but with one rather serious rip in his trousers, Blake lost no time in floundering past coal bins, mountains of stored trunks and other such things, and finally emerged into a court-yard that separated the two wings of the apartment house. Here, to his surprise and discomfiture, he discovered that the court-yard opened, through a small alley, out into the next street; that his acrobatic performance had been altogether unnecessary, since he could have used that means of entrance, which was sacred to the usage of tradesmen. However, he had gained his point, which was to get into that court-yard without being observed by interested parties.

Promptly seeking the shelter of an alcove, Blake now made an effective if not altogether startling change in his appearance. He had entered the premises apparently a man of business, and attired as such. By depositing his felt slouch hat up his back, flat, and drawing from another hiding-place a cap with a license number on it, he gained for himself quite an official air. At the same moment he duly constituted himself an inspector of fire escapes and looked around for the particular fire escape attached to this apartment house.

There it was, built against the west wall of the building, its last rung some two feet above his head. To Blake that would be an easy matter to handle. With one athletic spring he could be scrambling up it. But that was not the point. If Keene's theory was correct—and it was Keene's theory Blake was there to substantiate with hard facts—some one else had been up against that same problem, in the early hours of this morning; some one with not a semblance of Blake's athletic prowess. The problem, then, was, how had the other party accomplished it?

At this juncture Blake stopped and made an examination of the wall near the bottom of the fire escape. Nothing was his reward. It was sheer, hard brick, without a scrape or a scar. Even so seasoned and capable an assistant could be pardoned the swear word which Blake at this juncture released to the morning zephyrs.

Balked here, Blake promptly turned his attention to other means. He prowled into all the odd corners of the place, and finally came upon something which brought a good, healthy crow of delight from his otherwise impassive countenance. Back in the shadows of a corner of the wall was a ladder, a new one, too, and if one had not set out to look for just such a thing it would have escaped observation until the apartment house crumbled to ruins.

Whistling softly to himself, Blake placed the ladder against the wall and examined it carefully. All at once he stopped whistling. He had seen there what he had hoped, but scarcely dared to believe, he would see, and it gave him joy to behold it. With a chuckle he carried it back and replaced it where he had found it. Then, with a little run, he swung himself into the air, and his two hands caught the rung of the fire escape ladder.

With practiced ease he drew himself up and by dint of hard exertion and one or two epithets not necessary to a proper understanding of what occurred, he finally managed to acquire a foothold, and at last was standing safely on the ladder. Flecking the perspiration from his forehead, he glanced around him.

"There they go! All the way up!" he said to himself, and having seen all that he cared to see, he dropped to the ground again, threw the cap he wore up in the air, and sallied out of the alley-way. Straight to the front entrance he hurried and up to the elevator. Presently he stood before the mighty Burkehart himself.

"Well? Any news?" asked Burkehart, none too graciously. He himself had learned nothing, and he was fretting with impatience.

"I have a message from Mr. Keene," replied Blake, dutifully. "He asks that you bring Annette and come at once to his home. He says he is just about ready to spring the trap."

"Well, what's he found?" snarled Burkehart, angrily. "Don't keep me in the dark like this."

"I don't know what he's found," replied Blake, truthfully enough. "What have you found?"

"Not a damned thing," answered Burkehart.

"Have you—if I may be permitted to offer a suggestion—"

"Go ahead!" prompted Burkehart, with an amused and tolerant smile.

"Had you thought of the fire escape?"

Burkehart threw back his head and roared with laughter.

"That's the best joke I've heard to-day," he chortled. "What do you think we are down here—a bunch of pikers? Of course we've thought of the fire escape, young man. Inasmuch as the door was locked on the murdered man, there wasn't much else to think of. We are certain the murderer got away by the fire escape. But how he got into the place is quite another question."

"Yes—but—" put in Blake, modestly.

"Yes—but—what?" mimicked Burkehart, impatiently.

"Couldn't the murderer have come in by the way of the fire escape?"

Burkehart heaved a martyr's sigh, and looked at the questioner with a patience that was meant to be heroic.

"You poor slob," he cried, "don't you understand that there's a drop down there of a good many feet. How the devil could any man get up there without a ladder?"

"But suppose he had a ladder?" persisted Blake.

"But he didn't," cried Burkehart in exasperation. "We looked for one and couldn't find it."

"Yes," replied Blake, courteously. "But there was a ladder, you see. I looked for it, and did find it!"

Burkehart batted his eyes as if he had been dealt a blow. He blinked at Blake in silence for a while.

"Do you mean that?" he asked, slowly, when he had regained his speech.

"I want that ladder brought over to Mr. Keene's house at once," answered Blake. "It was hidden in a deep recess just off the court-yard. It is quite important as corroborative evidence."

Burkehart got up from his chair like a chastened hippopotamus.

"Two men will be demoted for this," he growled. "I sent Hickey and Sloan down there to search that court-yard and they didn't find nothing. A fine pair of boobs!"

He strode into the next room and hurriedly issued orders to have Annette Desiré, who had ceased her weeping and was now white and defiant, taken to the department automobile that was in waiting below. Then he called savagely for the two men whose inefficiency he had discovered, and roared a definition of their abilities that exhausted the dictionaries, ecclesiastical, slangish and profane. As a final humiliation he sent them back in the court-yard to find the ladder within five minutes under pain of being sent before the board under charges. They found the ladder.

As the automobile bearing the officers, the maid and Blake drew up before the mansion of the detective, Blake leaped from the car and opened the door with his key. Asking them all to be as quiet as possible, for the sake of the man so dangerously ill on the second floor, Blake led them down the long hallway into the laboratory of Keene himself. There they found Mrs. Stone carefully setting matters to rights; she having been sent home after receiving medical attention in the Dale apartment.

She pointed silently to an array of things that lay upon a table in the center. Three red candles were there, two notes, covered with printed characters, and a few other curious articles.

"Looks like something is in the wind," commented Burkehart. He made them all sit down and then turned to Blake, who was busying himself about a dozen details, the principal one of which was the bringing of the ladder into the laboratory without breaking any of the porcelain or bottles that lay at every hand.

"Gentlemen, I shall keep you waiting only a moment longer," promised Blake, and retired down the hallway. He crossed the reception room to the library door, and struck three times upon its massive oaken panels as he had agreed. He waited for an answer. But none came.

Again he rapped, three times, as had been their private understanding. And again there was no response.

Blake wasted no more time. He knew his master too well. Quickly he found his key to the library and opened it. He stepped into complete blackness, and a heavy odor of an anesthetic. Instantly he found the electric switch and turned on the lights.

The library was deserted. Gordon Keene had disappeared, and left not a trace behind.

CHAPTER ELEVEN
THE SEVENTH SHADOW

WHETHER IT WAS A MATTER OF MOMENTS OR HOURS that he was unconscious, Keene could not tell. He came back to his senses vaguely, gradually—very slowly. As out of a mist it seemed, he emerged into the light. His first sensation was of extreme weakness, nausea, and a weariness beyond expression. He did not care where he was, nor did he wonder what had happened to him. Every thing was indistinct, blurred and uncertain.

Then slowly the mists began to clear. Events began to shape themselves clearly in his memory; the darkened library, the circle of light, the shadow of the hands dropping ether on a face basket—and then forgetfulness. With a sudden surge of awakening he realized that he had been overpowered, that he was now a prisoner. For the first time he opened his eyes.

At first he could not comprehend his position. Something was covering his mouth, a thick, irritating cloth; he felt tired and cramped and sore. He tried to shift his position, and the effort cost him tortures. Exhausted, he sank back. He rested a few moments, and then, opening his eyes again, he tried to understand his position.

He was seated in a chair; of that he presently assured himself. His feet and his hands were secured tightly with bonds of some sort; that fact, too, he quickly realized. But where he was, or in what kind of place, he had not the faintest idea. He only knew that the place was dark, and in need of ventilation. His mind was now perfectly clear, though his head ached and he suffered from nausea. Failing to discover for himself the nature of his position, he decided to listen in the hope of hearing something that might guide him.

For a long time he heard nothing at all. Once he thought he heard the sharp intake of another's breath, as if some one were quite close to him, but it was too dark to see, and his hands were bound so that he could not grope. Again he fancied he heard a low murmuring, but it was only for a moment. For the rest, the stillness was acute.

Then, a whispered voice spoke directly in his ear. He could feel the hot breath of the speaker burning his cheek.

"You remember the note of warning?" whispered the mysterious voice, which sounded vaguely familiar. It told you the Dale girl should see her lover die before her eyes. He is about to die now. Marian Dale is at your side, bound and gagged as you are. Presently the door shall swing backward and you will both see. And then the rest of that prediction will be fulfilled."

Even as the voice ceased its words came true. A door opened slowly before Keene's eyes; it fell backward slowly, revealing to his amazed vision the interior of his own bed-room. In an instant he comprehended it all. There was an ancient Chinese cabinet which he had had placed in his room, because it was considered moth-proof, to contain his clothes. Both he and Marian Dale were prisoners in that cabinet that they might witness the appalling spectacle prepared by Marian's enemy.

As the door swung slowly outward, propelled by an invisible hand, Keene glanced to his right. His eyes met the suffering glance of Marian, whose mouth was covered with a handkerchief secured with twine, and whose hands and feet were lashed to a chair. He tried to convey to her by his look the hope that something might yet happen to save her lover and herself. But in his heart he feared, at least, that it was too late to save Jack Eastwood.

The door was now completely open, and he could see his room quite plainly. Neither the doctor nor the nurse were there; only the tossing figure of Eastwood lay beneath the crumpled coverlets of the bed. He was still delirious, still muttering in his fever. But his mutterings were silenced by that mysterious voice, which came again, and whispered, hoarsely:

"The physicians have come and gone and they say he will get well. He will not get well."

A hand suddenly appeared. It projected just far enough for Keene to discern it as far as the wrist and forearm; the rest was hidden by the edge of the cabinet in which he was confined. The hand held a small green vial, and drops of a fluid fell rapidly into a tumbler on the table at the bedside. Then the hand was withdrawn, and the whisper came again:

"That he will drink with his next medicine. Here comes the nurse!"

The voice died away, and Keene heard a rapid movement as of some one hastily escaping. The next moment Mrs. Stone came into the room, and bent over the restless figure of Eastwood.

"Nurse is mixing a broth for you, my boy," she whispered motheringly. "It's time to take your medicine now, and I've come to give it to you."

Silently she moved across the room and lifted a bottle, pausing to study its directions carefully. Then she poured out some into a spoon and emptied it into the tumbler. Keene gave one glance at Marian. Her eyes were wide with an emotion that was convulsing her entire body. She was about to behold her lover poisoned! And she could not make a move to save him!

Keene squirmed until his wrists bled in an effort to escape his bonds. His soul writhed and stormed in its utter helplessness. If he could make but a single sign; if he could move hand or foot, or make one outcry, he might save Eastwood from his fate. But he was bound so firmly he could not stir an inch; strain and struggle as he did with every ounce of strength left in his body, he could not move.

At that moment the ultimate pitch of horror came. On the wall above the bed there was a patch of warm sunlight. In its very heart there came now an ugly, venomous thing—the fatal seventh shadow that had crept to the wall at last. At the very heart of the sunshine it appeared; the cadaverous image of a human skull.

There it grinned at them both. The seventh shadow, with the cup of poison in the hands of the crooning old woman, and Jack Eastwood's parched lips parted to receive the fatal draught.

Something cold touched Keene's hand just then. There was the feel of metal, and of something that cut sharp and swift. A knife in the hands of some one unseen was severing his bonds; they dropped from his hands, and then from his feet. With an inarticulate cry the detective rose and staggered out of the cabinet. He reeled forward toward the bed and raised his hand just in time to dash the untasted cup of poison to the floor.

CHAPTER TWELVE
SINS AND SHADOWS

WHEN BLAKE CONFRONTED THE DESERTED LIBRARY, with the smell of an anesthetic heavy in the air, he knew immediately what had happened. Subconsciously he had feared it from the beginning. And something very close to a quiver of pain flickered across the stolid face of the young assistant. The long series of shadowy disasters that had culminated in his master's disappearance had torn away his mask in that brief moment and revealed him for what he really was—a man with a human heart who worshipped Gordon Keene.

But Blake's training had been too severe to allow such a temporary weakness to influence his course of action. It seemed merely to accelerate it. Blake's present business was not to mourn his master, but to find him. And knowing the class of criminals arrayed against him, Blake knew that the quicker he acted, the better it would be for Keene and all others concerned.

He set about his task, however, with a deliberateness that might have passed for slowness, if one did not understand the man. He examined the room carefully. Having learned nothing from this examination, he went to the book-case and threw back the curtains. One touch of his finger on one of the panel knobs served to cause an entire section of the books to swing back, ponderously but noiselessly, revealing a winding corridor. This was the secret passageway which Keene had constructed between his laboratory and his library; it greatly facilitated his work in having Blake overhear conversations with clients and in other delicate matters connected with the profession.

Blake sank immediately to his knees and crawled forward, his head bent nearly to the floor. And the assistant knew exactly what he was looking for. In the years that he had been associated with Keene, there had been an agreement between them what each would do in many different situations which they had foreseen. The abduction of one or the other had naturally been looked upon as a possibility at some time or another. And they had had an understanding that, in such a case, a trail would be left behind. It was for that trail that Blake was looking now.

He had scant hopes of finding it. By the smell of the ether in the air he knew that an attempt had been made to render the investigator unconscious. Could Keene have struggled hard enough to make the trail possible, to insure it, before he succumbed to the anesthetic? On that Blake was pinning his hope now.

Suddenly he was halted by something small and round and red that caught his eye. With a low exclamation he bent down closer and studied it. There was not a single doubt of what he saw. It was a small blot of crimson; a drop of human blood. He had found the trail!

For Keene and Blake had agreed to wear finger rings, with one prong in the setting always raised. That prong might prove their deliverance. For, in such an emergency it could be driven home in a finger hard enough to draw a flow of blood. Here was the blood-drop now. Blake scurried forward on his knees looking for another. One! Two! Three! They stretched away through the mazes of this corridor, losing themselves at the door of the laboratory, with which the secret passageway communicated. By pressing the knob of this laboratory door Blake was enabled to appear suddenly and dramatically before Chief Burkehart, who, with Annette Desiré and several deputies, was waiting for Keene.

"Humph!" growled Burkehart when he had gotten over his first surprise at seeing Blake appear in such an unexpected fashion. "You've got all the outfit, even to secret hallways, in this joint, haven't you? I've always said Keene was a model for all those story-book sleuths anyway. Well, where is he now, and why don't he show up? What's he got up his sleeve?"

"Mr. Keene is gone," replied Blake, soberly. "I can't find him!"

"What?"

Burkehart fairly bellowed the word in his rage. He jumped up and shook his fist in Blake's face.

"Do you mean to tell me I've been bamboozled by that interfering meddler?" he roared. "What do you suppose I'm doing anyway? I was a big ass to think he knew anything. He thought he had some fancy case, and now that it's fallen down he's skipped out. If I get hold of him, why, I'll—"

"Mr. Burkehart!"

Blake's voice was suddenly harsh and commanding. He pointed dramatically to the marble floor, where drop after drop of scarlet showed the continuation of the trail Blake had followed.

"That," said the assistant, earnestly, "will lead us to him. You wait here—let me follow it alone, will you?"

"Go ahead," snapped Burkehart, in disgust. "This is a devil of a mess, I say."

Up the rear stairs crept Blake, sometimes halting when the trail grew dim, but always eager, always confident, until at last he stood before the curtained entrance where the blood-drops ended. He threw the curtains aside.

He had come to the valet's entrance to Keene's bed-room. It had not been used in years, and now the Chinese cabinet of which Keene was so proud stood against it. But a whole panel had been torn away from the cabinet, and he could see right into it. He saw Keene straining at his bonds, and Marian Dale in a state of utter collapse. It did not take Blake a second to whip out his knife and cut those cords. He climbed through and followed Keene as the detective knocked away the cup from the hands of the astonished Mrs. Stone. Then the detective turned, his face radiant again, and shook the hand of his faithful ally.

"Blake," he said, "you're in like a man at the finish."

"You mean by that—" said Blake.

"I mean by that everything is ready. I have solved the mystery of the seven shadows!"

CHAPTER THIRTEEN
THE ACCUSING FINGER

TEN MINUTES LATER THE GROUP IN KEENE'S LABORATORY was complete. Arranged in a kind of semi-circle before him, there sat Marian Dale, Chief Burkehart, Annette Desiré, Blake and Mrs. Stone. The detective stood, facing them, a cigarette in his lips, his hands in his pocket, an easy and nonchalant air upon him that belied the fierce emotions that surged through him.

"Before I place the handcuffs on the guilty," he began abruptly, "I shall tear away the veil of mystery that has shrouded this bizarre series of events and show you the true inwardness of the deception. We have been grappling with a most unusual problem because it involved not only murder, but an organized system of terrorization as well. In this deliberate principle of throwing horror upon horror in the path of Miss Dale, there has been revealed an imagination and a mentality of most extraordinary caliber; a calculating intelligence beyond anything I have ever encountered. I will tell you the motive that brought that fearful capacity for evil into action.

"The motive was hatred and revenge. It was a motive that would not be satisfied with mere, swift death. It demanded slow agony for its abominable appetite. And it knew that the gradual increase of hidden, unknown horror is the greatest torture the human mind can undergo. That—without revealing to you the main-spring of the plot as yet—was the reason for these inhuman attacks on Miss Dale.

"In working out the case I found an underlying characteristic at the start. It was that one person had been present in the earlier stages at every manifestation. And it did not take me long to believe that this young woman here"—he pointed at the trembling, defiant Desiré girl—"was implicated. By stealing upon the fire escape, by hiding in rooms, by seizing countless opportunities given her, she was able to produce some extraordinary effects.

"But almost in the same breath I realized there was some one else behind Annette Desiré. Hers was never the mind that conceived this thing. Already I had discarded the rejected suitor idea, because it did not fit in with any of the facts in the case. I felt sure it was Annette Desiré who produced that dog shadow, and who, on the next day, poisoned the dog itself. I felt sure she made the figure of a highwayman. And I feel equally sure that she, or her superior, hired the thug who attacked Miss Dale the very next day. But easy as that was to reason, there came a stumbling-block.

"Marian Dale was brought here after midnight by the late Professor Rust. She had just seen the shadow of a reptile. Annette Desiré might have made that shadow, it is true. But could she have carried the snake into my house, inasmuch as she was not with Miss Dale, but had remained behind in the apartment? At first I suspected Rust himself, principally because he had a suspicious traveling-bag whenever he traveled, and in his fluster at receiving Miss Dale at such an hour, he evidently picked up his empty bag and carried it with him, quite unthinking. I did not have long to suspect the poor man before he was killed.

"How, then, had the snake been carried to my house? I know now what I was forced to reason then. But my assumption was based on a foundation fact which was true. It had been planned that the snake attack Miss Dale in her apartment. Miss Dale had left her apartment. What more natural, then, that her enemy follow and see that the shadowed prophecy was not discredited?

"I was then forced to conclude that the agency at work in Miss Dale's apartment had means of access into my own house. The mysterious telephone call to Eastwood to hurry here confirmed that suspicion. There was some one at work in my own house, who was firing shots, hurling daggers, and casting shadows.

"Now, the only way to look at a problem like that is a commonsense way. Before assuming some devious and complicated explanation, I worked to find a simple one. And the first thing I did was to ask myself: Who was near each time the shadows appeared? If I could find some one who was always near at that time, I would have a basis to work on.

"I found some one. Amazed and incredulous as I was at the beginning, the evidence began to accumulate as I considered it. Each fresh step pointed nearer to the truth. When Blake gave me the history of Miss Dale's parents, the whole thing became clear as day to me.

"By this time I was evidently considered a dangerous man by my antagonists, and so was slated for the fate which had already befallen Professor Rust, and which was threatening Jack Eastwood. When I was left alone in my darkened library, a light appeared on my wall and in it a shadow. I turned quick as lightning, but before I could see what had happened an ether basket was over my nose. But I had seen enough, then, to answer my last question. I knew then how the shadows were made.

"From the very first I had suspected a feminine hand in the entire business. 'Hell hath no fury like a woman scorned' is an old but a true expression. No man could be as cruel as a woman when she has turned her heart to ice and sets out to wreak revenge. This plot had all the earmarks of a woman at work. And the note, with the words 'Dawn is on the hilltops' had the ring of a woman about it. This was merely an impression, but events showed that I was right.

"I had at first hoped to glean something about those shadows by studying the movements of the moon, in connection with the floor-plan of the Dale apartment. As the moon moved across a room, it might produce a shadow which, as it moved farther away, would vanish. But that was merely a false trail, which led nowhere. The explanation was even simpler than that.

"The murder of Philemon Rust was, in the beginning, deeply puzzling, but as I got on the ground, with the background of my theory already sketched, it did not seem so mysterious. I felt sure Annette Desiré had been to my house to carry that snake, soon after Marian had departed. The information I got at the apartment house confirmed the fact that she had been out. What then had followed? Suppose that Annette was then advised to return home at once? As she nears her apartment she sees a light on her floor. Some one is there! As a conspirator she is afraid. She has a ladder ready for emergencies in the court-yard, and she puts it to use. The ladder and the fire escape stairs show her footsteps. She mounted the ladder and crouched at the window. She saw Philemon Rust, with a certain object in his hand!"

He faced the cowering Annette and fixed her with his gaze.

"You know what that object was!" he cried. "It disappeared, and you could not find it. As you struggled with him, as you slew him with your dagger, he threw it from him, and you could not find it. But I found it. It had fallen behind a picture. You should have been more careful. And that object which Professor Rust had sought for, and found at the cost of his life, will be the decisive factor in this case."

A low sob was the only answer from Annette.

"With Rust dead at her feet, Annette probably became panic-stricken," went on Keene. "She sought desperately for the missing object she treasured so highly, but it had gone. Then, giving it up, she got out on the fire escape again and hurried back to this house. She came to her secret friend here, to ask guidance and advice. And acting on this advice, she returned, complaining to the clerk she had lost her key. This was a deliberate invention; I had Blake search and he found the key in her pocketbook. But her purpose was accomplished; the clerk went upstairs with her; he opened the door; he found the body, and thus gave her the alibi she needed.

"With pictures which Blake found in the family papers in your apartment, Miss Dale—you must forgive us for that, because it was necessary—and with papers from the same place, which told us much of the unhappy family history, I was soon able to patch the story together. I am now able to put the facts plainly before you.

"Annette Desiré was your father's daughter, Miss Dale. She became your maid because this thing had been plotted years before; she came to you eagerly at a time when maids were hard to secure, and you wondered at it. She hated you. And her guiding counselor was her embittered, envenomed mother, who stands there beside her now; the woman who has conceived and brought about all this carnival of terror!"

The detective pointed a finger at the woman he accused; a gray-haired, old woman, whose blazing eyes now belied the meekness of her countenance. It was Mrs. Stone!

CHAPTER FOURTEEN
THE SHADOWS FLEE AWAY

A GASP OF AMAZEMENT CAME FROM THEM ALL. Annette Desiré fell forward, sobbing weakly. But her white-faced mother confronted them all, unafraid:

"I did it all," she said, in a low, intense tone. "It is true. I did it, and I'm glad I did it, and I wish I could do it over and over again. Why shouldn't I? Why shouldn't his daughter suffer as he had made me and mine suffer? I was his proper mate, his promised wife, but he threw me over because I was an actress, and married another. I swore I'd get even, and I've done it—for though that Dale girl isn't dead, she's known torment since I've put the shadows over her life.

"You're a clever man, Mr. Keene," she continued, facing the detective. "I admire the way in which you set out to solve the case. I came to work under you at the same time Annette went with the Dale girl, and I did it after the most careful analysis and a knowledge of the intimacy that existed between old man Rust and yourself. I knew that when our long-hatched plan began he would turn to you. So I was here, ready, when he did that very thing. You see, I looked ahead at everything.

"And you have deduced very nearly everything right, Mr. Keene. It is true that I handled the phenomena here, while my daughter did it at the other house. It was I who sent the snake stealing through the door at you; it was Annette who smeared the Dale girl's clothes with thorn root. It was I who, leaving Blake with Marian Dale in the laboratory, stole through the secret corridor, threw a dagger at you, after you had seen the dagger shadow. I did not mean to kill you. But if the terrorism we practiced to intimidate the soul was to succeed, it must never miss. If we had a dagger shadow, the dagger must appear. And it did, you see!"

She spoke with the most unmoved manner, as if she were discussing the subject of household groceries. Her coolness was appalling.

"And it was I," she added, "who made the poison shadow on the wall in the Dale apartment this morning. You remember that I appeared a moment later with the news that Eastwood had been poisoned and Marian Dale gone. I could have telephoned, of course, but I knew Annette was in the hands of the police by that time, and I just had to be near her."

Here Mrs. Stone paused for the first and only time during her remarkable narrative. But she soon regained her strength, and proceeded:

"All our plans had been worked out well, and yet, somehow, they missed. We wanted more than anything else that Jack Eastwood die before her eyes. Then we would know she was feeling some of the pangs we ourselves had felt. So I telephoned for Eastwood to come. Then, as Annette stole from the house, she fired a shot at him, and she can shoot the date from a ten-cent piece—yet she missed. It seemed as if Fate were moving against us. I cannot see why!"

The calm indignation of the woman was bewildering. Chills ran down the backs of those who heard her narrative; its facts so terrible, its telling so unmoved.

"I have no regrets," she finished calmly. "Except that Eastwood will get well and Marian Dale does not die."

A gasp came from Chief Burkehart. In all his years' experience in the police department he had never met a criminal of this type before. He rose to arrest her.

"Just a moment," interposed Keene. "There are two points yet to clear up, and we may as well finish the work now. The candles which helped produce the shadow were placed on the bureau by Annette from her position on the fire escape, on which she had crept around from her own room. Her thumb-prints are plain in the wax. They were lighted by affixing metallic potassium flakes to their wicks and spraying water on them, see!"

He turned to the three crimson candles on the table beside him, and dipping his hand in a saucer of water sprinkled them freely. Each candle-wick sputtered and blazed into light.

"A simple laboratory experiment," explained Dale. "Almost as simple as—the shadows themselves!"

He lifted an object from the table and held it before him.

"This," he said, "is what Professor Rust had found when Annette discovered him."

It was a small pocket flash-light and over its lens had been stuck a tiny paper silhouette of a highwayman holding out a revolver. Pointing the flashlight at the wall opposite, Keene touched the little knob and instantly a circle of light appeared on the wall, and in its center the figure of a highwayman.

"Note how small it is," he said, easily. "It was done so for a reason."

With a sudden, quick movement, he dashed at Mrs. Stone, and before she could struggle free from his clasp, he had released the fastenings of her high-puffed gray hair, and it fell behind her. As it cascaded down, he snatched something that gleamed dully in the center of her hair.

"There is where the apparatus was concealed," he said, triumphantly. "And this will complete our evidence. By innocently touching her hair, as if to rearrange a stray strand, she could press that button, flash on the shadow, and before any one could see where it came, she had turned it off again. The whole thing was hidden in her hair, and to make a new shadow, one had only to cut out the figure in paper, tear off the old one and stick the new one on the face of the lens."

Mrs. Stone smiled at him bitterly.

"Yes," she said, "but it sent chills to the soul of all who saw it."

A silence fell upon them all. Mrs. Stone began mechanically to rearrange her tresses. At last Keene spoke.

"Mrs. Stone," he said, "you are a splendid example of high intellectuality ruined by evil emotions. You, nor your daughter, will ever be punished for what you have done. You will be sent to the asylums."

Again Mrs. Stone smiled her bitter smile.

"We have counted on that," she said, haughtily.

Then Burkehart and his men led mother and daughter away.

Two hours later Jack Eastwood opened his eyes. He was very weak, and he lay very still. Bending over him, her cool hands soothing his brow, her lips close to his cheeks, was a wan-faced but happy girl. He saw her and he smiled. And she smiled back at him, oh, so joyously.

"Jack!" she whispered, "the shadows have gone from our lives forever.

The sunshine will aways be with us now, dear Jack. Oh, it's wonderful! Wonderful!"

And Gordon Keene, who stood in the doorway, and who, by the way, is a confirmed bachelor, thought it was wonderful, too.

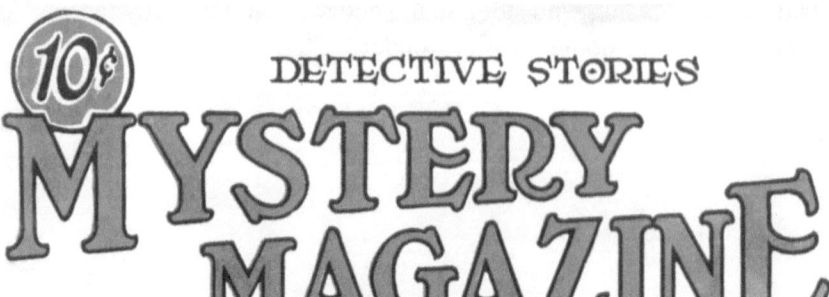

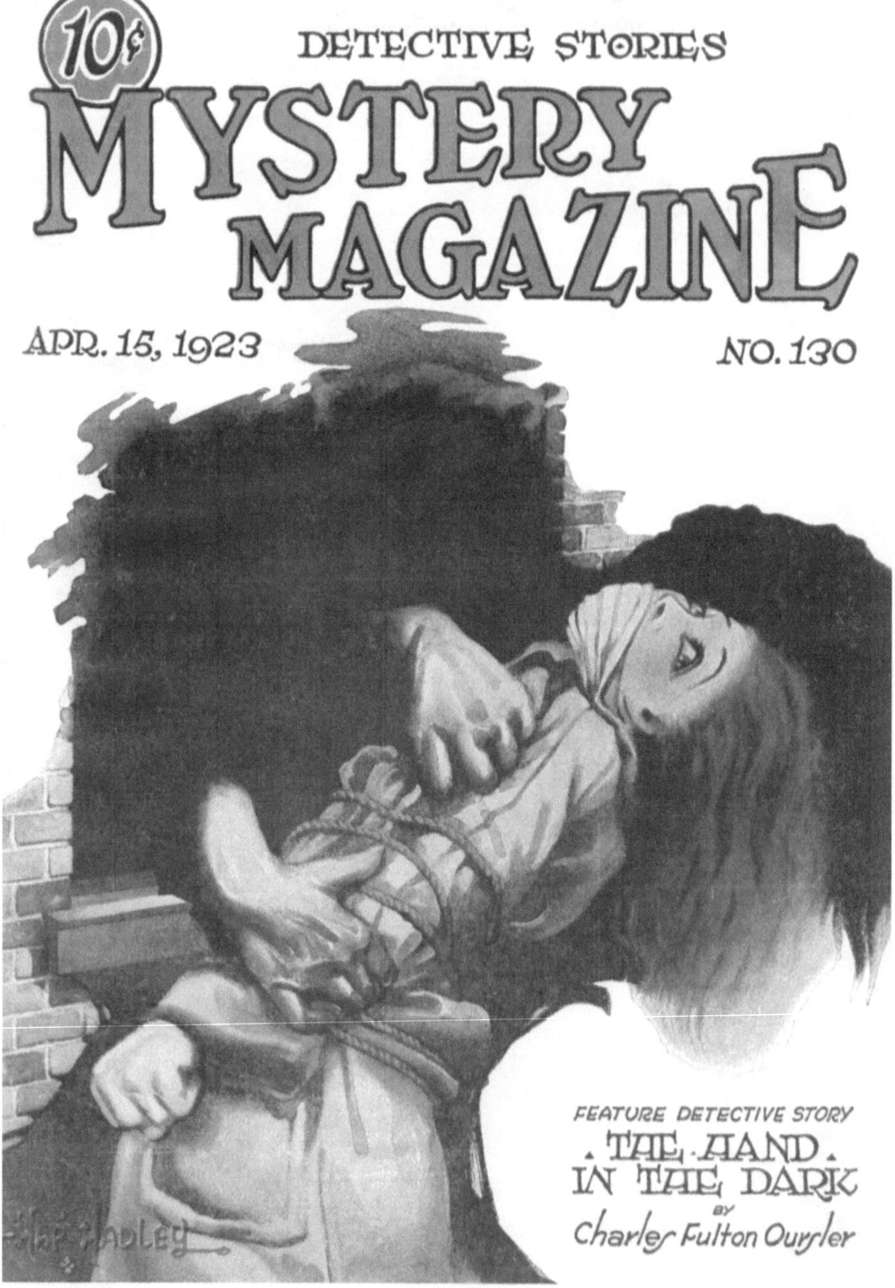
10¢
DETECTIVE STORIES
MYSTERY MAGAZINE
APR. 15, 1923
NO. 130
FEATURE DETECTIVE STORY
. THE HAND .
IN THE DARK
BY
Charles Fulton Oursler
HAP HADLEY

Cover art by Hap Hadley

The Hand in the Dark
by Charles Fulton Oursler

CHAPTER ONE

I HAVE NEVER FOUND OUT HOW MRS. REMSLOW LEARNED MY ADDRESS. She had been in England for years. We had not corresponded. There had been a time when I thought she and I would be married; in fact, with the optimistic folly of a very young man, I actually deluded myself into believing that she was in love with me. A proposal was forming on my lips the very night that she told me she was going to become Remslow's wife.

All of my friends are aware of it, so there is no reason for me to conceal the fact that this disappointment in love made me a most unfriendly man. My little income was sufficient to keep me. I left Anita—I cannot avoid calling her that in my own thoughts—in a daze. Through the ensuing months, and even years, part of that daze persisted. I moved my lodgings from East Sixty-second street to a quiet part of Forest Hills, where I boarded with an old man and his wife. I gave up the opera, the concert, the theatre. The art galleries knew me no more. I spent my time tramping over the Long Island wastes, the seashore and my room, crowded with its books.

Yet one snowy afternoon in early February old Painter, the man with whom I boarded, tapped on my door and informed me that a lady was waiting to see me in the living-room below.

I was completely surprised. Having no friends, not even acquaintances, I could not imagine how it could come to pass that I should have a woman visitor. At first I decided to refuse to meet her. Then my old habit of curiosity, one of my strongest traits, prevailed. I promised to be down in a moment.

The early dusk filled the old house with vague purple shadows as I descended the stairs and entered the living-room. One glance and I recognized her.

"Anita!" I exclaimed. Her name escaped me before I could command myself. The shock was tremendous; my feelings were swirling.

She rose and came toward me, and my amazement turned to a shocked pity. It was not that her beauty had faded. I do not think that would be possible. But it was the defeated evidence of shame on her fine features which struck me. When I had known her first she was nobly beautiful. Now she was like some haunted ghost, furtive and frightened.

She held out her hand with a faint shadow of her old poised grace, then suddenly drew back, covered her face with her hands and began to sob. This naturally unmanned me. Any woman in tears is a destroying spectacle, but the woman one loves, and one so sadly changed, weeping, is a sight to shake the strongest.

"What has happened?" I asked her tenderly as I led her to a chair.

In a little while she was able to speak to me, and then she asked me an astonishing question.

"John Hunter," she said, "have you heard what I have become?"

I shook my head, not trusting myself to speak.

"I am a spirit medium!" she told me.

In utter confusion I stared at her. A spirit medium? I could not understand. Spirit mediums were associated in my mind with police-station stories in the newspapers, with broken-down houses in shabby streets and ignorant women in blowsy attire. How could this cultured and lovely woman be a spirit medium?

"I see that you are shocked," she said. "Certainly it is very shocking to people like us. But it is what I deserved, I guess. I know you, John, for what you are. If you thought I had come here to complain against my husband you would not listen. And yet that is what I have come here to do!"

"Is he dead?" I asked.

"Oh, if he were only dead!" she exclaimed. "I have wished my husband dead a hundred times!"

"Anita!" I exclaimed, aghast. "Anita, you do not mean that!"

A slight noise in the dark shadows at the other side of the room arrested my attention. Old man Painter suddenly loomed up out of the gloom. The inquisitive old gossip had been sitting there listening all the time. But now he seemed to feel that he had better be leaving, and without another word he shuffled out of the room. I heard him mumbling to himself as he passed down the hallway to the back of the house.

"Don't mind him!" I said. "He doesn't know you, and he's half dead, anyway. But—you mustn't talk about your husband like that, you know!"

"I must!" she persisted bitterly. "It is he who has made me what I am to-day. He lied to me. He pretended to be very wealthy. He blinded me and dazzled me with his bland ways and his suave insinuations. Oh, John, if I only had it to do all over again! He took me to England, and there I learned the truth. He was practically penniless. He had married me, deliberately intending to make me do the very thing that I am doing now—be a medium!"

"What do you mean by that?" I asked.

"I am a liar, a cheat, a vile fraud, and I am making dupes of the rich people who come to me, paying me to call back their sacred dead from the graves. I haven't one single ounce of real mediumistic power, if there is such a thing in the world. I am just a fake! But he has taught me a hundred clever tricks; he drilled me in it, he beat me, he starved me, he threatened my very life, until he had me cowed. But even then I would have run away if it had not been for the disgrace at home. My people thought I had made a great match. I could not go home and face them. And so I stuck it out. I made tables rise in the air; made the spirits write messages on clammy slates; I materialized the faces and the forms of the dead, until I feel as if I were living in a cemetery and sleeping in a grave. Oh, the horror of it, and the shame of it, is too deep for words!"

"Aren't you afraid of being arrested?" I found myself asking.

"Remslow can take care of that," she said. "He has paid his graft to the police departments of every large city in the British Islands and on the continent. But he went too far when he brought me back to America. I fought him like a tigress. I swore I would throw myself into the sea. But he knew that I did not have the nerve. He knew he had broken me forever, or he thought he had. And so here I am!"

"And did you think that I could help you?" I inquired, forcing myself to remain detached and aloof, though I longed to take her into my arms and caress her. I found that I loved her now more deeply, more passionately, than I had ever loved her before. But she was Remslow's, and could never be mine.

"You can help me!" she cried. "To-night we are giving our first American séance. Some of the smartest people from Park avenue are going to be there—at the Giltmore. Remslow has been busy all day getting information about the people who are to be there so that he can surprise them at the meeting. There is one little Scotchman with him and a deaf man named Ham, and I am afraid of them all. And, oh, John, I know that something terrible is going to happen!"

"You are hysterical!" I chided. "You are simply upset. What can possibly happen that would be so terrible?"

"Read this!" she gasped, fumbling in her hand-bag. "I found it on my bureau this morning!"

She passed me a folded note of paper, which I opened and read:

You have prayed very long to be released from your husband.
To-night you shall have your wish. In the dark séance he will perish.
You will kill him. You think you will not, but you will. You can't help

attacking him, because you will be the instrument of a will stronger than your own. When the lights are out and the spirits of the unseen dead hover with silent wings around you, Remslow will die by your hand. I swear it by your strong, brave lover lad.

I crumpled the note contemptuously in my hand.

"This should not alarm you," I protested. "It's the work of some silly crank who wants to annoy you!"

"No! No! No!" she cried excitedly. "It is much more than that. There is something deadly, something sinister, something too strong for me to resist behind it, John. I have proof of that!"

"What proof?" I demanded almost roughly.

"John," she said, speaking with manifest effort, "perhaps it sounds shameless, but I've known all along that you loved me. I knew it that night when we parted; I told you abruptly of my engagement, because I could tell you were about to speak. But what you have never known, John, was, except for a few months of mad infatuation with Remslow, I've loved you with all my heart and all my soul. Your image has been constantly in my thoughts. I've made you a god! And always I have thought of you as my strong, brave lover lad. That dear phrase has sung through my mind like a sweet song of old remembrance. But my lips have never spoken those words. No one has ever heard them in all the world except you! And yet that phrase is written in this note. That is what terrifies me, that is what makes me believe it is true, that is why I have come here, John—because I need you!"

"What can I do?" I cried, fighting manfully against the impulse to snatch her madly in my arms.

"I want you to come to that séance tonight. Oh, I know that you've made yourself a recluse, denied yourself to your friends. I know it may seem strange for you to come out as soon as I am back in New York. But we've got to overlook those little things. I've got to know that you are in that room when the lights go out. If you are there I shall not be afraid. Won't you come?"

I took her hand and kissed it.

"I shall come!" I promised.

CHAPTER TWO

THE SÉANCE OF MADAME LASCAIRE, as Anita was known professionally, was held in one of the gilded little meeting rooms on the tenth floor of the hotel. Chairs had been placed in rows, perhaps a hundred in all, and before the meeting began they were all filled. The walls were concealed by hanging velvet draperies.

The curious part of it was that I had never before seen Remslow.

When I went to the Hotel Giltmore that evening, I did not know whether he was fat or thin, hairy or bald, red-faced or sallow, ugly or handsome.

Yet I knew him the moment my eyes fell upon him.

I arrived early. There were only two or three guests seated when I came to the door of the private meeting hall where the séance was to be presented. At the door a thin, mouse-like man, with his left hand continually held to his ear, accosted me with a whispered request for my ticket of invitation. About this there was no difficulty; Anita had been foresighted enough to bring one to me, and so I passed in without difficulty. As I entered the well-lighted apartment I saw a man sitting rigid in a chair, facing the rest of the seats, and I knew without asking that he was Remslow.

He was a large man, with a squarish head, crowned with thick tufts of gray hair. His forehead was massive and forbidding, jutting out like a boulder over the deep caverns of his little eyes. The huge shoulders, the thick, powerful arms, the mighty expanse of chest, together with the short legs crossed in front of him, gave him something of the appearance of a human gorilla. I raged inwardly at the very sight of the fellow. To think this was the brute who had tyrannized over Anita!

I sat down quietly and waited. Gradually the seats began to fill up; the hall became crowded with women, perfumed and in exquisite evening gowns, with well-groomed men smiling attentively at their airy whispers. There was a general atmosphere of nervous anticipation. These wealthy, bored society people had come, hoping to be shocked, eager for a sensation.

And all the while Remslow sat there, staring into space like a Hindu mahatma in evening clothing—a white Yogi from the Himalayas, communing with the infinite.

It was well on toward nine o'clock, and Remslow had not changed his position, except once I heard him utter a deep and profound sigh. This pose produced on me a most disagreeable sensation. True, he was acting his part well. There was something terrible in his rigid attitude, as if he were in a trance. But I knew he was a charlatan and a brute, and I wanted to thrash him before them all, without waiting for the séance.

Presently Anita appeared, conducted through the doorway at the rear by the man with the hand at his ear. From a chattering couple next to me I gathered that this man, Harris by name, was the personal secretary of Remslow and always opened the meetings. I surmised that he did more than that. My personal opinion was that he secured information about the private lives of the customers, and gave it to Remslow, who delivered it dramatically at the proper moment.

But this was only a passing fancy. My eyes were now all for Anita. She was wearing an exquisite gown of black-spangled satin, cut low at the neck, an attire which accentuated her unnatural pallor and the frightened luster of her eyes. She did not glance at me, though I was sitting conspicuously on the end of the second row, within easy reach of the silent Remslow, if by any foul chance I should be needed.

There was a vacant chair beside Remslow, and it was to this that Harris led Anita. She did not glance at her husband, but sat down quietly, relapsing instantly into a pose almost identical with his. Plainly she, too, was acting the part of one entranced. I shuddered with revulsion at the sight; a fierce determination seized me. By one means or another I meant to part those two who sat so oddly before me. Anita should endure his tyranny no longer. This should be her final séance. I did not know what I was going to do, but I meant surely to do something.

Mr. Harris, his hand still cupped behind his ear, took a position just beside Mr. and Mrs. Remslow, and in a tone that reached barely above the proportions of a whisper, he said:

"Ladies and gentlemen, I have only a word of introduction to say for those who are not familiar with the ordinary manifestations of psychic phenomena. Both madame and monsieur are powerful mediums—batteries of psychic force. But madame is the most expressive; monsieur is a stronger reservoir of force. Together they sit before you. Madame, using her own powers and drawing upon those of her husband, will give out messages to you. We ask no questions, but we shall be glad to answer any that you may ask. That is really all. Are you ready, madame?" and then just at that moment Anita looked at me. Perhaps the light of disapproval was too clear in my eyes. She seemed all of a sudden rebuked and ashamed. For a moment she could not speak. Then she rose, her face glowing with resolve.

"No!" she said. "I will not go on with it. I will not! Let him say or do whatever he pleases. I refuse!"

The startled audience heard her in absolute silence for the fraction of a minute. Then, without warning, the lights in the séance room went suddenly out. We were plunged into a darkness.

A confused and startled murmur came from the crowd, which was not checked until several minutes later by the returning illumination. The lights came on again, but before that a terrible suspicion had flashed through my mind. I remembered the warning words in the note which Anita had received: "When the lights are out and the spirits of the unseen dead hover with silent wings around you, Remslow will die by your hand!"

I could not refrain from leaping from my seat and rushing toward him, when the lights came on. But halfway there I halted in dismay.

Remslow was moving; his body was slouching forward soggily, and even as I watched it pitched down drunkenly and fell in a sprawling hump at my feet.

One glance told me all that I then needed to know.

Remslow was dead; he had died in the dark; the dread threat had been fulfilled.

But by whose hand?

CHAPTER THREE

THERE WAS NO QUESTION THAT REMSLOW WAS MURDERED.

A dagger had been thrust straight through his left side into his heart.

The moment that we turned him over on his back, bared his agonized face, and saw how he was slain, the terrible significance of this struck me like a blow.

The weapon had been plunged in Remslow's heart from the left side. Anita had been sitting at his left. No one else was near to him. Harris had been on the other side; the nearest sitter in the audience was too far away to be seriously suspected.

My mind, racing like lightning, summed up the circumstances like a column of figures, and the total frightened me. As the crowd made way for one bearded man who kept muttering that he was a physician and please let him through, I glanced at Anita. Her eyes were looking into mine, and there was in them a kind of dull and hopeless woe. No triumph was there, but only a great fear.

I knew in that instant that she was utterly and completely innocent. And I knew that she would soon need a friend. The look in my eyes must have been a tender promise that I would be that friend, for her eyes kindled with gratitude and with thanks.

On that instant I determined that come what may, be the circumstantial evidence what it might, Anita should never be sorry that she appealed to me in the hour of her trial.

Naturally there was a great deal of shocked confusion after the first reaction of numbing fright. Women began to get hysterical, and their escorts began to hurry them toward the door. But here they found their progress barred.

The hotel detective had been in the room all the time and was now ready to take charge. He was a tall man, with a black mustache and beady eyes— the typical hired sleuth, I thought, with enormous feet and tiny brains.

"Nobody's going to leave this room!" he shouted. "A murder has been committed in this here place, and nobody's going to leave this room. I don't care who it is who wants to get out. Charlie Murphy couldn't get out of here this minute, not if Tammany Hall was on fire. The police have been notified, and you'll all stay here until the police come. There ain't nobody going to leave this room!"

He stood squarely in the doorway, and nobody thereafter suggested leaving the room. Instead the crowd divided into small and chattering groups, talking in low tones, while the doctor and some volunteers covered the body of Remslow with an overcoat, until such time as the authorities would give permission to move it.

And all the while Anita sat still in her chair, cowering back, pale, a little disheveled, with eyes glittering and lips trembling. I attempted to approach her, but by an almost imperceptible gesture she bade me not to.

And, too, all the while Harris stood, pale and glowering, where all along he had stood with his left hand cupped to his ear.

The situation was getting so strained that I think every one was relieved by the entrance of three bluecoats, led by Inspector Gale in plain clothes. But the thing that happened after that was a startling surprise.

Inspector Gale gave only a contemptuous glance at the dead body, from which the overcoat was rapidly lifted as he approached. His eyes were fixed accusingly on Anita, and he strode up to her with a menace in every motion of his body.

"So!" he exclaimed. "Your husband has been murdered, eh?"

Anita only looked back at him, like a wounded and frightened fawn.

"I guess you would like us to think it's a mystery," snarled the inspector, edging his rough tone with sarcasm. "They tell me our friend Remslow was struck down by a hand in the dark. No one can fathom the mystery, eh? Well, think hard, woman. Think hard! Know who did it, do you?"

He caught her roughly by the wrist. This was more than I could endure. I sprang forward, saying:

"Look here! You have no right to talk to this lady like this!"

"You go to thunder!" said Gale. "I know what I am doing. You just wait. Your turn is coming. I guess maybe you had a hand in this little deal, all right!"

"What do you mean?" I demanded.

"You had a motive, all right," he shot back. "You love this woman and she loves you. And she said this man beat her. And she said she wished him dead a hundred times. Well? Didn't she?"

CHAPTER FOUR

THE NEXT FEW HOURS REMAIN IN MY MIND as perhaps the most terrible in my life; not so much because of the unjust suspicions with which Inspector Gale plainly regarded me personally, but because of the way he treated Anita.

Gale was the kind of officer who gets his evidence by bullying witnesses, suspecting everybody, and ploughing along roughly until some one comes across with a confession. This was the plan of campaign which he proceeded now to put into immediate operation.

There is no denying that he knew how to organize the inquiry on the spot. One of his men was dispatched to telephone for additional assistance from headquarters and for the coroner. Others began taking the names and addresses of every one present, and then sending them, one by one, under guard into another room which the hotel manager had instantly placed at his disposal. I noticed, with some uneasiness, that he paid no attention either to Anita or myself during this procedure; he did not look at either of us, in fact, until we two were left alone with him and the dead body of Remslow.

Then Inspector Gale folded his arms in front of him and glared malignantly.

"How did you two ever expect to get away with a raw thing like this?" he demanded.

"Speaking both for Mrs. Remslow and myself," I replied, "I can say that we resent your implied accusation. If you think either of us are involved in this terrible crime, you are on the wrong track! We may as well come to an understanding about that without any more delay!"

"We will!" he replied heavily. He continued to stare at us, while he fumbled until he had found a cigar, which he lighted.

"We will!" he repeated. "And the way we will come to an understanding is for me to let you know some of the things I have already found out. As, for instance, that you two are old sweethearts. Didn't think police headquarters would ever know that, did you? Or that Remslow, here, treated his wife worse than he should, I guess. Didn't think a detective would ever find that out—huh? Or that Mrs. Remslow had said, not ten hours ago, that she would be happy if he was dead—what? Or that she came to see you out in Forest Hills this afternoon—what? Well, why don't you deny those accusations? I thought you wanted to come to an understanding about this matter. Why don't you?"

"Some of the statements you are making are true," I admitted, far more shaken than I cared to let him know. "But I do not see that they have any particular bearing on this case."

"Oh, you don't!" mewled Inspector Gale sarcastically. "Well, I do, and I think the grand jury will agree with me. If they don't bring in a double indictment of conspiracy and murder in the first degree, I'll go into the insurance business. Why, it's as plain as the nose on your face. One or two little details need clearing up, and that won't take long. But why not confess and have it over with? The jury will be inclined to be more lenient if you come out with it!"

"I think you ought to go into the insurance business," I said suddenly, "or anything else except the detective business!"

"What!" he ejaculated angrily.

It had occurred to me while he was talking that Inspector Gale was showing himself a very poor investigator. I was a layman. I knew nothing of detective work, except those stories of imaginative fiction in which a romantic, almost super-brained detective solves a mystery that seems too baffling for any one to unravel. But Gale's methods seemed to me to be very irregular. I suspected where he had got the information which made him accuse us. Old man Painter, with whom I boarded, had overheard a part of my interview that afternoon with Anita. Painter had a son who was on the police force. He and I never liked each other especially. No sense of personal loyalty to me would have made him keep quiet about what he had heard. Probably he had told his son at dinner all the conversation he had overheard, and the son had likely informed some one at headquarters.

It made the situation distinctly unfortunate, of course, but why should Gale stop there? Why should he be focusing his energies on making two people confess, when he might be making an examination which would start suspicion in an entirety different direction?

The real murderer might be getting farther away with every wasted moment!

"I mean," I told him, "that you are basing a case on very flimsy evidence. You have nothing tangible with which to convict us. I tell you we are both innocent. Whether you believe us or not, your professional experiences ought to tell you not to hold up your work until our guilt is definitely established. Have you looked at the dagger with which Remslow was killed? Have you given the body anything more than a most cursory examination? Have you questioned any one else except ourselves? You have not, and that's why I believe you would make a damn fine insurance agent!"

"You 'tend to your business and I'll 'tend to mine," he retorted after a moment. "But since you make the suggestion, I will take a look at that dagger!"

He drew back the overcoat from the still form of Remslow and bent down to examine the wound.

But, after a moment of muttered confusion, he leaped erect and stared at us wildly.

"The dagger is gone!" he gasped.

CHAPTER FIVE

"GONE!" BOTH ANITA AND I EXCLAIMED. Such a thing seemed incredible. No one, except the physician, had been near the body since the lights flashed on. Who could have taken it?

"Are you sure there ever was a dagger?" I asked Inspector Gale.

He looked at me in a kind of defiant exasperation.

"What are you talking about?" he rasped. "Of course there was a dagger. Didn't you see it?"

"No!" I answered truthfully. "Did you see it, Anita!"

She shook her beautiful head quite dolefully.

"No," she said. "I just couldn't bear to look after that first horrible glance, and then I saw only his face—and the blood!"

"But there must have been a dagger!" fumed Inspector Gale.

"Of course!" I concurred, but inwardly I was not so sure. An idea was stirring around in my brain, which was getting me excited. I knew that Anita's life and my own were actually in jeopardy. Circumstantial evidence was already woven around us, and if Gale could find another coincidence which might tend to add to the case against us, it might go hard. I was determined to do what I could to save Anita. But I did not intend to take Gale into my confidence. I had no confidence in him, in a mysterious affair such as the Remslow murder. I began to believe I might play quietly at the role of detective and save Anita before it was too late.

What I swore to myself to do, if it were humanly possible, was to clear up the mystery before any of us left the hotel. I did not want a single whisper of suspicion to be published against the woman I loved.

Therefore I allowed Inspector Gale to bend down to the corpse again and renew his examination of the wound. I felt sure that he would not see the significance of that which I had already seen regarding the vanished weapon.

Moreover, he did not know, and apparently no one had thought to tell him, that the lights had gone out just at the predicted and psychological moment. Whatever old man Painter may have traitorously divulged about the talk Anita and I had had, he did not know, and had no means of knowing, of the note which she had shown me.

That note contained a definite prophecy, and the prophecy was fulfilled. No spirits had written the message. It came from human hands, and those hands were now stained with blood. I was utterly sure that the writer of that warning message was also the murderer of Remslow.

In my hands then there were clues of which Inspector Gale had no knowledge. Perhaps it would have been wiser, even more honest, if I had come out with them then and made a clean breast of them. But that I could not bring myself to do. I did believe he was acute enough to see their importance or even to accept them as genuine. To tell him about them would only block any of my own efforts. I decided to remain silent.

"There is nothing here," muttered Inspector Gale, rising, a picture of disgust. "I am going to have the two of you searched, and if you have that knife on your persons it won't take long to find it. Well?"

"We haven't got any knife," I assured him impatiently.

"Maybe!" he said. "Meanwhile I'll take a look around this room!"

He threw back the overcoat on the body and then stood off to measure the room with his eyes.

"I'll start here! I guess if that knife is around here, it won't take me long to find it," he muttered, and walked toward the opposite end of the room. As he passed us I looked at Anita with my eyebrows uplifted contemptuously. I thought Gale the most unbusinesslike or the most unprofessional and apparently incompetent bungler of an officer I had ever met.

She seemed about to speak to me, when suddenly a light came into her eyes which frightened me. It seemed as if some impending disaster had suddenly become clear to her. As I opened my mouth to ask her what was the trouble every light in the room suddenly went dark.

"Turn on them lights! Who did that?" yelled Inspector Gale.

He shouted out blasphemous curses, until after a while the lights again came on, mildly and quietly, disclosing a new and horrible state of affairs.

The body of Remslow had been lifted from the floor and was put again in the chair where he was murdered.

Anita had utterly and completely disappeared.

CHAPTER SIX

"WHAT ARE YOU TRYING TO PULL OFF HERE?" shouted Inspector Gale, rushing over to me with balled fists.

If the situation had not been tragic, I should have laughed at him. His face held such a mixture of fight and fear. The Remslow murder was already on his nerves. Things were happening which he could not explain. And he was taking the first opportunity to strike back at this mysterious unknown something by accusing me.

"Don't be an ass!" I exclaimed. "Something terrible must have happened. Where is Mrs. Remslow?"

He glanced wildly about.

"My God!" he gasped. "She's *gone!*"

"Yes, and she's probably in danger!" I cried bitterly. "While you are loafing around this room trying to fasten the crime on her, the guilty man or woman is playing a game without any hindrance or interference. Have you never thought about searching behind there?"

I pointed to the walls. For the first time, I believe, since he had come into the room Inspector Gale observed the singularity of the draped curtains. Ostensibly these hangings of gray velvet had been hung in front of the walls and their windows for the better preservation of "psychic influence." They completely hid the walls, and now, as Inspector Gale followed my pointing finger and rushed over to look at them, he saw that they were suspended from rods jutting out a full ten inches from the walls, leaving that much of a little curtained corridor between the walls and the curtains.

"Somebody might be hiding back there!" he exclaimed, and put his hand on a fold of velvet, where there was a part in the draperies.

"You stay there!" he ordered, and then a glint of suspicion came into his hard blue eyes.

"How do I know this isn't some new kind of trick?" he muttered. "Healy, come here!"

These last words he uttered in a shout, and immediately the door at the other end of the room opened and a policeman in uniform, a short, thick-set Irishman, stepped in, closing the door behind him.

"Guard that man, Healy," ordered Gale, pointing to me. "There's some rotten business going on here. Don't let him make a move. I want to see what I can find behind these curtains!"

"Yis, sor," answered Healy dutifully. "I'll blow daylight through him if he makes any cracks!"

"You do just that," concluded Gale, and passed through behind the curtains. "It's dark as night in here," he called, his voice muffled by the velvet hangings. "I suppose there is a switch in here, and that's how they turned the lights on and off so nice. Good God!"

"Need any help, chief?" called Healy as he heard this last exclamation.

"No! But I've found something, all right. I think I see the whole game now. You hold on to that man there; don't let him stir!"

Healy clutched my arm and stuck out his jaw, his eyes glowering at me savagely. Healy was a man who liked to obey orders. I had the fancy that he almost wished I would try to escape. But I was too much keyed up, wondering what had happened to Anita, what Gale had found, and what could be the solution of the mystery, to think of giving battle to a policeman who, after all, was doing nothing more than his duty. We could hear Gale stamping about behind the curtains and see the bulge of his figure as once or twice he backed against the draperies.

Perhaps five minutes had passed. For the last two minutes at least we had heard nothing from Gale. The silence and the figure of the dead man, which had been moved so mysteriously back into the chair, began to make an impression on even the stolid Healy.

"Say, chief," he called finally, "is there anything I can do for you?"

There was no reply.

"Chief," bellowed Healy, "is there anything gone wrong?"

Only silence answered him.

The policeman gave me a push away from him and covered me with an automatic.

"I don't know what is happening in this place," he said, "but I'm of a mind to find out, d'ye hear? Walk over there and pull down them curtains. Pull them all down, and if you make a break I'm goin' to shoot to kill. Get busy!"

He had no need to threaten. I was as eager as he to pull down those shroud-like draperies and see if anything lurked behind them. Was some new and appalling disaster confronting us? I sprang forward quickly and, seizing one of the soft folds of velvet in my hand, tore them to the floor.

Nothing but a wall covered with a mirror was revealed.

Around the room I ran, yanking down those priceless curtains with impatient hands. But they disclosed nothing. Inspector Gale had gone the way of Anita; he had disappeared, totally and completely, and the only clue was an open window that looked out upon a sheer drop of a hundred feet to the sidewalk below!

CHAPTER SEVEN

HEALY WAS CROSSING HIMSELF AND MUTTERING AN AVE MARIA.

I clapped him suddenly on the shoulder.

"Healy," I said, speaking briskly and clearly, "you are dealing with something here that is outside your line. That dead man in the chair there was a spirit medium!"

"God help us!" gasped Healy.

"His widow, Mrs. Remslow, disappeared from this room not five minutes ago. She just vanished like a shadow. It was to find her that Inspector Gale ventured behind those curtains. You see what happened. He too vanished. What do you make of it, Healy?"

"God help us!" he repeated vaguely.

"Well, what are you going to do?"

"I'll have to—let them know outside," he murmured vacantly.

"And disgrace the inspector?" I asked sharply.

"How's that, sor?"

"Why, don't you see? Inspector Gale, I am sure, is still alive. But some one behind those curtains overpowered him, and now he's a prisoner—somewhere. He'd like it better if we found him and rescued him, without making him ridiculous!"

It was a very weak argument. I do not think it would have worked on any one else. But on Healy it did make the impression I was working for. I knew that if Healy summoned the others from the outer room I would be arrested, and no more opportunity would be given me to try to rescue Anita and solve the mystery. This double problem, first of rescuing the woman I loved and then clearing her name, and indeed my own, was of such monumental consequence that I think I would have strangled Healy into unconsciousness before I would have allowed him to call his fellows and thus make me powerless.

But fortunately my ruse worked.

"He told me to watch you at all costs," he reflected aloud and dubiously. "And yet the inspector is an awful proud man!"

"You can watch me," I argued. "But I believe I am the only man that can solve this whole thing now. Listen to me!"

As rapidly as I could I explained the situation to Healy as I saw it. The whole situation was so peculiar, so out of Healy's daily experiences, that I am not sure to this day how much of it he understood. Yet to me the solution had been near at hand, almost from the moment that Remslow had been found dead. I was certain that the guilty man or woman was in hiding behind the curtains. This gave him easy control of the electric switch and complete temporary concealment.

"Do you know what those curtains were really put up there for?" I asked.

Healy shook his head. He hadn't the faintest idea.

"When these poor dupes came in here to attend this séance," I explained, "they had to check their overcoats and other wraps in the little cloakroom on the next floor. That was done for a purpose. After they were all seated in here a confederate of Remslow—probably the little Scotchman in his party of whom I have heard, a very small and stealthy man—went through all those overcoats, hats and wraps, getting initials and chance mail left in the pockets and so forth and making memoranda for the use of Remslow. Now, he had some way of getting into this room without being seen. With all that information written down, he sneaked in here behind those curtains, and in the dark he slipped out and passed the memoranda to Remslow. By some trickery of his own Remslow managed to read the memoranda without being noticed, and thus he was able to astonish a great number of people who couldn't imagine how he got all that private information about them. Before I came here to-night I read up in a book exposing spiritism. Do you see?"

Healy nodded his head doubtfully. He was like a man slowly recovering from a profound drunk. I was speaking as rapidly as I dared, because every minute was precious, and yet I had to make my theories clear to this man. Without his cooperation I could do nothing.

"Now," I concluded, "the question is, how did the confederate get into this room without being observed? When we find that we'll find out where he took Anita and where he took the inspector. How could he get in and out without being seen?"

At first it seemed like an unfathomable puzzle. The walls were obviously solid. There was only one door. It was out of the question for Remslow to have prepared trapdoors and secret panels in a rented hotel room.

"There it is!" I suddenly exclaimed, and pointed at the open window.

"How? It can't be!" gasped Healy.

"Come over here!" I cried. "I'll show you!"

CHAPTER EIGHT

I HAD REALLY NOTHING AT ALL TO SHOW HEALY except an open window, which he had already seen for himself. But to me that open window was conclusive. Gale had been near it when we last had heard from him. Moreover, Anita's situation, just before she had disappeared, was within easy access to it.

When we looked out of the window, however, we found only air between us and the pavement of the courtyard!

How, then, had the window been used?

The question was torturing my mind as Healy turned to me, a sneer curling his thick lips. He was about to place me under arrest and call for help, when a slight noise below reached us both. Simultaneously we leaned far out of the window. We were just in time to see a head darting back into the open window immediately below us.

"Did you see that?" I cried excitedly.

"I saw a head!" said Healy without enthusiasm.

"Well, man, that's the point. I believe that Gale and Mrs. Remslow are prisoners in the room below us!"

"And what d'ye believe that for? Ain't the man what's rented the window below us got a right to poke his head out his window if he feels like it?"

"Healy," I said solemnly, "the man whose head we saw is one of the assistants of the dead man there!"

"Aw, can that stuff!" blustered Healy, more than ever determined, I could see, to end his parley with me. "It's dark, and you couldn't see his face, anyhow. How could you tell?"

"The man had his left hand cupped around his ear," I said solemnly.

Healy looked at me in surprise.

"Well, and suppose he did, and what of it?"

"That's a habit with the man I suspect. He's partly deaf, and he keeps his hand to his ear almost all the time," I told him. "He was listening, because we were talking at that open window. Now he's probably taken the alarm. Come on downstairs with me!"

My excitement had subtly communicated itself to the stolid policeman. His eyes took fire from mine.

"It will mean a promotion if you are there at the finish. And you can take the credit for solving the mystery," I promised him.

"I'll fix it," he decided, and without another word strode across the room, opened the door and passed through, closing it and locking me in. I was left alone with the dead body of Remslow, the medium.

But I did not tarry long.

In one bound I darted across the room and seized a coil of rope lying on the table. It was a length of window cording placed there to be used in tying Anita during some of the spirit tests in the séance.

My long outdoor life along the Long Island shores had put me in first-class physical condition, so that I had no fear of the undertaking which had formed itself in my mind. It was an easy task to secure one end of the rope around a steam pipe near the radiator at one end of the room.

I thrust the other end of the rope out of the window and let it fall.

Then I clambered out of the window and let myself down.

CHAPTER NINE

I WAS JUST IN TIME.

The one thing I had feared and dreaded was almost accomplished while I was in mid-air, dangling between the street and the star-flecked sky.

The gaunt figure of Harris, the man who kept his hand at his ear, appeared at the window again. But this time his hand was not at his ear. His arms were clasped around the limp figure of Anita, corded and bound and tied to a rope.

He was about to lower her out of the window!

As I came swirling down the dangling rope my feet touched the windowsill just as he held out her form from the gloom in his arms. I took him completely by surprise, and before he knew what to expect I kicked him in the face.

He sprawled backward in a heap, and the next instant I had leaped into the room. An extraordinary sight greeted me.

On the bed lay the corded, fettered figure of Inspector Gale. His mouth was stuffed with a gag, but his eyes were rolling furiously, as if entreating me to release him.

Leaving Anita helpless on the floor, Harris leaped to his feet and flung himself upon me with the fury of a madman. Never have I encountered such supernatural strength in any human being. It was as if seven devils of violence were in the man's body, flailing his arms, pounding his fists, and lending a dreadful force and power to every muscle of his lean, strong body.

A thumping and beating at the door came to my ears as I struggled with all my will and might against the furious onslaught of my assailant.

Then a click sounded at the door. Healy had used a skeleton key. He came at the right moment, not a second too soon, and rushing up behind Harris, clipped him neatly on the back of the head with the butt of his automatic.

He fell silent and still, and he remained silent and still long enough for me to release Anita and for Healy to untie and ungag his fallen chief.

Then, under Gale's merciless direction, we trussed up Harris, not leaving even an arm free to cup his hand around his ear.

CHAPTER TEN

THE MOST SENSATIONAL LIES AND EXAGGERATIONS appeared in the newspaper account of the affair, but the true facts, thanks to the grateful cooperation of Inspector Gale, never reached the public.

Gale did have the manliness not only to apologize but to admit that I had solved the mystery and captured the murderer. For of course Harris was the murderer.

When I first accused him of being the murderer Gale looked at me blankly and said:

"That is impossible. He was standing to the right of Remslow, and Remslow was killed from the left. And besides, where was the dagger?"

"The method of his killing was very simple," I replied. "The little Scotchman, whom I have never seen until a few minutes ago"—this conversation took place some hours later, after the excitement had died down—"was an innocent tool. He told me how Harris had hidden him behind the curtains, with instructions to turn off the lights when he gave the signal. Then, with his cat-like tread, Harris slipped around, killed Remslow with one thrust, and returned to his former position before the lights went out!"

"And the weapon?" demanded Gale.

"He hurled it through the air, and it stuck in the velvet curtains, where no one noticed it until I pulled the curtains down," I smiled. "But that was a piece of information I kept to myself until the proper time. You will find it right where I left it!"

"Well, I said if I was wrong I'd go into the insurance business, and it looks like I ought to do something like that," confessed Gale good-naturedly enough. "But what I can't understand is the motive for this crime!"

It was not until Anita was quiet enough to talk that we were able to solve this final tangle in the problem. The true motive was hate—the hate of a madman. There was no doubt that Harris was a lunatic. That was proved to the satisfaction of the district attorney at the trial, and Harris was committed to an insane asylum without further trial. He hated Remslow because he madly believed himself to be a real medium, and resented Remslow using him as a tool and never letting him have an opportunity to exercise what he considered his genuine gifts. How he had learned the secret way in which Anita used to think of me—her "lover lad" which he had used in his note of warning—was never entirely cleared up, although Anita believed that he had heard her crying to herself, and perhaps in her frequent moments of hysterical grief at Remslow's treatment she had uttered the phrase aloud. He was cunning enough to catch its true meaning.

Because she had once spurned his advances he hated her as well and planned to cast the crime on her. When all the other witnesses were being taken out of the room he managed to slip unobserved behind the curtains. From there it was easy for him to turn off the lights, grab Anita and choke her into unconsciousness and drag her behind the curtains. A rope-ladder was already at the open window, having been placed there under Remslow's direction. It was used for his confederate to come upstairs with the information gathered by going through the wraps of the guests at the séance. He carried her down the ladder, and was returning when he discovered Inspector Gale at the window.

With his maniacal strength he overpowered Gale, knocked him unconscious, and carried him down as well. His madness by this time had reached such a pitch that reason and caution had almost deserted him. But he did tear down the rope-ladder, and thus it was missing when Healy and I came to the window.

Why he did such a singular thing as to replace the corpse of Remslow in the chair he refused to explain.

But his intentions were plain enough. He was going to complete his murderous plans by throwing Anita out of the window. Then he meant to escape. And as none of the police knew that Remslow had rented the room beneath the séance hall, he might easily have got away. Gale was sincere when he said that I got there just in time.

Anita and I were standing together in Gale's private office late that night when Inspector Gale was saying good-night.

"I understand," he said thoughtfully. "I know how much you two love each other. You are going to be happy, after all. I suppose it is indelicate for me even to refer to it, but I wish you well. And I'm sorry I was such a brute!"

He shook hands warmly.

"By the way," he said to me, "what business are *you* in?"

"I have a little income," I explained, "but it is all invested in the same line, so I can truthfully say that if I am in anything at all it's the insurance business!"

He grinned at us as we went out into the night—and into the future that was ours!

10¢

DETECTIVE STORIES

MYSTERY MAGAZINE

FEB. 15, 1924

NO. 150

DOUBLE FEATURE

"THE FOOTPRINTS ON THE CEILING"

by

CHARLES FULTON OURSLER

and

"BY THE BREADTH OF A HAIR"

(Two Part Story)

by

ARTHUR B. REEVE

and

MARGARET W. REEVE

Cover art by Hap Hadley

The FOOTPRINTS on the CEILING.
by Charles Fulton Oursler

CHAPTER ONE

THE HOUR WAS MIDNIGHT.

Outside the library windows of the home of Eric Garth, private consulting detective, a November storm of wind and cold rain moaned and howled.

The logs on the hearth sputtered and crackled cozily, spitting red sparks upward with each angry gust of the storm.

Eric Garth put down his fountain pen with a sigh of relief. He shoved aside the papers littering his desk, glad that the notes on a case just completed were at last set down, ready for the typist in the morning.

"Now," he reflected, "I shall smoke a pipe and then go to bed."

Perhaps there was a pang of regret in his mind—a tinge of loneliness. Sometimes Garth believed himself the loneliest of men, although he kept the opinion carefully to himself. He was an orphan and a bachelor. At the age of thirty-five he found himself the most successful private detective in America, with many warm friends. His life held for him the applause of the world, the consciousness of great success and all the money a man could decently spend. But there was one thing lacking.

He would never admit, even to himself, what it was. There was a lack—something that he missed, a loneliness nothing could fill, but beyond that his stubborn mind refused to go.

Now, as he lighted his pipe and sank back gratefully in the big armchair by the fireplace, this loneliness stole upon him even more poignantly than he had ever known it before. The knock that came softly to his door a moment afterward was unexpected, but it was welcome because it drove away his lonely thoughts.

"Come in!" he called.

The door opened softly and a small, yellow man in a blue dressing-robe stood before him. He was Kaji, the personal attendant of the detective. Kaji was a Japanese.

"Yes, Kaji? I thought you were asleep."

"Kaji never sleeps when the great master is awake," replied the Jap, his face impassive. "There is a visitor below."

"A visitor! At this hour?"

"She is an old woman. She came in an automobile. There is a chauffeur at the wheel of the car and another person, I know not what kind of individual, seated in the sedan. But the old woman is in the reception-room. She is crying."

"An old woman crying in the reception-room?"

"Yes, great master."

"Suppose you bring her in here, Kaji."

A few moments later there came through the door a little old woman, not more than five feet high, bent and wrinkled, but with an air of indomitable respectability about her. There were undeniable tears on her withered cheeks, and her black-gloved hands twined together excitedly as she curtsied to the detective.

Eric Garth studied her keenly. Her little gray suit was of modish cut, her hat fitted snugly down over her gray hair and her nose was neatly powdered. Under other circumstances her blue eyes might have had an extremely knowing and modern twinkle.

"Won't you sit down?" asked Eric Garth, offering her a chair.

The old lady sat down with a gasp and immediately plunged into the business of her call.

"You are Eric Garth, are you not? I am Mrs. Amy Andrews. I am the companion of Miss Louise Greenwood, of 14000 West End Avenue, and oh, dear Mr. Garth, do help me, or I don't know what will happen to us!"

Her eyes were distended with anxiety and her voice shook so as to make her words almost inaudible. Garth said in his most soothing tones:

"Now just sit still a while, and then tell me all about it. Kaji shall bring you some water."

After she had sipped the water and smoothed her hair she gave Garth a grateful look and launched into her story. She had lived in the household of Amos Greenwood since the birth of his daughter Louise, in the capacity of nurse and governess to the child. A close attachment had sprung up between the little girl and her nurse, and Mrs. Andrews developed into more of a companion than a governess. Louise was now an orphan, both parents having died several years before, and was under the care of her uncle, Benson Drummond, while Mrs. Andrews remained to look after her charge.

Mrs. Andrews then dramatically announced that she was convinced the apartment they were living in was haunted.

"But, my dear Mrs. Andrews, how can an apartment be haunted? I'm afraid your nerves are a little upset," said Garth, patting the old lady's hand reassuringly.

"They *are* upset, and the apartment *is* haunted. If you had lived through the scares I've lived through this past week you'd swear the place was haunted, too. Why, I can't sit down to sew or read without hearing those sounds!"

"Sounds?"

"Yes. I wouldn't call them noises; they're not loud enough. They're just sounds."

"And what are the sounds like?"

"Of bare feet pattering around! And I've seen footprints on the ceiling."

Garth leaned forward and gazed into his visitor's eyes long and earnestly, as if to assure himself of her sanity. He seemed satisfied with what he saw, for he leaned back in his chair again and said:

"Go on. Tell me more about these bare feet."

Mrs. Andrews's voice shook as she said:

"Wherever I go, in the bedrooms, in the kitchen, in the living-room, I think I hear those bare feet following me. They patter along, sometimes in front of me, sometimes behind me. I lie awake at night listening to them. I feel that I am going crazy! We heard them so clearly tonight I couldn't bear it another moment; and so I thought of coming to you for help, and brought Louise with me. Louise is almost hysterical from the sounds."

"Oh, the young lady is with you? Where did you leave her?"

"Down in the car."

"Suppose we go down to see her."

He assisted the old lady with her neat little coat, and together they descended to the street. A beautifully appointed gray sedan was parked at the curb. As the detective and Mrs. Andrews stepped from the doorway of the apartment-house a tall girl, closely wrapped in gray squirrel, was in the act of leaping from the car, a look of horror in her large, gray eyes. The chauffeur, a tall negro, was trying to pull her back into the car.

They ran toward her, and Garth caught her as she stumbled from the running-board. She threw herself into Mrs. Andrews's arms and began to sob convulsively. Garth got them both into the car and drew the gray silk curtains. The tall girl was now crying softly, and Mrs. Andrews was patting her shoulder and murmuring:

"Louise, darling. Louise, honey. Look, I've brought Mr. Garth. He's a detective and he'll help us. Look up, dear, and speak to Mr. Garth."

Louise lifted her head. Several honey-colored curls were escaping from the squirrel toque on her head, the large, gray eyes were swimming in tears and the small, full mouth was trembling piteously as she tried to greet Garth politely. Garth thought her the sweetest and most beautiful girl he had ever seen.

"What is the trouble, Miss Greenwood? Has anything happened in the last few moments?"

She pointed mutely to the mudguard of the machine. They looked.

Plainly outlined on a slight film of dust was the imprint of a bare human foot!

The grilled lanterns hanging beside the portals of the apartment-house threw a pale, yellow light on the dusty impression of five long toes, the indentation of the arch and the round of the heel. A drop of rain descended lightly and spattered on the tip of the great toe. The two women were trembling violently.

Garth whipped out his magnifying-glass and bent down close to the footprint, peering at it long and earnestly. At last he whirled and confronted Mrs. Andrews and Louise.

"You say you have been hearing the pattering of bare feet all over your house?"

"Yes, yes!"

"And they follow you everywhere, no matter where you go?"

The old lady nodded, her eyes glued intently on those of the detective, as if hoping in them to read a solution and the promise of help.

With a final glance at the footprint on the mudguard, Garth said:

"Now let's hurry up to your apartment. I imagine there'll be something there to interest us."

He seated the women carefully. Louise was dabbing at her eyes with a scrap of white lace, and Garth concealed a sigh of sympathy for the tall, graceful girl with the honey-colored curls. He slid his large bulk into the back seat next to Louise, and was in the act of leaning back luxuriously when he straightened up suddenly and looked at the girl.

"Miss Greenwood," he said, "what have you in your pocket?"

"Why—nothing!" she replied.

"Yes, you have. You have something in your pocket."

"But—I never carry things in my pockets. I hate bulgy pockets. I carry a bag. See, this is my bag."

"I'm sorry, my dear young lady, to seem rude and insistent. But you *have* got something in your pocket. Take it out, please."

Louise favored him with her iciest stare and made no move. So Garth, being always a man of action, plunged his hand into the gray squirrel wrap. His eyes suddenly lit up with a curious glow. He slowly withdrew his hand. It was clutching something. All eyes were riveted on what he was holding. Old Mrs. Andrews swayed and fell back against the cushions of the car. Louise gave a smothered cry. Garth held the object up to the light.

It was the wax model of a human foot!

Chapter Two

Garth turned the object over in his hand and then asked Louise:

"What do you know about this thing?"

"Mr. Garth, believe me, this is the first time I have ever laid eyes on it. I can swear to that."

She was holding one slim hand against her throat and the words came with great difficulty.

Garth addressed her again, with great gentleness.

"Miss Greenwood, I am deeply sorry to distress you, but you must give me all the help you can. Otherwise, how can I help you? Now I have a request to make of you. Just put your thumb on the heel of this wax foot."

The girl complied. Garth took out his glass and peered intently through it at the foot. There were a dozen other thumb-prints on the wax cast, including the latest one, and they were all identically the same! They were, all of them, the thumb-prints of Louise.

The detective whistled a few bars of "Suwannee River," scratched his ear and finally said with a little sigh:

"Well, let's go on up to your house."

It was a silent trio who alighted at the door of a gray brick apartment-house on West End Avenue. The silence continued as the elevator bore them to the top floor and still continued as Mrs. Andrews let them in with a latch-key. As the hall-door closed behind them and they found themselves in a softly lighted reception-room, Garth's quick eye espied some one slip into a door at the end of the room beyond the one in which they were all standing. Mrs. Andrews led Garth quickly to a chair in the large room beyond.

He sank into it comfortably and cast an appreciative eye about him. The color scheme of the room was ivory and rose. Soft rugs and glowing lamps made for material comfort, while a few small etchings and Japanese prints delighted the eye of the soul.

Louise had shed her wrap and was standing, nervously tense, beside a wrought-iron lamp, her slender fingers braiding and unbraiding the silken fringe. Mrs. Andrews had perched herself on a low stool near Garth. Suddenly Garth sat bolt upright and said:

"Mrs. Andrews, bring here to me every single soul in this place, one by one. Don't leave any one out!"

The little old lady smilingly extended her hand to an electric button near by. In a few seconds two neat maids stood primly before them. Garth fired a volley of terse questions at them. They both denied having heard of any footsteps and seemed utterly astonished at his questioning, and, at the sight of the wax foot in Garth's outstretched hand, they both shrieked and clutched each other frantically. He finally dismissed them and turned again to Mrs. Andrews.

"Now bring on the rest of the folks."

"There is no one else important here, Mr. Garth. Those two maids are all the servants we have."

He made no reply, but rose ponderously, heaving a prodigious sigh. He strode across the room. Mrs. Andrews also rose and fluttered beside him, a little cry on her lips. She laid a restraining hand on his arm, but he shook it off. He continued his long stride until he reached the door at the far end of the next room. The two women were at his side, Mrs. Andrews tugging at his sleeve and saying:

"Listen—there's not a soul here. Nothing is in that room, I tell you! It's—"

But the sleuth had already flung wide the door and was straining his eyes into the interior of the room. The light was extremely dim, a sort of twilight, and Garth could make out nothing. Then suddenly a weight struck him against the chest and a swiftly moving object brushed past him and darted across the two intervening rooms to the hall-door. Garth whirled around.

It was the bent figure of a youth running in an ungainly manner, his body curved forward as if shielding something precious from the gaze of the world. His awkward loping gait brought him finally to the door leading to the public hall, and while he was fumbling with the lock Garth caught up with him and swung the boy around.

It was a remarkable face which the detective was gazing down upon. Pale and drawn, its two outstanding features were the mouth and eyes. Flabby, pinkish lips hung loosely in a foolish grin, the grin of an imbecile. But the eyes were a velvety brown, large and lustrous, and appeared to Garth to mirror all the tragedy this earth has ever known and some of celestial tragedy as well. They now filled with tears and dropped from Garth's wondering face to the thing he was clutching in his hands.

Garth made a dive for it. There was a short struggle, a piercing shriek from the boy, and Garth held aloft a crudely improvised doll, made of a whisk-broom wrapped in a handkerchief of pale green silk. Mrs. Andrews snatched the toy out of Garth's hands and restored it to the moaning boy. She then drew the youth's cowering form into her arms and faced Garth indignantly.

"Why can't you let him alone? He has absolutely nothing to do with this business. Can't you see he's—he's"—her voice trailed off into a whisper—"he's half-witted? He's my poor little son who isn't right in his head!"

She began to weep softly.

Garth fell to stroking his chin with one hand, while the other smoothed his ruffled black locks. He did not know what to make of this new phenomenon. Could the mysterious pattering be ascribed to this half-witted boy who played with dolls? If there were such a possibility, what of the girl Louise's thumb-prints all over the wax foot? And there was something else. Ah, yes, the footprint on the mudguard of the car!

"Hell's fire!" ran his thoughts as he stood there, "I haven't been so stumped in years."

He looked around for the boy. He was moving around the room in a most peculiar way. He would slide up to each piece of furniture in turn, look furtively all around him, then, grinning craftily to himself, would touch lightly the table or chair or lamp in front of him. He completed a circuit of the room and then stood broodingly, his doll cradled in his arms, staring at nothing with those great tragic eyes of his.

Garth walked to the table nearest him and examined the boy's finger-prints. He went to all the furniture and did the same. Then he slowly drew the wax foot from his pocket, and slowly he examined it beneath his faithful glass. He grunted. Back and forth several times from furniture to foot he looked. No. It was beyond all doubt not true. The thumb-prints on the furniture and those on the wax foot were entirely different. Yet why had old Mrs. Andrews tried to hide the half-witted boy from the detective?

And if Louise were herself responsible for the mysterious pattering sounds and the footprints, why did she do it?

It was a pretty question.

Why?

CHAPTER THREE

AS GARTH WAS SITTING ON THE ARM OF AN OVERSTUFFED ARMCHAIR and thoughtfully stroking his neat, silk-clad ankle, the hall-door opened and shut and a second later a man entered the room. He was a round, rosy little man, with a smiling countenance fringed by fluffy white hair. He brought with him the smell of the crisp outdoors, and as he shed his brown overcoat he beamed benignly at the assembled company out of twinkling blue eyes.

"I say, I say," he remarked cheerfully, rubbing his hands, which were reddened by the wind.

Mrs. Andrews rose and presented the men to each other.

"Mr. Garth, this is Mr. Benson Drummond, the uncle of Louise. Mr. Drummond, this is Mr. Garth, who is going to help find where the footprints came from."

The rosy little man gave Garth a swift, piercing look, then became all twinkles again. He walked over to Garth with short, mincing steps and held out his hand.

"I say, this is a pleasure. Come into my study, will you? What abominable cold weather this is! Louise, my pet, how are you?"

Instead of replying, Louise suddenly threw back her head and laughed loudly, and as suddenly she began to sob wildly and with utter abandon. The square of lace in her fingers became torn to shreds, she clutched frantically at the throat of her dress as if she was choking and her entire frame was racked and shaking.

Drummond strode over to her and, putting his strong arms about her slender figure, spoke to her in a low, gentle voice:

"Poor little thing, this is too much for you to bear. You are to go to bed at once. And you are absolutely not to worry or fret. Mr. Garth is here to help you, and he won't leave this house until he has helped us all. Now go into your room and lie down."

Still with his arm about her, he led her to the door. Garth had to admit that his brain was reeling. Surely this lovely, frail creature could harbor no guile in her breast. Her eyes were too honest. They were good eyes—he had seen enough of all kinds of eyes to know that. And yet what was one to think of a girl who went about with a wax foot concealed on her person? Lord, but he wished he could see a chink of light somewhere. In the meantime—

He turned back to Benson Drummond. The little man was standing in the doorway waiting.

"I say, Mr. Garth, do come into my study a while, will you? I suggested to Mrs. Andrews today that if there was more trouble she get you. Right this way. What say you to a glass of nice Madeira? Here we are. This is my little retreat. I say, old man, that chair over there is the most comfortable. Do take it."

Exactly like a fussy, puffing little steam-engine he towed Garth to his destination, a big, soft easy-chair drawn up to a low mahogany table. Having made his guest comfortable with a glass of rich brown Madeira, Benson Drummond lit a cigar and spoke:

"So they did call you in to help 'em look for footprints, eh? I am skeptical about the subject, Mr. Garth. What is all this fuss about footprints, pray? The dear ladies have been somewhat overwrought lately; from what cause I am at a loss to say. But their conversation is footprints, footprints, footprints, eternal and everlasting and unending footprints! Gad, sir, I give you my word that I have seen no footprints and heard no footsteps. To this I swear. Yet, damn it! I would rather see the walls lined with footprints and have them resounding in my ears than listen to these women much longer. The long and short of it is, my dear Mr. Garth, that these dear little ladies of mine are hysterical, and need a long rest or a holiday, or both!"

Garth twirled the stem of his wine-glass in his fingers. His eyes roved casually over the room, taking in its luxurious yet subdued furnishings, and coming back every now and then to rest on his chubby vis-à-vis. Who could have introduced this disrupting influence into this hitherto calm and orderly household? Mrs. Andrews, Louise and Benson Drummond were all obviously gentlefolk, living the serene existence of gentility. They were "nice people"; this much was very patent to any observer. And yet—

"Mr. Drummond, you declare without reservation that you have never heard a single footfall, or seen a single footprint, around this house or in the vicinity of any one of its inmates, that you couldn't explain?"

"Oh, I swear it, old chap. I say, you simply must believe me. I never, never, never—"

Here the good old gentleman began to choke and grow purple. Garth poured him another libation of Madeira, which Mr. Drummond quickly poured down his dry throat.

"As I was remarking, I never heard or saw anything. I must believe it is only the vaporous imaginings of those hysterical women—or lose my own reason—for Mrs. Andrews is as clay, my good sir, in the hands of my ward Louise. She has a half-witted son, you know, and perhaps—but it is Louise who is primarily responsible for this nonsensical footprint bogey."

"May I ask the young lady's age?"

"Certainly. She is twenty-one."

"But didn't I understand you to say that she is your ward?"

"That she is! That she is! Little Louise is my ward. Adorable child!"

"She can scarcely be twenty-one and at the same time be your ward. What is the answer?" was Garth's dry comment.

For answer Benson Drummond left his chair and went to the door. He assured himself that it was closed and that no one lurked without. Then he drew his chair close to Garth's and leaned forward portentously.

"I say, here's something that will explain much. Listen to me. I make no intimations regarding little Louise, who is the apple of my eye. I raised the child from babyhood, sir; when my dear sister died she commended her little orphaned daughter to my care. She has been my most precious charge all these years."

Mr. Drummond was temporarily overcome by his feelings and held a handkerchief to his eyes. Then, leaning still farther forward, he resumed:

"I watched the child so carefully. Saw her blossom from long-legged childhood into the graceful, blooming creature you now see her to be. I say, how I did watch over that girl!"

"Why did you have to watch her so carefully? Wasn't she healthy?"

"Physically, yes. A perfect flower."

"Only physically?"

"That, my friend, is what I do not know. To all outward appearances she has until lately lived her little life, secluded but happy, untouched by care. Then along comes this footprint abomination, making my life a trial. The long and short of it"—his voice sank to a whisper—"there is insanity in her family. Her grandfather died in a private asylum. He, too, had footprint delusions!"

"There is insanity in the family!" Garth was endeavoring to keep his face immobile, and took a quick sip from his glass.

"Alas, yes. Her mother's father—"

A piercing shriek filled the air and arrested the words on Mr. Drummond's lips. Both men leaped to their feet and dashed out into the living-room. The two maids and Mrs. Andrews, wide-eyed and disheveled, were scurrying at top speed into the bedroom of Louise Greenwood. Benson Drummond and the detective got there at the same time, and all piled into the room. The girl was lying on the floor near the bed, unconscious. Her face was ashen, even under the rosy glow from a silk-shaded lamp on the dressing-table. Squatting beside her, rocking back and forth, was the half-witted youth, cradling his doll and staring vacantly at the toe of Louise's pink slipper.

"Hell's fire!" muttered Garth, pushing forward. He bent over the girl's prone form, slipped his arm about her and lifted her very tenderly to the bed. The warmth and softness of her body caused him to sigh sharply. He involuntarily tightened his arms about her before laying her on the lacy coverlet. By this time the servants, Mrs. Andrews and Mr. Drummond had all swarmed about the bed, and the air was filled with exclamations and the sound of weeping. Through it all the boy sat on the floor, unmoved, impassive, in a world of his own.

Garth straightened up from a lingering survey of Louise's face, and as he did so looked up at the ceiling. A spasm of astonishment crossed his face, but he said nothing. He had seen a miracle.

The ceiling was covered with footprints traveling around in a wide circle, and every single print was of the right foot!

CHAPTER FOUR

PANDEMONIUM HAD BROKEN OUT IN THE BEDROOM, and Garth held up his hand.

"Never mind anything now but Miss Louise. Get her feeling better before you do another thing. Quick, now!" He addressed the two cowering domestics, who straightway fled.

It was the intention of Garth to empty the room as quickly as possible. Fortunately, no one else had looked at the ceiling; of all those who had been in the room he alone knew that it was marked with the footprints of what he was beginning to call in his mind the "damned thing."

"I would suggest," he said quietly, "that we carry Miss Greenwood into the library. Something has disturbed her here; when she returns to consciousness she will feel better if she is in a different room."

He stepped forward as if to lift her in his arms when Drummond interfered.

"I will do all the carrying that is to be done here, Mr. Garth," he said sharply.

"By all means," agreed the detective, reddening.

He stood aside while the gray-haired uncle lifted the lovely girl in his arms. Awkwardly enough he carried her down the hallway to a couch in the library where he had been conversing with the detective.

"Go with them," whispered the detective authoritatively into the ear of old Mrs. Andrews. The aged woman gave him a bewildered look and then glanced at her half-witted boy, still crooning to his doll.

"Leave him here," said Garth, still in a whisper.

Mrs. Andrews hesitated only for a moment. Her sharp eyes seemed to study the detective and appraise him. Whatever she saw there satisfied her. Without another word she turned and walked hurriedly out of the room.

Left alone with the half-witted boy, Garth's first move was to turn his eyes again to the ceiling. There they were—that appalling circle of human footprints—every one a right-foot print, clearly printed on the ceiling paper in a faded red color, like pale blood. It was as if some uncanny creature with the power to walk upside-down had hopped in a wide circle on one foot around the ceiling—hopped on a foot that was wet with some red and ghastly fluid.

What could be the meaning of this incredible mystery! Into what lurid plot had he been dragged at the very moment when he, in his loneliness, had meant to smoke a peaceful pipe and go to bed? Such things couldn't be true! The whole idea was monstrous. The print on the mudguard of the car—and then the wax foot in the girl's pocket. The girl! She was worth it all. Somehow Garth trusted her. He liked her eyes—she—

Even in her distress, even in the midst of all this mystery, he fancied to himself there was something in her that might make him forget his loneliness.

"Ha! Ha! Ha!" laughed the half-witted boy.

Garth jumped, thoroughly startled.

"What's the matter? What are you laughing at?" he asked, looking full into the boy's queer face.

"Somebody's been walking upside-down. That ain't right," said the boy with a hideous leer.

"You mean—" began Garth.

The boy pointed upward with a white forefinger, long and thin.

"Them!" he said. "I won't look at 'em again. I've seen 'em before. They make me—*afraid!*"

Garth looked from the grim footprints on the ceiling to the face of the boy in great perplexity. His mind seemed stalled like an engine. It was stiflingly hot in the room; he gave a curse and opened the window. The thing was getting on his nerves. The sound of the voice of Louise recalled him to himself, and turning he saw that the half-wit had slipped away.

With a farewell glance at the footprints on the ceiling, he turned and walked down the corridor. When he reached the library he saw that Louise was conscious again. She was sitting, propped upright, against pillows on the couch. Her uncle was standing near, his good-looking face thoroughly worried. Mrs. Andrews was on her knees beside her charge, weeping piteously. The maids and the half-witted boy were not there.

At the sight of the detective Louise cried out:

"Oh, Mr. Garth. I'm so glad you're still here. You must help me—I feel as if I am losing my mind!"

"What has happened?" asked Garth quietly. "But before you tell me, why not wait and get thoroughly quiet?"

"I can never be quiet until whatever the thing is that pursues me is driven out of this house!" cried Louise on the verge of hysteria. "I shall go mad—I know I shall go mad!"

Drummond exchanged a pitiful and significant glance with the detective. Plainly he was thinking of the girl's grandfather who had died in an asylum.

Garth drew up a chair and seated himself beside Louise.

"Then tell me what happened," he suggested. "It may ease your mind just to tell it."

She flashed him a grateful glance from eyes which thrilled him whenever they encountered his own.

"I had got into bed," began Louise, her voice trembling, "and though I was still very nervous I was so reassured by your being here that I felt sure I would be able to compose myself and later to go to sleep. But as I lay there I began to fancy that I heard those pattering sounds—like bare feet. Just to be as brave as I could I had turned off the light, but on hearing those sounds I grew frightened again and turned on the light. There is a button close to my bed. I lay back and looked up at the ceiling and then—"

She began to laugh hysterically, and the sound of it filled Garth with the greatest pity he had ever known for a human being.

"And then—" he prompted gently.

"There were footprints all over the ceiling!" she cried. "I know you won't believe me, but there were—I saw them, I tell you, I saw them!"

Drummond clapped his hands together impulsively.

"You imagined that you saw them, Louise," he said. "Such things couldn't be."

"Did you look at the ceiling, by any chance?" demanded Garth, angry at the man's tone.

"I did!" said Drummond stoutly. "I did look at the ceiling when we all went in there. And there were no footprints on the ceiling. Of course there weren't."

"You are mistaken. I think you just imagine you looked at the ceiling," retorted Garth. "I looked at the ceiling and I—"

"So did I," interrupted old Mrs. Andrews.

"And what did you see?" asked Garth.

"I saw the footprints," sobbed the old woman.

"So did I," said Garth.

Drummond threw out his hands in a gesture of thorough exasperation.

"You are all like a lot of lunatics!" he cried. "The idea of saying such things! It couldn't be true. I want to tell you, Mr. Detective, that I do know what I am talking about. I *did* look at that ceiling—and there were no footprints, or anything else, on it. This thing must be infectious."

"The argument is very easily settled," said Garth evenly. "I am not disposed to make light of what Miss Greenwood says she saw. She is a sensible, normal woman and she has seen a very terrifying thing. I, for one, know that she is telling the truth, because I saw the same thing. But in order to settle the dispute let's look at the ceiling again."

"There's no reason why we should do any such thing," protested Drummond vigorously. "It's nonsense to even suppose that a thing such as that could happen."

"Do you object to looking again?" demanded Garth.

"Why should I, Mr. Garth—except that it is all nonsense."

"The room is only a few steps down the hall. Come with me and I'll show them to you!"

Drummond hesitated a moment, then gave in.

"All right," he said. "Anything to oblige you, Mr. Garth."

The two of them walked down the corridor without a word. As they came to the door Garth said a strange thing.

"I should like to go in first, Mr. Drummond, if you please?" he suggested.

"Why not?" asked Drummond, plainly surprised.

Confidently Garth stepped into the room and looked up at the ceiling.

Then he received the greatest shock of his career.

The ceiling was bare. There was not the slightest trace of even one footprint left upon it.

CHAPTER FIVE

"WHO'S LOONEY NOW?" asked Drummond insolently.

Garth did not reply.

His mind was busy—bitterly busy—with the ripening intention of solving this mystery at all hazards and at all costs. He realized now that he was fighting no ordinary criminal. For by the very token of those disappearing footprints he knew that he was on the trail of a crime and that behind the crime was a scheming intelligence so crafty, so malignant, so daring, that it would take all his skill and all his cunning to defeat it and to save Louise from—

He dared not take Drummond or any one else into his counsel. This mysterious apartment was not the place for expressing opinions or revealing his theories.

"Mr. Drummond," said Garth, "I am afraid you win. At the same time there is a mystery here. I am not a fool. Neither is your niece. Something is at work here. Do you want me to solve it or not?"

"I do," said Drummond seriously. "Only I am afraid you detectives are all alike. You want to solve a mystery. I do not think there is any mystery here!"

"But surely, Mr. Drummond—"

"No mystery at all," insisted Drummond, lowering his voice and glancing over his shoulder down the hallway. "I am afraid the mystery is all in the mind of my unfortunate niece. Her grandfather was mad. And now—"

Tears were in his eyes.

Garth could not disregard that theory. Lunatics did just such things, he well knew. Yet he could not bring himself to believe such a horrible thing against the lovely girl whose eyes even now warmed his heart. Even with the evidence of the wax foot he had found in her pocket fresh in his memory he could not believe it.

"But old Mrs. Andrews saw the footprints, too," he reminded Drummond.

"She says that she did. But did she? She has a half-witted son who gives me the creeps. Where did he get his insanity if not from his mother? I think the old woman is crazy, too!"

"Do you think I am?" demanded Garth.

"I never trusted a detective in my life," said Drummond coldly.

The insult brought a red flush to Garth's cheeks. His hands clenched into balled fists. Then he smiled, but if Drummond had known Garth he would have remembered that smile.

"Very well, Mr. Drummond," said Garth quietly. "Do you wish me to withdraw from this case?"

"I would like to summon an alienist," said Drummond.

Garth passed him without a word and returned to the library.

"Miss Greenwood," he said earnestly, "I have come to the conclusion that you are entirely correct in all that you have told us. You have seen the very things you have described; I have seen them, too. I would advise you to come with me; I have friends who would willingly open their homes to you and where I can promise you nothing will disturb you!"

"She shall not leave this house!" thundered Drummond, who had followed Garth swiftly into the library.

"Why not?" cried Garth.

"You know why not!" shouted Drummond, rapidly losing his temper. "I am this young woman's guardian and I will not permit it!"

"How old are you, Miss Greenwood?" asked Garth tensely.

"I am twenty-one, Mr. Garth."

"Then you are of age, your own mistress and you can do whatever you please. Your uncle has not the slightest authority over you. I tell you to come with me; he tells you to stay. You will have to decide!"

Bewildered, Louise looked from the angry face of her uncle into the calm eyes of the detective, whom she had met for the first time that night. Only for an instant she hesitated. Then she rose from the couch, breathing deeply, proud and capable.

"I shall take your advice, Mr. Garth," she said. "I shall go with you!"

CHAPTER SIX

OLD MRS. ANDREWS WENT WITH THEM. Drummond blustered and swore, but Garth knew how to dominate even such an excitable and outraged character as Drummond. Before they had departed the uncle was reconciled. He was only looking out for the best interests of his niece, and it was a great deal to expect him to approve her leaving, in the early hours of the morning, with a stranger.

"Where are you taking her?" asked Drummond when the summoned taxi was at the door of the apartment-house.

"To the home of Mrs. Whitfield, the novelist, 244 Riverside Drive, Apartment One-B," replied Garth evenly. "Mrs. Whitfield is one of my good friends. She has based one or two of her novels on my humble exploits. She will welcome your niece."

"Very well, then," acceded Drummond with more grace than he had hitherto shown. "When am I to see my niece again?"

"She will return here when this mystery is cleared up," replied Garth.

"And when"—Drummond was sneering—"and when will that be, may I ask?"

"No man can tell that," replied Garth, "but I shall be back here at ten o'clock tomorrow morning."

"What for, in God's name, Mr. Garth?"

"To solve the mystery, Mr. Drummond. Good-night!"

As Garth had predicted, the gray-haired and majestic Mrs. Whitfield was ready with a welcome for the distraught young Louise and her old nurse when the party reached their door considerably after two o'clock in the morning. Garth pressed the hand of Louise in parting and promised her that all would be well. Her parting glance lingered with him on the way home. In fact, he remembered it for the rest of his life.

Garth did not sleep that night. His mind was too filled with the mystery of the affair. Step by step he reviewed the incidents. He had brought with him the wax model of the foot which he had found in the pocket of Louise. This he studied with the most intent curiosity. After a while he put it aside, put a fresh log on the fire and gave himself up to sheer meditation.

Over and over in his mind he recited the details of what had happened from the moment old Mrs. Andrews entered his study. At each successive incident he paused, waiting to discover if it was not freighted with some significance. It was dawn before he found the one clue which he had wished for. It came at the memory of what had seemed, at the time, to be a most trivial detail.

"Of course!" he muttered with chagrin. "What a fool I was not to notice it!"

With a bound he reached a bookcase and began hunting for a volume at which he had not looked in many years. A few minutes' search found him exactly what he wished to know. He chuckled with a kind of subdued hilarity. He was getting somewhere; all sorts of clues were opening up.

For the next three hours Garth was an exceedingly busy man. He went to a certain store and had a long talk with its proprietor. What he learned there brought a smile of approaching triumph to his lips. From there he sought out a man in overalls with whom he had a brief conversation and took down an address. He called on a firm of real-estate agents and from the manager gleaned some facts of a highly confidential nature. Immediately he went into a telephone booth and called up two men in Wall Street, who asked him to call again in five minutes. One after the other he called them again in the time specified, and by that time his smile was almost a grin.

There remained but one more call for him to make, and this was to a firm of decorators not far from the house on West End Avenue where Louise Greenwood had been tortured by such abominable and evasive mysteries.

This last Garth regarded as conclusive. The case was clear. With that one clue to work on he had followed the trail through a winding maze, but it led resolutely and unmistakably back to one source.

At last he was able to unravel the mystery of the footprints on the ceiling.

CHAPTER SEVEN

PRECISELY AT TEN O'CLOCK, as he had promised, Garth rang the doorbell at the apartment of Benson Drummond, and it was Drummond himself who opened the door.

"So!" he said not very politely. "You did come back. Well, I hope you have come back to apologize?"

"I have," replied Garth with a forgiving smile. "I have come back to apologize for my great stupidity. I should have seen through this thing at once. I have been a great ass, Mr. Drummond. But now I'm ready to explain all the mystery!"

"Indeed!"

"Indeed. Yes, sir. I have not much time, so I would suggest that we get down to business. Let us go to the room of your niece at once!"

"What for?"

"I want to show you those footprints on the ceiling."

"There aren't any footprints on the ceiling."

"Yes, yes, there are, Mr. Drummond."

"I don't believe it."

"I don't ask you to. I ask you to let me show them to you."

"Oh, very well, then."

They spoke no more until they both stood in the pretty little bedroom where Louise Greenwood had dreamed the sweet dreams of girlhood until this terrible mystery had made them all nightmares and hours of cowering awakeness.

"I ask you to look at the ceiling, Mr. Drummond."

"I am looking at it, Garth. And there's no footprints on it, as you very well know."

A cold wind, the remnant of the storm of the preceding night, struck them chilly through the open windows. Garth pulled down the window and turned on the heat.

"Now let's watch the ceiling," he proposed.

"And make fools of ourselves? Not me! I've played with this thing long enough, Mr. Garth—altogether too long, in fact. I've got to get down to my business."

"How is your business?" asked Garth casually.

"What does that matter to you?"

"Isn't it a fact that you are trembling on the verge of bankruptcy—and, perhaps, discovery?"

Drummond grew ghastly pale.

"What do you mean?" he growled.

"Just what I said. Aren't you?"

"You impertinent, damned scoundrel, I'll—"

"Easy, Mr. Drummond. It is the business of a detective to know everything. I know your business is in a bad way. You've been a fool to let it get that way, but you have. And you've done something you ought not to have done, Mr. Drummond. You've borrowed your ward's money, for which you were the trustee, to try to save your business, and that went, too. It's a bad mess, Mr. Drummond."

"I'll break your damned—"

"Look!" cried Garth suddenly.

Drummond looked up at the ceiling. The blood-red footprints were there again—a wide and lurid circle of footprints over their heads.

"Do you see them, or don't you?" snarled Garth.

Before Drummond could reply Garth had sprung upon him. Like lightning a pair of handcuffs were on the man's wrists and Garth had flung him backward upon the bed.

"Now, you damned old thief and hypocrite," said Garth sternly, "lie there and look at the footprints of your own making while I tell you the facts that you already know. Your business was going to smash through your foolish speculations. I more than suspect that it was because you wanted to buy diamonds and furs for a dancer at the Summer Garden that you plunged so recklessly. A business man ought to keep away from that sort of thing, Drummond—especially the guardian of a good, pure girl like Louise. At all events, I know that your business is in a bad way and that you are suspected of misappropriating funds from the fortune left to Louise by her father. I got that from confidential sources in Wall Street in five minutes over the telephone this morning.

"And now I'll tell you just what you did. You sat down and realized that you were pretty well at the end of your tether. What made it worse for you was the fact that Louise was just of age and could legally claim her inheritance. You would have to render an accounting to her of the money you had used.

"Were you man enough to do that? Were you man enough to throw yourself on her mercy, tell her your plight, and offer to work for the rest of your life to make a restitution? She would have forgiven you. She is just that kind of a girl. But you were too big a coward to play a man's part, even after you had acted like a crook. No! You sat down and contrived a villainous plot against an innocent and helpless girl. You determined to play sly and frightful little tricks on her and then accuse her of being insane. She had a history of insanity in her family, and you would play on that and crush her. She would say she saw footprints on the ceiling—and then there would be no footprints there. That would be case enough, with your tricks, to railroad her into an asylum. Your guardianship of her money would have to be continued for life—and you would get her money. You monster!

"So you decided to have this apartment redecorated. You didn't ask the real-estate agents to pay for it. You *volunteered* to pay for the job yourself; I got it from the agents this morning. You hired your own paperhanger. I talked with him this morning. He tells me you insisted on him showing you the rolls of paper which were to go on the ceiling, and that they remained in your possession for two nights; that you delayed the job for two days, for what reason he did not know.

"But I know. It all became very clear to me when I remembered last night that the footprints did not disappear until I opened the window. They were affected by heat and cold. That gave me the clue. It all became clear and simple after that. Of course, I have known of magic inks since I was a kid. We used to write love-notes to the girls with them. Mix up a few chemicals and you have a colorless liquid. Write with that liquid and the paper remains blank. But heat the paper and the writing plainly comes out—to disappear again as soon as the paper is cold.

"That is what you did. You mixed a mess of those chemicals. I talked with the druggist up the street—the man you bought the chemicals from. He remembered the transaction perfectly; he couldn't understand why you wanted such large quantities of chemicals. And then you dipped your wax foot in the ink and printed the footprints.

"Oh, you were clever. You knew what to do. You knew Louise never turned the heat on in her bedroom—a sensible, physical-culture girl. Therefore your footprints were safe until you chose to turn on the heat, unknown to her, and your magic footprints appeared.

"You made the print on the mudguard of the car. You put the foot in her pocket. You did everything you could—probably pattering up and down in the halls in your bare feet, in your cunning way, to terrify that girl and make her appear insane. But it didn't work.

"Drummond, you are under arrest!"

But Louise insisted that Garth let him go. She wept over her rascally guardian, and consented to lose the money he had stolen from her if he would leave the country.

He is now in Australia, and writes to Louise that some day soon he will pay her back. As far as such a man can repent he has repented, but such men can't go very far.

As for Garth, his loneliness is at an end. He has a wife whose name is Louise, and they love each other very, very much.

Bibliography

"Arthur Garfield Hays Dies at 73; Counsel to Civil Liberties Union." *New York Times*, Dec 15, 1954.

"Authors of 'The Spider.'" *NYT*, Mar 27, 1927.

"Court Finds 'Spider' Was Not Plagiarized." *NYT*, Mar 29, 1930.

Ernst, Robert. *Weakness Is a Crime: The Life of Bernarr Macfadden*. Syracuse University Press, 1991.

"Fulton Oursler, Author, Dies at 59." *NYT*, May 25, 1952.

"Grace P. Oursler, Novelist, Editor." *NYT*, Dec 17, 1955.

Hersey, Harold. "My Friend Fulton Oursler." *The Author & Journalist*, Jul 1927.

Locke, John. "Harold Hersey: Tales of an Ink-Stained Wretch," introduction to *City of Numbered Men: The Best of Prison Stories*. Off-Trail Publications, 2010.

Macfadden, Mary, and Emile Gauvreau. *Dumbbells and Carrot Strips: The Story of Bernarr Macfadden*. Henry Holt & Company, 1953.

"Meet the Editor: Fulton Oursler, Editor of *Liberty*." *Writers' Journal*, Mar 1940.

Oursler, Fulton. *Behold This Dreamer!* An Autobiography by Fulton Oursler, Edited and with Commentary by Fulton Oursler, Jr. Little, Brown and Company, 1964.

———. "I Am Looking for a Writer." *The Writer's 1934 Year Book & Market Guide*.

———. *The True Story of Bernarr Macfadden*. Lewis Copeland Company, 1929.

Oursler, Will. *Family Story*. Funk & Wagnalls Company, Inc., 1963.

Schallert, Edwin. "Weird Thriller Is 'The Spider.'" *Los Angeles Times*, Jun 26, 1928.

" 'Spider' Author Loses Suit." *NYT*, Mar 17, 1928. Oursler v. Brentano.

" 'The Spider' in New Suit." *NYT*, Jan 25, 1928.

"Third Plagiarism Suit Filed Against 'Spider.'" *NYT*, Sep 7, 1927. Robert H. Rohde.

Wood, Clement. *Bernarr Macfadden: A Study in Success*. Lewis Copeland Company, 1929.

Index

PULPWOOD DAYS: Volume 1: Editors You Want To Know
Edited by John Locke • 180 pages, $16

> *Numerous articles from the writers' magazines by and about pulp editors, with ample biographical profiles. Editors include: Frank E. Blackwell (*Detective Story, Western Story*), Ray Palmer (*Amazing Stories, Fantastic Adventures*), Edwin Baird (*Weird Tales, Detective Tales*), and many more.*

GANG PULP
Edited by John Locke • 19 stories, 294 pages, $24

> *Hardboiled stories of the criminal underworld from the first year (1929-30) of the gang pulps:* Gangster Stories, Racketeer Stories, *etc. These violent tales came under immediate censorship pressure; the history is explored in an in-depth essay. "A remarkable work of popular-culture scholarship"*—MYSTERY SCENE, *Fall 2008.*

THE GANGLAND SAGAS OF BIG NOSE SERRANO
Volume 1: Dames, Dice and the Devil
Volume 2: Horses, Hoboes and Heroes
Volume 3: Hell's Gangster
By Anatole Feldman • Introductions by Will Murray
Each: 4 novels • **Volumes 1-2**: 266 pages, $20 • **Volume 3**: 224 pages, $18

> *The complete Big Nose Serrano novels from* Gangster Stories, Greater Gangster Stories, *and* The Gang Magazine, *1930-35. Feldman was the best of the gang pulp authors, and Big Nose was his most inspired creation, the berserking king of Chicago gangsters.*

AMAZON STORIES
Volume 1: Pedro & Lourenço
Volume 2: Pedro & Lourenço
By Arthur O. Friel • Introductions by John Locke
Vol 1: 10 stories, 222 pages, $18 • **Vol 2**: 10 stories, 286 pages, $20

Collects Friel's first twenty stories from Adventure *(1919-21), following the strange experiences of two Amazon Basin rubber workers as they explore the jungle. The best of pulp adventure fiction.*

GROTTOS OF CHINATOWN: The Dorus Noel Stories
By Arthur J. Burks • Introduction by John Locke
11 stories, 194 pages, $16

The complete adventures of Dorus Noel from All Detective Magazine *(1933-34). Burks' Manhattan Chinatown is a place of dark mystery, riddled with secret passageways, menaced by hatchetmen. Introduction discusses the history of* All Detective *and the career of the Speed-King of the Pulps, Arthur J. Burks.*

THE GOLDEN ANACONDA: And Other Strange Tales of Adventure
By Elmer Brown Mason • Introduction by John Locke
10 stories, 260 pages, $20

Ten fantastic stories set in the exotic corners of the world, all of them known to their globe-trotting entomologist author. Includes all five Wandering Smith stories from The Popular Magazine; *and five tales from* All-Story Weekly, *topped by the horror-laden two-part saga of Borneo, "Black Butterflies" and "Red Tree-Frogs." All published, 1915-16.*